DATE DUE

MAR 14 2000	
MAR 23 2000	
MAR 31 2000	
APR 17 2000	
FEB 27 2001	
JAN 20 2005	

BRODART, CO. Cat. No. 23-221-003

Medicine Hat

Also by Don Coldsmith

Trail of the Spanish Bit
The Elk-Dog Heritage
Follow the Wind
Buffalo Medicine
Man of the Shadows
Daughter of the Eagle
Moon of Thunder
The Sacred Hills
Pale Star
River of Swans
Return to the River
The Medicine Knife
The Flower in the Mountains
Trail for Taos
Song of the Rock
Fort de Chastaigne
Quest for the White Bull
Return of the Spanish
Bride of the Morning Star
Walks in the Sun
Thunderstick
Track of the Bear
Child of the Dead
Bearer of the Pipe

The Changing Wind
The Traveler
World of Silence

RIVERS WEST: *The Smoky Hill*

Runestone

MEDICINE HAT

A Novel

Don Coldsmith

University of Oklahoma Press
Norman and London

To the women
who have influenced my life
and made it good.

All of the characters in this book are fictitious, and any resemblance to actual persons, living or dead, is purely coincidental.

A novel in the Spanish Bit Saga
Time Period: Mid-1700s, shortly after *Bearer of the Pipe*

ISBN 0-8061-2959-X

Published by arrangement with Bantam Books.

Published by the University of Oklahoma Press, Norman, Publishing Division of the University. Manufactured in the U.S.A.

Introduction

Among the horses of the American West, there is a rare, but recognized, color marking, the "medicine hat." It is most commonly encountered among the breeds associated with northern mustang stock, which in turn descended from the Spanish Andalusians.

The medicine hat occurs on an animal with a white or light base color, such as a light roan. The ears are dark, red or blue-gray, and a narrow strip of this color runs across the top of the head, joining the dark ears as a single unit. Viewed from front or back, the animal appears to be wearing a headdress like that of a holy man, a fur cap with the animal's ears still attached . . . a "medicine hat." These animals have few other markings, possibly only dark "points," such as stockings, mane, and tail.

The spiritual, religious, and magical power of the American Indian's medicine is not easily understood in European cultures. There is no word in English that implies all of these things. "Medicine" is a poor attempt at translation. Most important is the implication of strength and power obtained through spiritual gifts. These are nurtured by the growth of *self-respect* and *humility*, which in many other cultures are actually inconsistent with each other.

But imagine an animal, a horse, already sacred to one's culture, which is born wearing the medicine hat of a holy man. . . . This would be an event of great importance, worthy of worship, perhaps.

This is the story of a young holy man and his wife, challenged to a quest for new spiritual experience by such a horse.

DON COLDSMITH

1

Pipe Bearer, I am called. I was given this name by my grandfather, the holy man Singing Wolf, to honor my deed in saving his sacred pipe when the Big Whirlwind struck our band. Ours is the Southern band of the People, who are called by others the Elk-dog People, because we were among the first to be given the horse.

My parents are Dark Antelope and Gray Mouse. You may remember my father as a skilled tracker among the People.

But those are not the things of which I would tell you tonight. I would tell of strange things that we have seen and learned, my wife and I. You know my wife, Otter Woman. . . . Otter is also of the People, the Southern band. We were childhood sweethearts. . . . Ah, I try to tell too much, and the story of our quest itself is so big. . . . Forgive me.

Now, around a story fire, as you know, I would begin with Creation, and follow the story of the People down to the time when this happened. But this is among friends, and you know those things, so I will go ahead with our story.

It began a few moons after our marriage. The Moon of Awakening, maybe. . . . No, Otter says the Moon of Greening. No matter.

We had wintered well. The Southern band was very poor after the Whirlwind, and we needed a big buffalo kill that fall, to provide lodge skins, for shelter against the coming winter. We were blessed with a great hunt at the Medicine Rock. So many buffalo that we were able to trade meat and even skins to the Growers in that area. It was hard work. . . . Yes, Otter, I know. That is not the story I started to tell. I will go on.

We had no children yet. . . . Yes, Little Bird, come sit on my lap, but you must be quiet, like the others. Yes, I know you love to hear this story. . . . There. . . . We had no children. . . . Ah, I said that.

It was the dream, the night-vision that started it. It was one of those in which you know that it is a dream, and you seem to be watching it and are in it at the same time. Yet it seemed to be a poorly formed vision. Colors and shapes were shifting and changing. There seemed to be a mist over everything, like that on a crisp fall morning. You know, when it rises like smoke from the water and layers out among the trees . . . like that.

My vision seemed to have no beginning or end. It was just there. Horses, magnificent horses, moving through that mist, plainly seen and then swallowed up among the trees along the stream or in the blue misty prairie. Ah, it was a wonderful vision. You know how the People have always been with horses. My family . . . an ancestor once . . . No, forgive me, my friends, let me go on.

There was this one animal in my dream that I will never forget. It was tall and strong, the sort of horse that . . . well, that one *dreams* of. His back was short, his chest deep. The slope of his hip was good, his tail set low, and the great muscles in his hind quarters showed strength and power. His head was well formed, and . . . But first, his color: white, or light-blue roan. I know, some do not like a white horse, for it is easily seen. It is a disadvantage sometimes, and I feel that way myself. But this horse was not all white. The mane and tail were dark, and all four feet, up to the knees and hocks. It was much as we often see in yellow horses. Like that.

But I have left until last the truly unusual mark of this dream-horse. *It was wearing a hat!* You know the fur cape that some holy men wear? Well, the wolf-priest of our allies, the Head Splitters. The skin of the animal's head, ears sticking up? It was like that. A medicine hat.

Well, anything may happen in a dream. It is a look, maybe, into the Other Side, that of the spirits. But no matter. Yes, this horse wore a medicine hat, and I tried to look more closely. It was of dark fur, and at the back blended into the mane, and *aiee!* I saw that this medicine hat was part of the animal itself. The dark gray-blue fur was that of the horse's head and ears. The entire poll was dark, blending into mane and forelock.

I now realized that I was in the presence of a spirit-horse, one with a powerful medicine. I did not know the meaning then, or why I had been chosen. I was made to think that there was something that I must do.

"Yes, Grandfather," I said, trembling a little as the horse turned to look directly at me. "What is it? Where? How?"

The horse turned and wheeled away, disappearing into the fog without a sound. I felt that I should follow it, and I would have done so, except for one thing. I woke up. I was trembling, sweating, and a little afraid.

"What is it?" whispered Otter sleepily.

"It is nothing. A dream," I told her.

"It is good. Go to sleep," she told me.

But I lay there in her arms, in the darkness of the lodge for a long time, wondering. *What is it? What does the dream say?* I knew that I was being called to something. In some way the spirits were trying to get my attention.

My grandfather, the holy man Singing Wolf, who crossed over only last season, was my adviser and mentor. He was no help. He listened and asked a few questions, and finally spoke.

"I do not know, Pup. . . ." Grandfather always called me by my childhood name. . . . "I have heard of such a horse. To the north, I think. The Lakotas or Crows, maybe . . . I do not remember."

"What should I do, Grandfather?" I asked.

"I do not know, Pup," he repeated. "You are a capable holy man now. You will surely be shown."

"Should I cast the bones?" I asked him.

"I am made to think not," he told me. "If you wish, but you do not have much on which to base it. I would wait."

And so I did. It was not easy. I was impatient. *Maybe*, I thought, *it is only a dream, and no more.* But somehow I was made to think that it was more important than that. Was it a call to travel north to look for such a horse? I did not know.

The next occurrence was not long in coming, though. And as always where things of the spirit are concerned, it was in a completely unexpected way.

Early one morning a young man came to the door of our lodge and shook the deer-foot rattles to indicate his presence.

"Uncle, I would speak with you," he called.

I was younger, of course, and I was still unused to the term of respect. "Uncle" had always been used for men older than I. I was beginning to hear it because of my status as a holy man, and was still a little bit uncomfortable with it. I stepped outside, wondering why this young man had sought me rather than Singing Wolf, who was by many years superior to me in skills and understanding.

"It is one of your mares, Uncle," the boy told me. I recognized him now as one of those whose duty it was to herd the horses.

"Yes?" I asked him.

"She has a new foal," he told me.

It is not unusual, of course, for one of the horse herders to let someone know of a new foal. That is only right. But early in the morning, not long after dawn? I had still been in the robes. . . . We had been married only a few moons, and . . . What? Oh, yes, Otter. . . . I have to tease her a little, you know. Let me continue.

"Is the mare healthy?" I asked.

"Oh, yes, Uncle. But the foal . . . "

"It is deformed? Dead?"

"No, no. It is healthy. A beautiful colt. It is special, somehow. You will see."

Well, I followed him, still puzzled as to what he was talking about. Otter had crawled out of the robes and slipped into her dress to go with us.

It was one of my best mares, one that I had taken in trade from the Growers. There was a story involved. They had obtained her from a trader who had bought her from the Pawnees, who had stolen her from someone to the north of them. Lakotas, maybe, it was said. That did not impress me at the time.

What did impress me was the foal. *Aiee*, what a horse! Yes, I know what you think. I am about to tell you that he was marked like the one in my dream. But no, he was not. In fact, I did not even think of that at the time. Only that this was one of the most perfectly formed newborn colts I had ever seen.

He was an unimpressive color, it is true. His coat was a nondescript mouse color or sandy brown. Many foals are born like that and will usually shed their fuzzy baby hair to reveal their true color. This one I presumed to be a black. He had no markings at all.

I watched him nursing at his mother's milk bag, butting her playfully when it did not flow fast enough. He would pause and stare at us for a moment, then run to the other side, bucking a little as he ran to hide behind his mother.

A foal is always a joy to watch, and we stood laughing at his antics and playing with him for a long time. There was an odd thing happening. As you know, we have many horses. We did have even then. We had maybe twenty foals even that year, just starting out. We enjoyed all of them, but this one was special. We handled him, rubbed him all over, and he seemed to enjoy it. The mare tolerated it well, seeming proud of what she had done. Some mares . . . *Aiee*, I remember one old grouch who would draw blood on anyone who came near her new foal. She was dangerous. And, you know, the rest of the year she was so calm and easygoing. . . . Yes, yes, I will go on.

Both Otter and I, and later Singing Wolf, when he saw this foal, had a strange and excited feeling. The spirit of this animal seemed to reach out and speak to us. Unfortunately, it was in a spirit-talk that we could not understand. A sort of think-talk. I see you nodding. You have felt this too, no?

The colt grew rapidly, filling out muscle to flesh out his fine frame. He continued to be easy to handle, probably because we did so early. I am made to think that it is important, to touch a foal soon after birth, to let the spirits mix, so that he sees they mix well without harm. Do you not think so? But let me continue.

It was the next moon before I began to realize that there might be some connection between my dream and this foal. When the fuzzy baby hair around his face began to shed, the color underneath was white! At first I thought that he had eaten in a sloppy way and had milk on his nose. Then I looked more closely, and touched, and *aiee!* This was his true color! Not clear white, but a light-blue roan, and even then I did not think . . . But as he continued to shed, a bit more every day, I began to realize . . . his dark points, his markings . . . *Yes!* I will never forget the day when, as I approached the pair, he looked around from behind his mother and I saw at last what was happening. This *foal* was wearing the *medicine hat*! This was the horse in my dream. Or maybe another like it.

I hurried to bring Singing Wolf. He had seen the colt before and felt its power, but he, too, had failed to recognize . . . Of course, he had not had the dream, either. He stood looking at the animal for a long time, saying only "*aiee!*"

Finally he turned to me.

"Pup," he said seriously, "I am made to think that now you could cast the bones!"

2

The casting of the bones brought another puzzling thing.

You may not be aware how this is done. It is part of the holy man's gift among the People. There is a skin, painted with designs that have special meanings and special spirits.

The bones are not really bones, except for a few of them. Some are stone, wood, shell . . . fetishes and small carved figures whose spirits relate to those of the skin I spoke of. These "bones" are placed in a special cup, shaken to mix them, and tossed out on the skin. The important part is interpretation, and that must be learned by years of study and experience.

Anyway, I cast the bones, in the privacy of our lodge, with only Otter Woman present. She had begun to learn as my assistant, you know. The bones skittered and bounced, and, as always, seemed to come alive for a moment. Maybe they do. I cannot say. But they appear to do so, and this time they were exceedingly active. The little fetish that represents the horse, especially . . . *aiee*, that one seemed to take on a life of its own! It leaped across the skin and skittered to a stop almost at the edge. I saw that it was *beyond* the border of the usual signs and symbols.

Ah! My grandfather would say that I am telling you too much. The older holy men have always made much of the *secrecy* of the spirit-gift. And that is probably as it should be. I have a tendency to explain too much of what I am doing in the ceremonies. Some things are not meant to be explained or understood. It is better when a little mystery remains, no?

I see my wife, Otter Woman, giving me a sidelong glance, there. She is reminding me that I also tend to talk too much sometimes anyway. But I am telling a story here, Otter! I cannot do so without talking!

Well, we have had our chuckle, my friends. And I thank you, Otter. I will try to stay with the story. Where was I? Oh, yes! The bones . . .

The pattern of the bones on the painted skin was exceedingly strange and unusual. Some of the objects are heavier than others, so some usually can be expected to bounce farther. . . . Ah, I have done it again! Forget that. . . . It is enough to say that the bouncing fetishes came to rest in completely unexpected places. It was very difficult to interpret. In looking for a general pattern, I found none of the signs for which I sought. Again, it is hard to explain without explaining, no?

So an overall description, the one I should have given at first. I sought to impress you with how unusual it was. There were indications of a far journey and of a horse, as I said. Signs of danger . . . They are always there, because is not life itself fraught with danger? Then some of the other indicators . . . man, woman, strangers, customs other than our own. Strange creatures. Enemies . . . It was a little frightening.

And over all, I still had no idea of what I was meant to do. There was the strong suggestion of a quest. But for what? I was made to think that I must learn more about the horse with the medicine hat. Yet I knew not where or how, much less *why*.

One pattern seemed to emerge, though, in the casting of the bones. When a holy man does this ceremony, he faces to the east. This deals with the future, so the rising sun . . . well, you know these things. . . .

Now all of the pattern established by the skittering, bouncing bones and fetishes had a tendency to move to my left farther than usual. *North!* Did this establish a *direction* for the quest that I now felt I must take? Or was it only that I am right-handed and *cast* to the left? Maybe I tossed a trifle harder than usual, because of my uneasiness over this odd sequence of happenings and the importance that it seemed to hold.

Then it finally came to me, that in the whole plan of things, it would not matter. The fact that I am right-handed would be known to those in whatever realms of the spirit are involved. That would be taken into consideration and allowed for, as we would allow for a side breeze in shooting an arrow. Such things would be a very small problem to the spirits.

So I began to see the strong suggestion of a quest to the north. Yet I still had no clear call, and no idea what I was to search for. I was impatient.

Singing Wolf always said that during my apprentice years. "You are impatient, Pup." He always called me by that childish name, Wolf Pup, even after I became Pipe Bearer. He was more likely to do it if I was being a bit childish. It was a mild scolding, maybe.

Well, I am still impatient, though I am better about it now. At that time I was younger, and eager to begin whatever it was that I was meant to do. And I did not know. I talked to Singing Wolf about it, seeking advice. I was further frustrated when his advice did not please me.

"Wait," he said. "If this is a thing you are meant to do, you will be told. So wait!"

Aiee, that was hard, my friends. I knew that it was a quest, and that I must do it, but I knew nothing more. I must wait for a more definite sign. I could not have done that either, without the support of my wife, Otter Woman. She managed to remind me what I must do. And if all else failed, she always had the ability to *distract* me. I could forget everything else for a little while in her arms.

Now, where was I? The thoughts of Otter still distract me, no? Ah, she blushes!

Ah, yes . . . I was waiting for a sign. I was expecting it to come as the first sign of all this had, in a dream. There was none.

"Are you sure?" Otter would ask me. "Maybe you dreamed and have forgotten when you came awake."

"No," I said. "This dream, when it comes, I will not be *able* to forget."

So it did not come. Did you ever notice, friends, that many times it is so? Something that we expect, or even think we *know* must happen? When it finally does, it is in some completely different and unexpected way than we thought. Sometimes I am made to think that the spirits have a wonderful sense of humor. Is it not so?

Now, when the signs came, telling of my quest, it was nothing at all as I had expected. It was in common and everyday things. Maybe my spirit-guide needed to remind me again that I must be observant. One grows lazy about that very easily.

It was a warm evening late in the Moon of Greening. I was restless, and I had been watching the geese fly northward. *Maybe that in itself is my sign*, I thought. But no. When I thought about it, I realized that geese *always* fly north in that moon. And always there is a stirring in the human spirit that seems to be an urge to go with them. I have thought about that many times. . . . Well, that is not my story, is it?

My purpose in walking out of the camp on that evening was not a very important one. I was restless, and went for a walk. Otter was cooking, and the sun was low. A wonderful sunset . . . I found myself near the horse herd and thought that I might take a look at the foal that seemed to hold such importance in this mystery. Why, I had no idea. Even now . . . Well, let me go on.

I found the colt and his mother, and watched them a little while. I was impressed once more with the quality of this animal. He was growing rapidly. The dark mousy hair was nearly gone, and his true color, brighter and new, was reflected in the setting sun. A light, *very* light blue roan, and with the dark points and the medicine hat.

"Can *you* not tell me about it?" I asked him, but he only snorted, bucked, and sprinted away in a big circle around his mother. My eyes followed him, and only a short distance beyond, I suddenly realized that there was a coyote sitting and watching.

Not that such a thing is unusual, of course. Since Creation, Man and his brother Coyote have shared the kill. Our Old Man of the Shadows, the trickster, loves to appear as a coyote. Here, of course, was no kill, and the animal seemed only to be watching out of curiosity. He is certainly not a danger to a colt of several weeks' age.

But there is another thing. My medicine animal is a coyote. As you know, some of our neighboring tribes do not reveal such a thing to others. Among the People, even, there are some to whom that is a private matter. Yet I have no qualms in revealing my helper. That is as it should be. We cannot all think exactly alike, and *should* not, or nobody would ever learn anything, no?

Yes, Otter, I will stick to the story. . . .

The coyote stared at me, and I felt its spirit reach out. Even then it took a few moments for me to realize that this was no ordinary coyote, but *my spirit-guide*. The look in the eyes, the quality of his fur and his appearance in the odd slanting rays of the setting sun . . . It is hard to describe. . . .

I had the strong impression that he was laughing at me. That has happened before. Usually, when I have been feeling overconfident, sure that I know more than I really do. I am fortunate, maybe, to have a medicine guide who keeps me humble. I usually need all the help I can find, but I forget that.

"*Ah-koh*, Uncle," I said respectfully, and waited.

The coyote cocked his head to one side and seemed amused.

"What is it that I must do?" I asked.

My answer, you understand, does not come in words. The guide sends a *thought* into one's head. I am sure you have felt this, sometimes. In this case I knew from experience that my guide would make me work for any information I might receive. And I am made to think that he loves to tease me.

"Why do you wait?" This thought popped into my head.

"I . . . I wait for a sign, Uncle," I mumbled.

I had the impression that he was laughing at me, inside. Somehow I always feel childish and a little bit stupid in the presence of my guide. But after he is gone there is an uplift. . . . I get ahead of my story, here.

"What more sign do you want?" came the thought. "The dream, the horse, your bones . . ."

I began to see. I had been given all the information that I might need. I had been waiting for a plan to be given me, and that part was to be mine.

"Must I do your thinking, too?" the thought struck me, placed there as if my guide had spoken aloud.

"But Uncle, I . . . ," I stammered.

The coyote rose, stretched and yawned, and turned away up the slope and among the rocks. In an instant he was gone. Not in the distance or behind a rock or clump of grass. Just *gone*. One moment he was there, and the next he was not. It happened so before, when I was visited by my guide.

What? How often does my guide come to me? *Aiee*, I do not know! Not often. When I need him, I think. But never, ever when I expect. Maybe when I need to be reminded of my own shortcomings, or when I become too proud. . . .

Anyway, the coyote was gone. The evening was turning purple with the shadows as the last flicker of fire from Sun Boy's torch slipped behind earth's rim. In the far distance I heard the chortling cry of a coyote. Not my guide, but an actual flesh-and-blood coyote. Or is there any difference? I do not know. But I thought that the creature was laughing at me, in my lack of understanding.

Another coyote called an answer, and something struck me. *Both* were to the north.

Yes, maybe I did have all the signs that I needed. The medicine-hat horse, *twice* . . . once in my dream, then in a foal born to my own mare. A mare from the *north*. The bones, a toss suggesting north. Coyotes singing, geese . . .

I had not seen a pattern emerging here, until the coyotes . . . well, my guide . . . It had been necessary, almost, for my guide to paint me a picture. But at last I understood. Not completely, but enough to make a start. I was to make a quest-journey, to the north. Somehow, sometime, and somewhere, more would be revealed to me.

3

Thank you, my husband. . . . It is good for me to tell part of the story, friends, because it is not mine or that of Pipe Bearer, but *ours.* Is it not so with any event that affects a person? It also involves his family and those around him.

Now, as my husband has said, there were strange events going on that spring. I was aware of part of it. The horse . . . ah, what a foal that was! I knew that Pipe Bearer . . . ("Pup," I always called him, as his grandfather did, and for the same reason. It is a pet name since our childhood.) I knew that he was struggling with a big decision. He conferred often with his grandfather, and when Pup cast the bones, I could see that he was troubled. I was there, as he has said. I had begun to learn much of the holy man's ceremony and ritual and was beginning to understand something of the bones.

I *saw* that ceremony, and even I could tell that this was very unusual. I will never forget the way the little fetishes seemed to come alive and jump around. *Aiee*, it was a little bit frightening. But as the wife of a holy man, I had also begun to become accustomed to such things. One sees things happen that are outside the usual happenings, around the lodge of a holy man. Something occurs that is not of the usual world. One thinks *I know that cannot happen, but I just saw it happen*. Yes, you chuckle, but you know I speak truth! You have seen.

Well, it was that way when my husband cast the bones that spring morning. I had an idea what they were telling him, and I was alarmed. I could already tell that he was considering a quest of some sort. In fact, he had mentioned it. Pup had been greatly troubled by his dream, and we had talked of it.

But after the casting of the bones, he became different. He was withdrawn. For the first time since our marriage, he was distant, and he wanted to walk alone to think and pray. I was hurt a little bit, because I wanted to be a part of everything that happened to him. But in this I was feeling shut out, maybe. I knew that there are places in the life of a holy man that even his wife may not go with him. Yet this was my first experience with it, and I was hurt. We had been so close, always.

I went to talk to Rain, who was the wife of Singing Wolf. They were the grandparents of my husband, you know. We lived with them after our marriage, while Wolf Pup learned the ways of the holy man. And while I, of course, learned the ways of the holy man's wife. Ah, Rain was a help to me! She knew and understood the problems, not only of a holy man's wife, but of any young wife. I still miss her counsel, though both are gone many seasons now. . . . But I will continue the story.

I went to Rain and told her of my hurt. Always before we had shared our joys and sorrows, Pup and I. I felt that I was losing him, and to what, I did not know.

"Yes, Otter," this wonderful old lady said, "I know. It is the way of men, sometimes. Especially men such as ours, who have been given gifts of the spirit."

"But he is troubled, and I cannot help him," I told her.

"Yes, you *can*, child," Rain told me.

"But how, Grandmother?"

"Well, one is to let him be alone to think. He needs that right now. He is working with a problem and needs to listen to whatever guidance he may be trying to receive. So just be patient, but do not ask him to explain."

"You said that is one way, Grandmother. There are others?"

"Of course. One other, anyway." Rain's old eyes twinkled as she told me this. "Even with his problems, he is still a man. And you are a woman. Quite a woman, I am made to think," she teased me. "You can distract him sometimes. I *know* this." We had lived in their lodge. . . . Yes, I said that before. But she went on: "You will know when, in the privacy of your lodge. You can do much to help him, but do not push him too hard. *Let* it happen. . . ."

Ah, I see my husband laughing. Yes, he remembers. We chuckled about this later, and his grandmother's advice to me. I was made to think that, even at her age . . . Well, never mind. Let me go on.

When Pup finally had the experience that led to his decision, it was very hard for me. He must go, he said, on a quest to the north. He did not know where or why. Now, even though I already knew that the wife of a holy man must make many sacrifices, I was not prepared for this. Yes, I was angry, and I felt abandoned. We had been married only a few moons . . . less than a full season.

I sought the advice of Rain again.

"I have failed," I told her. "He is leaving me!"

"Nonsense, child," the old woman said. "It has nothing to do with you."

"Then why . . . ?"

"It is a call. Something he must do. That is all."

"But how can I . . . Rain, I cannot move our lodge alone when the band goes to the Sun Dance, and to summer camp. I *need* him."

"Yes, child, and for other things, too. I know. I could tell you . . . Now, look! Others could help with your lodge. Your brothers, the family of your husband. But maybe there is a better way."

"What is that, Grandmother?"

I realized that Rain was studying my body. Especially my belly.

"You are not with child yet?" she asked.

"No . . . we have been married only . . ."

The old woman waved a hand to stop me.

"It is not that," she said bluntly, "but if you were, it might make a difference."

"What difference? I do not understand."

"All the difference, child. If you were pregnant, it would be a bigger responsibility for him. Since you are not, it is no matter."

"Then what . . . ?"

"Go with him, child! Go on the quest with him!"

Now, I had not even thought of that. You know that among the People it is not unusual for a young wife, before they have children, to hunt with her husband. Girls learn the use of weapons in the Rabbit Society with the boys. There are even young women who go on war parties sometimes. But I had not even thought of this.

"Do you think that he would let me go with him?" I asked.

"I am made to think," Rain chuckled, with the twinkle in her eye, "that you can convince him."

And it was so. We planned it carefully. At first no talk of that possibility. Only mention, at carefully chosen intimate moments, of how *I* would miss *him*. Then playful teasing, a mock refusal of activity in the robes. I told him how much he would miss *me*, and that he must learn to do without me. Of course I did not carry through with that threat, but it made him think.

"Your lodge and your bed," Rain told me, "must look to him like the most desirable place in the world."

That, I must admit, was not difficult, because he already thought so. But what if I had pouted and been angry about his leaving? Ah, you see? Rain and I continued to plan.

Our object, mine and Rain's, was to make Pipe Bearer believe that it was his idea for me to go along. That is one of the ways of women of the People, to make our men feel so. A way of all women, maybe, but I cannot speak for all. Maybe not all women are as clever as women of the People. It is known, of course, that our women are prettier. At least, that is what the old men say. Who am I to argue the truths of the elders? Ah, yes, I joke. I will stick to the story.

Ah, my husband, I see you looking puzzled over there, as if you did not know that women plan such things. But you know. . . . And we know each other. . . . We did not know each other as well then as we do now, with many winters and a lodge full of children.

We had only a few days to plan, while the two holy men, my husband and his grandfather, planned the quest. It was necessary for him to decide what to take, how many horses, such things as that.

Rain and I were preparing some odds and ends for him to take. A pair of extra moccasins, a new shirt . . . I had decorated the shirt with both quills and the new glass beads of the French trader. A man should have a means to dress up a little if the need arises for ceremony. If not, well, he may wear out one shirt on such a trip. He should have another. Gray Mouse, mother of my husband, helped us to prepare a pack of dried meat and pemmican for his journey. We worked together on that, but on the rest of the plan, only Rain and I. . . .

Singing Wolf suggested that Pipe Bearer should have some reason for travel. He had such reason, of course, but it might be hard to explain. Especially to those who speak another tongue. And, of course, there is danger there. The northern tribes are mighty warriors. Well, that is apparent by the hand signs. Some of the strongest are Lakota, and you know their sign: "People-who-cut-your-throat" . . . *Aiee!* And *they* have enemies. Crow, Blackfeet . . .

But I get ahead of my story. Anyway, it would be dangerous at best. Singing Wolf suggested a disguise. My husband could pretend to be a trader. Traders are usually immune to local politics, because they are useful. True, anyone *could* kill a traveling trader, but the word would soon be out, and no one would come to trade there. So Pup could appear to be a trader, and no one would question. He could then pursue anything he could find out about his quest as he went.

I thought that this was an excellent idea, and I mentioned so to Rain. Yes, she said, it seemed so to her, too. There was the twinkle in her eye, and as I look back, I am made to think that maybe *she* suggested this to Singing Wolf and let him think of it. But this I am only guessing.

"When the time is right," Rain told me, "we will let them notice that most traders have a wife!"

But another problem arose. A trader must have something to trade, and we had nothing. The Southern band had been impoverished by the destruction of the Big Whirlwind. We had been able to recover and to winter well, but still there was little to trade in the entire band.

Pup's story, Singing Wolf suggested, could *be* that of the tragedy: It had been necessary to undertake trade for the purpose of recovery. A few furs, said to be already taken in trade, a few robes. These could be borrowed from family and friends. But, still . . . It was Stone Breaker, boyhood friend of Wolf Pup, who came forth with the suggestion that solved the problem. Stone Breaker was, and still is, the expert maker of arrowheads and spear points. Knives and scrapers too, of course, but the artistry of his points is famous. Yes, I know that the metal knives and arrow points are becoming popular. Still, many prefer the artistry of the crafted edge. There are those who say it cuts better, too. But these are things for the old men to argue. I know only that our friend Stone Breaker, who took the name and the craft from his father and his father before, was quite helpful. He brought a pouch of twenty or thirty knives and small points. They were of our fine-quality gray-blue flint from the Sacred Hills.

"You have traded all the rest for the furs you will carry," he explained. "Or so says your story."

This man is a good friend, and this appeared to be exactly what was needed. One pack horse, loosely packed, as if by an amateur. A man who is not really a trader, but driven to it by circumstances. That part would not be hard to pretend! My husband could appear to be inept quite easily.

Oh, never mind, Pup. You can have a say, too. You see, my friends, Pup and I have come to understand and appreciate each other quite well. The pack horse is a private joke.

But the story . . . We must get this quest started, no? Here, Pipe Bearer! You tell this part!

4

Well, it was as Otter has said. I was preparing to portray a trader as I traveled north. I would take a horse to ride, and a pack horse, with what pretended to be trade goods. What *was* trade goods, actually, but the goods of a very poor trader.

But there was a problem. I had been tormented from the first about whether to take the foal who wore the medicine hat. To try to inquire about such a horse, to ask people who speak different tongues, would be difficult. Especially in hand signs. Can you imagine trying to ask about a horse wearing a fur hat . . . ? Well, you see!

It would be much more effective to have the colt along. Imagine again . . . I could lead the animal into a camp or village and watch the people for a reaction or recognition. Let *them* ask the questions. Or if there were none, I could then inquire. Hand signs would be simple: Point to the colt and give only the sign for a question. It is the same, of course, for what, where, how, when, even "Do you know anything about this?" If they use the same hand signs there, *and they must*, I thought, I would only be asking, "Tell me of this colt if you know." It would be better to take him along.

But now rose other problems. To take a nursing foal meant to take his mother. I could ride the mare but did not want to do so, for a number of reasons. My size and weight, of course. The roan mare could handle that, but it would be hard on her, and I wanted her in the best condition to feed the foal.

I thought of using her as the pack horse but hesitated to do so. A mare of such quality, used as a pack animal, would not be good. A stranger would see this and think, "*Aiee*, how stupid can this trader be?" Both I and my roan mare should have more pride, no?

There was yet another danger, however. I had traded fairly for the mare, but she had probably been stolen, maybe more than once. And from someone to the north. There was a possibility that when I reached the north country, someone would recognize the animal. She *was* special, you know.

After long soul-searching, I felt that it was a risk that I must take. Maybe I could talk my way out. The risks were worth the advantages, but I still had the problem of *how* to take the mare and foal. Ride one horse and lead two, plus a loose foal? It could be done, but with difficulty.

I talked of this with Singing Wolf, who sat, silently lost in thought as he usually did while he pondered a problem. He half closed his eyes. Finally he nodded slightly and spoke.

"I am made to think that you should take him with you."

I had already realized that, of course, and said so. My grandfather nodded again.

"I know," he said. "Let me think on this, Pup."

This time he was quiet for so long that I thought he was asleep, with his eyes squinted, half-closed, you know. But finally he moved, cleared his throat, and spoke.

"Let us sleep on it."

Naturally, I was disappointed. I had sought my answer right then, while we talked. He saw my disappointment.

"You are still too impatient, Pup," he said.

Then he rose and walked away, stooping to enter his lodge. I was irritated and did not sleep well that night.

But next morning, before I had even left the robes, Singing Wolf was at our door, shaking the door rattle and calling my name. And, yes, he actually said, "Pipe Bearer."

"A moment, Grandfather," I called, scrambling up. One does not keep an elder waiting.

I ducked through the doorway and stood in the chill morning air, still trying to come awake.

"I am made to think," Singing Wolf said, "that I know how to solve your question."

His eyes were shining, and I could tell that he was excited. Almost like a child at the Sun Dance.

"How? What?" I stammered.

"You should take Otter Woman with you!"

"*What?*"

"Of course. Think about it. You ride any horse you like, and lead a pack horse. Let Otter ride the mare, and the foal will follow."

"But . . . Grandfather, I had not thought to take Otter with me. There may be danger."

"Of course. There may be danger here, too. But you will be together. And think, Pup: How many traders have you ever seen who travel *without* a wife? Sometimes more than one wife. It will help to give the idea that you are a trader, no?"

Now, I was having a hard time grasping all of this. I was still half-asleep. I did not know at the time, of course, that this was part of a plan. Otter and my grandmother had waited for the right moment, when the question would arise. They knew that Singing Wolf always talked over his problems with Rain. So they had planned and waited.

When Singing Wolf had been wrestling with this problem of mine, my grandmother had watched, waited, and finally inquired. He explained the dilemma that I faced. Rain then seemed to ponder a long time and finally suggested that he take someone to help with the horses. This seemed like a good idea, but *who*?

You realize that I knew nothing of this until much later. I learned the whole story from Otter.

"Who could go with him?" my grandmother pondered. "A person of smaller weight could ride the mare. One of the young men, maybe? *Aiee*, mostly the traders who stop with us have a helper, no?"

"Yes. Usually it is his wife," Singing Wolf answered.

Then, according to Rain's story, the eyes of Singing Wolf grew big and round. This big . . . He let out an exclamation.

"*Aiee!* Of course! I should have seen it sooner. Otter can go with him, Rain! She will make a believable trader's wife."

It was late at night, but Rain had all she could do, to prevent her husband from rousing us to tell of his marvelous idea. I am made to think that Singing Wolf always thought that the idea was his. *I* thought so, until Otter told me, later. Otter could keep still no longer and wanted to share the joke with me.

Aiee, my friends, it is frightening, no? Who knows how many ways our women conspire against us to accomplish what they would have us do? Yet, is it not a joy to let them do this to us? Yes, Red Dog, I see the doubt in your eyes. And you are thinking that it works well when a husband and wife are such good friends as Otter and I are to each other, no? But how did we become such friends?

Ah, let me see, now, as the laughter quiets down. . . . Where was I in my story? Oh, yes!

Singing Wolf left, and I cautiously approached Otter about the proposed plan. I did not know, of course, that she and Rain had thought of it and had worked on this from the start. Otter seemed reluctant for a little while but allowed me to talk her into this plan. I thought, of course, that I was a marvelously convincing talker. And, of course, she allowed me to think so. Ah, well . . .

With this altering of the plan, the preparations took on some change. We would need more supplies, which were no problem. We must pick our horses and make certain that they were in good condition. They were thin, of course, from the winter. But the grass was coming on, and the horses looked better every day. More sleek and thrifty.

This condition of the horses would be very important, you see. Our horses must spend about half the time eating, or they would begin to lose weight and could not travel well. On a trip such as this, that could be very dangerous. What sort of country would we find to the north?

Otter began to ride the roan mare a little. To become acquainted with each other, and to develop the trust that is needed between horse and rider . . . You know how important, my friends!

This also let the colt become used to following his mother. It would save much trouble, maybe, if he already knew that. We would not have to spend the first few days helping him to learn it.

It was a sight to see, friends, the beautiful mare, ridden by a beautiful woman. And the colt . . . he seemed to catch the excitement. They would travel along across the rolling prairie. . . . I rode with them sometimes, to condition my own horse. . . . The colt would run in circles around his mother, bucking and kicking high. Sometimes he would rush at my horse and then shy away at the last moment. Maybe a playful kick as he passed. Ah, what spirit, my friends. I could see that here was a fine hunter or a war horse in the making.

Finally came the day. We would leave at sunrise the next morning. My mother was sad, but she knew that we must do this thing, go on the quest. I had been called to do this. Singing Wolf prayed and offered tobacco, a pinch on the morning fire.

"I have cast the bones," he told me aside. "I am made to think that the signs are good. Some strange signs, but . . ."

"*What* strange signs, Grandfather?" I asked him.

"Nothing that I can recognize," he told me. "You know, Pup. You had the same thing, no?"

Well, that was true. I *had* experienced the same, the trouble interpreting my roll of the bones. But I had assumed that it was because of my inexperience. I did not want to say too much, and neither did my grandfather. As you know, it is not good to anticipate bad things, and it may even cause them to happen. So neither of us wanted to say much.

Regardless, though, Singing Wolf did seem to feel strongly that there was a favorable tone to the spirit of this quest. I felt this, too, and so did Otter. It was exciting, the thought of new country, new sights and sounds and smells and customs. The quest for new *knowledge*, when we come right down to it. Yes, that was how it felt. We were on the edge of great truths, and I felt good about it. It was good to know that my grandfather did, too.

"But be careful!" Singing Wolf advised. "There are always dangers in the path of anyone who is not alert."

I was impatient, of course. I was younger then and felt that my grandfather should know that I would be careful. Is it not always so when a young person comes of age? It is a part of leaving the lodge of one's family, no? He thinks he knows everything, and his parents know that he does not but are unable to tell him. In my own case, Otter and I had already established our lodge, yet did not know . . .

There was a sight that we saw on our first afternoon of travel. At the time it was only amusing.

A pair of young eagles were just learning to fly. We saw the nest in a tall cottonwood, and the parents circling above, calling to their young. One of the young birds was sitting in a little tree, not much higher than a man can reach. I thought that maybe it was hunting rabbits, but then I saw the other eaglet. It was standing on the ground, and I realized that the young had just left the nest, probably that morning.

They were great ungainly things, awkward in motion like a young man when he starts to grow and his voice is changing. They looked larger than the parent birds. Then the one on the ground took to the air, trying with all his might to fly to a tree about a bow shot from where we were riding. He was tiring quickly but managed to sweep upward to grasp the low branch of a sycamore.

But he was exhausted. Though he had managed to reach upward and grab with one foot, he did not have the strength to pull himself up. So he just hung there, head down, by one leg, not knowing what to do next. The parent birds circled and screamed.

Finally as we sat laughing, the eaglet seemed to decide that there was nothing much that he *could* do. His grasp loosened, and he fell like a rock, landing with a thud.

He was not injured, of course. He fell from no higher than my head. He got up immediately and flew to a lower perch on another tree. As I said, it was quite amusing, the embarrassed look on the face of the young bird.

Later, I came to think that it had been a sign, a warning as we tried our own wings in the country to the north.

5

We traveled well. The colt was old enough to be able to keep up with a normal rate of movement. Actually, he was strong enough to do better than that. With all the circling and running ahead and back, that foal probably covered each day three times the distance that we did.

But it was no time at all until we fell into a daily routine. Sleep, get up, and travel, with short rest stops, of course. Make camp before dark, hobble the horses for the night. It was much like when we were first married, and we were enjoying each other, and the joy of just being together, with no one to intrude. Coyotes sang us to sleep each evening. We snuggled in our sleeping robes against the chill of the spring nights, and we woke to the morning songs of birds.

We did see some people from time to time. Villages of Growers. We stopped to talk to them sometimes, telling them that we were going north to trade for a season. It is strange, my friends. At first I thought that we would find that people would doubt our story. I was prepared to have to convince the listeners of our mission.

It was not like that at all. No one even questioned such a tale. It was as if no one cared. No, not that, either. It seemed that the Growers assumed that if we wanted to do such a thing, it was no concern of theirs. Would that be a fair description, Otter? Yes, thank you.

We did no trading at first, did not even open our packs. After all, people who live near us have access to most of the goods we do, no? The people we met just seemed to assume that it was so.

It was a little different, the first time we encountered a real trader. We had reached a good camping place, one where there was a big spring, and evidence that here was a traditional stopping place for travelers.

Our People usually travel with the whole band, or in hunting parties, who go only a day or two from the main camp. But we were beginning to learn something about this travel. A trader, for instance, or a person on a long quest, is following a trail, no matter how faint. Somebody has followed it before, no? Maybe deer or antelope, or a lone buffalo. But each has looked for the easiest walking, so they seek out the same path, the one that is best. Some of these become well-worn roads, like the Southwest Trail, which leads to Santa Fe and the towns of the Spanish.

But you know this. What I was trying to explain, which we had not known before, was that on the smaller trails, everyone has about the same speed, that of a walking person or a walking horse. Everyone moves about the same distance in a day. So it is not unusual to arrive at a place each evening where someone else has camped. In fact, we soon came to expect it. Someone who passed that way before had located the best camp site and the best water.

I wondered sometimes when the *first* traveler stopped there. Many lifetimes ago, probably. The spirit of some of these camping places does feel very old. Maybe they go back all the way to Creation. Well, no matter. I was only voicing some thoughts.

What I had started to say was that the first time we encountered other travelers was a surprise. I do not know why it should have been, but we had been distracted by each other and our shared solitude. It was as if we were the only two people in the world sometimes. In some of the Creation stories of other tribes, you know, there are only two people at first, First Man and First Woman. We felt like that, when we would go a day or two and see no one. Sometimes we even avoided an area where we suspected there would be a village. Yes, just to pretend a little longer, I suppose. A childish game, maybe, but what joy we were sharing, starting out together.

But on this evening we had just made camp. We started our fire and offered a pinch of tobacco to recognize the local spirits. This was a camp site where two trails seemed to cross. Both were faint. We were following the north-south road, and the trader came from the west along the other.

We heard the horses approaching from about a bow shot away, and I glanced around to see to our weapons and the safety of our animals. We were in an area where there are more trees, near the River of the Kenzas, and we could not see as far as usual.

The man rode into the camp, waved a hand sign in greeting, and swung down from the saddle.

"We saw your smoke!" he signed.

He was of middle age, appeared friendly, and seemed not to think it out of the ordinary at all to encounter someone else at his intended camp site. We came to realize that in fact it is not unusual.

Behind him a woman who appeared to be his wife dismounted stiffly and began to establish their camp. Each had been leading a pack horse, and it was easy to see that here was a trader. A *real* trader, and I was a little anxious about how they would regard us.

I need not have worried. A trader, by being a trader, must be able to meet people well and quickly. We learned a lot about that in a very short time. This man ran a quick glance over our horses, our packs, and ourselves, and seemed to have learned what he needed.

"I am called Trader," he said in hand signs. "That is also my nation. How are you called?"

In this way we learned that they were Arapaho, the Trader People, and not potential enemies. We began to relax.

"We are of the Elk-dog People," I signed. "Southern band."

The trader smiled broadly and spoke aloud, and in our tongue.

"It is good! We know your Mountain band and speak your tongue."

He glanced at our packs and asked casually, "You are traders?"

I was about to begin our explanation about what we were doing, when a light dawned in his face, and he spoke yet again.

"Ah, yes! Yours was the band that was struck by the Big Whirlwind. Last season, no? Your people told us."

"That is true, Uncle," I told him.

"Ah! That must have been hard. You lost everything, no? Lodges?"

"Yes. We had very little. A good hunt in the fall. We were able to winter well."

"If you are alive, you have wintered well . . . a saying of ours . . ."

I was made to think that he wanted to ask more but did not want to seem impolite. I decided to help him.

"I am Pipe Bearer. This, my wife, Otter Woman. We decided to trade a little."

"You have no children?"

"Not yet. We have been married only a few moons. Times were hard in our band, and it seemed a good time to try something."

The trader nodded. "Why not? But have you trade goods?"

"Not much. We . . . the whole band, that is, traded meat and skins to the Growers after the hunt. Mostly meat. We needed the skins for lodge covers."

"Of course. So now . . . ?"

He was probing for information now. It probably seemed to him that something was not quite right. There must be more to the story. I hurried on.

"This was just an idea, to get out of our own area to trade. We had a supply of flint knives and points. . . . Here, let me show you!"

I had packed a few points for easy access and drew out a pouch to show him.

"Ah, yes," he said. "The blue-gray! Good stone! Did you do this work?"

"No, no, Uncle. A friend . . . Stone Breaker, he is called."

"I can see why. He is truly skilled. But many want metal knives and points, now. It is not like the old days of trading. For what do you trade?"

"Anything of value, Uncle. Otter Woman and I are new at this, as I said. We only hoped to find a few furs, something to trade to the French to the east of here."

"And how does it go?"

I shrugged, hoping to make it seem casual. I pointed to our packs.

"Not bad . . . not good, either. But we have just started."

"Where do you go?"

It was just at that moment that the medicine-hat colt came running past, bucking and kicking. Otter had released the mare, who was rolling luxuriously in the grass.

"*Aiee!*" the trader said softly. He was obviously greatly impressed by the colt but said nothing at the moment.

"You are going . . . ?" he resumed the previous conversation.

"We had not decided. Somewhere north."

"North of the River?"

"Yes, probably. Maybe to the Platte or beyond."

He nodded. "You know the Pawnees? Horn People?"

"Yes. Not well. Do you trade with them?"

"We do. They are enemies to many. They are different, Pipe Bearer. You can trade with them, but their customs are strange. Be careful."

I was made to think that this was merely an open and friendly caution. The trader said no more about the horse, and I saw no reason to call attention to it.

We camped near each other, and the women quickly began to visit too. It was a pleasant evening.

The next morning, as we prepared to part, the trader brought up the subject of the horse.

"Would you sell the roan mare?"

I was startled. "The colt is a suckling," I protested. "He must have milk!"

"Of course. I would take him, too. He is not much, but he may grow up to be acceptable. I have some goods, and you need something to trade to the Pawnees."

Now, by the way that he was talking down the qualities of the colt, I realized that he was not really interested in the mare but would trade for her to get the foal. So he must know something that we did not. I longed to ask him, but it was necessary to play the game.

"That is true," I said casually. "But my wife rides the mare, and we need the other horse for packs. No, I cannot trade."

He thought for a moment and then spoke. "I am probably crazy, but I like the mare. I will offer trade goods and your choice of any of my horses for your mare. And her foal, of course."

Well, the mare was good. There was no doubt about that. But I saw that the horses of the trader couple were the best of animals. I smiled, and he realized that he had overplayed his offer.

"No," I told him. "The mare and foal are not for trade."

Now he smiled ruefully. "I had to try," he said, turning away.

"Wait," I called. "Tell me of this colt."

His eyes widened. "I thought that *you* must know. I have seen only one horse with such a marking, the medicine hat. That was many seasons ago. It was considered a sacred animal."

"Where? By whom?" I asked eagerly.

"The north, somewhere. I cannot remember which nation. Shosone, maybe . . . no, Lakota . . . ah, I do not know."

"So you only wanted him to trade."

"Yes, of course. To someone he has great importance."

"But you cannot remember who?"

"That is true. But others in the area would know. You knew some of this, no? That is why you travel north?"

"Yes, partly. Well, we are on a quest." I saw no harm in telling him such a thing. He had been very helpful.

Now he nodded understanding. "But be careful."

"Of course."

"No. Especially so. There are those who would steal the colt, because they know his importance, better than you or I."

"Who?" I blurted. I was made to think that I could trust this man, now that we were no longer horse trading.

"Anyone! First, Pawnees. They know horses well. Then as you go beyond the Platte, any people you encounter. Especially hunter tribes. Buffalo hunters. Growers, not so likely. Of course there are fewer Growers to the north. But anyone who wants to take the risk . . . a quick trade."

"I thank you for the warning, Uncle. May you have a good season."

"And you! Whatever you seek. One other thing . . . keep a close eye on *all* your horses. To steal horses is to prove manhood among many tribes. So be careful!"

6

It is as my husband has said. That unexpected evening with the Arapaho trader and his wife was very important to us, though it did not seem so at the time. But we had been allowed to see a real trader and his wife. We saw how they did things, some of how they thought.

I had talked to the wife while the men were discussing horses, and it helped me greatly. The woman was of one of the northern tribes, and told me of their country. Open, big skies . . . much like our Sacred Hills, she said. To be in the country of the People, our people, always made her long for her home.

I wondered about that. Usually when a man marries into one of the other hunter tribes, *he* joins *them*, you know. But she did not explain further, and I thought it would not be polite to ask. That is their way, and no concern to me.

She did tell me more about the Pawnees. She and her husband were on good terms with them, though many neighboring people consider them enemies. The biggest problem, she said, is that the Pawnees occasionally steal a girl from another tribe. There has always been some of that, of course. Sometimes a girl is "stolen" willingly, as a wife.

This Pawnee custom, however, is part of their religion, the woman told me. Whatever anyone's religion, of course, is his own problem. Like everyone else, the People have customs, and things that are forbidden. We do not kill bears, but our allies, the Head Splitters do. That is *their* problem.

I mention this only to tell you of the difference with the Pawnees. The trader's wife talked of this in great detail, because it is so foreign to any custom of her people or those of her husband. Well, to ours, too. Every few seasons the Pawnees must find a new bride for their Great Spirit, Morning Star. She is treated with great honor, but when the ceremony is held, the bride is killed with a sacred arrow. She cannot become the bride of Morning Star unless she crosses over, you see.

But what causes the anger of their neighbors is this: The bride is not one of their *own* maidens, but one stolen from another tribe. When another's worship begins to harm *me*, *aiee!* It is no longer his problem, but *mine*!

I told her that we had heard rumors of this custom, but not in this much detail. We have had contact with Pawnees, have even traded with them some. One of our kin even had a Pawnee wife a few generations ago. But this . . .

The woman told me that there was nothing to fear. This was not the year that they would need the ceremony. They had held it only two seasons ago. Besides, they would want only a maiden. Still, I felt that I would be very uncomfortable around the Pawnees. But more of that later.

The other thing that was of great interest was the woman's reaction to the medicine-hat colt. I had seen her face at her first glimpse of the colt and saw that she must consider it of great importance. She tried not to show that, of course. At least not until after her husband had made his try to buy or trade for it. When we saw that there was to be no trade, both of us were amused at the serious way our husbands had tried to maneuver. We laughed about it, but not to them, of course.

But I learned from her, more than Pipe Bearer did from the trader. A horse with this medicine-hat marking is known to her people, and is very special. Very *rare*. To them, she said, this would be a sacred animal.

"What must its owner do, among your people?" I asked her. With any good fortune comes responsibility, does it not?

No special requirements, she said. It was, to her people, mostly an honor to possess such a horse. Prestige, maybe political power. To a leader, riding such a horse into battle, for instance, would not only protect him, but inspire his followers. And surely, good luck and success would follow in whatever he might attempt. So we began to understand a little more of the medicine of the horse who wears the hat.

When we parted that morning, it was on good terms.

"May our trails cross again!" the woman told me, and my heart was made good toward her. She recognized our youth and our innocence and tried to help us.

Our husbands, too, felt good toward each other, I think. They had been able to talk of horses and trade, and when they found that there was no trade to be had, the subject was dropped. It is so with traders, and we were beginning to learn.

We moved on to the north, and the Arapaho couple to the east. I really hoped that we would meet again.

Our biggest problem now was how to cross the river. The big river, the Kenza. We knew that it was only a day's travel or less from where we camped with the trader. As it happened, Pipe Bearer had asked about it, and the trader had told us.

"Turn west a little," he suggested. "You should find a trail. . . . This one you are following divides, and the east branch leads to some villages along the river. Kenzas, mostly . . . South Wind People. Their big town is four, five sleeps to the east. Well, near the French trading posts. You know that area. The other branch will take you to the river crossing . . . some sandbars and an island. We have not crossed there for a season or two, and the sand shifts, you know. Oh, yes . . . you will have to swim the horses part of the way, but the river will not be high."

"How do you know this, Uncle?"

The trader shrugged, as if anyone should know such a simple thing.

"Too early. The snow melt has not filled the rivers yet, and there have been few spring rains in the country of my people."

It was as he said, but the river still looked wide and deep. We could see, though, that it was a matter of one step at a time. From the south bank across a shallow riffle to a long sandbar. From there a short crossing to an island covered with a thicket of sand plums and a willow or two. Then on. . . . There was only one place where the main channel flowed which required a short swim. The horses took it well.

I had been concerned about the colt, but *aiee*, I need not have been! He plunged in after his mother. I was riding her, you know. That foal swam so strongly that he scrambled up the bank *ahead* of us!

We crossed and camped on the north side of the river that night, to have a good start in the morning. We could see that the country here was quite different from that to the south. There were more trees among the rolling hills, and steeper but smaller hills. Still some open grassland, though.

Our friend the trader had suggested that we go straight north from there. It was only a few days' travel, he said, to the next big river, which the French call the Platte.

"It is easier to cross," he mentioned.

My husband had asked him about the Pawnees.

"Mostly farther west," the trader said. "One town, a few sleeps west of here. They are on a river that runs into the Kenza."

"What is it called?" Pup asked.

The trader laughed. "I cannot recall what they call it. Some of those who live upstream call it Dung River."

"Its water is bad?"

"No, no. Very good, most of the year. Only when the buffalo, the great herds in the fall come south, they reach the river very thirsty. They stand and drink and their great numbers foul the water. It tastes like dung for a while. But that is mostly upstream, and if you go north toward the Platte, you will not even see that river."

"And you said that there are more Pawnees on the Platte?"

"That is true. How far west on the Platte will you go?"

"Ah, we do not know, Uncle. Where we are guided."

"Yes." The trader nodded. "I did not remember. This is a quest, no? The horse?"

"Yes. We . . ."

"No matter!" The trader waved a hand. "The Skidi, or Wolf band of the Pawnees, live to the west, many days' travel. If you want to find them, go north to the river and then follow it west. If you want to avoid them, go on to the north. We trade with Pawnees and have no trouble, but some avoid them. Do as you are made to think."

Later we thought that his had been very good advice. One must do as he thinks best. But the general idea of the country to the north for the next days of travel had been explained to us quite well.

On the morning after we crossed the Kenza, we talked of our plans.

"I am made to think," said my husband, "that we have little need to trade with Pawnees."

He was probably thinking of the fact that the mare I was riding had come through the hands of the Pawnees and might be recognized. I doubt that it would have made any difference. Horses change hands often. But there was the foal. He had felt that his quest must lead us farther to the north. The answers to his questions were to be found among the tribes living there. Why waste time trading with Pawnees, who quite possibly would not have information useful to us anyway? It is possible, too, that the sensibilities of my husband were offended by the Morning Star custom of the Pawnees. But he did not say.

We decided to head northward, and if we encountered Pawnees, so be it.

We found that there was a trail that led northward. There is always some travel, and it would be foolish to think that no one had come this way before. A crossing of the river, the easiest place, is used by all, and so a trail leads to and from it. Anyone heading to the north uses it.

Likewise, a day's travel brought us to the same area that other travelers had reached. There was good water, and grass for the horses. We could see the blackened spots from old fires. Fuel was a little scarce, but we did not need much of a fire anyway. We were not cooking, but using our dried food.

Somehow this night seemed to be the one on which our great adventure started. We had crossed the river and were in new territory. Yes, I know that we were still in the country of our own Northern band, but they were farther east that season. Neither Pipe Bearer nor I had been here before, and it was new country to us.

Because we had seen no people, there was a feeling that we were the only ones on earth. It was a special night, with a red moon rising at sunset. The excitement of our quest kept us awake as the shadows purpled the dark places, contrasting with the silvery moonlight that flooded the open country. There was a feeling of expectancy, as if something was about to happen.

We sat on our robes for a long time, watching the play of light and shadow. The night carried a slight chill. . . . It was not yet summer, of course. We cuddled close to share the warmth of our bodies, with a robe drawn around the two of us. The sensation of our caresses became more and more pleasant, and we drew even closer.

Aiee, Pup! Do not become so excited. I am only telling a story. No, I need not tell all to our friends here. Are you afraid I will reveal all our secrets?

I was only about to say that we settled down in our robes for a perfect ending to one of the most beautiful evenings of our lives. The moon rose higher, the Seven Hunters made their circle around the Real-star, and Kookooskoos, the hunting owl, called to his mate in the timber below us. We snuggled close, and it was good.

You see, Pup? I did not reveal all. I am made to think . . . Well, *you* tell them, then, about the Pawnees.

7

Ah, my friends, I was not certain where Otter was going with her story. What can I say after such a description? But, yes, we have had many wonderful times together, and that was one of the most memorable.

In fact, we slept well. So well that it was daylight when we woke. One of the horses nickered, and I sat up, alarmed. Had something alerted them? I glanced quickly around and rolled out of my warm bed to check the animals. We had hobbled them before nightfall. I immediately saw the direction in which they were looking, and at about that time I heard an answering cry. Horses were approaching. At least one horse. Now, the cry of that horse was reassuring. If anyone meant us harm, they would surely muzzle their horses to prevent such a cry.

Several other possibilities flashed through my mind. Those who approached did not know of our presence. . . . It might be a wandering loose horse or a wild horse. . . .

Over all of this was one thought that I could not shake: An enemy could have easily crept up to our camp and stolen all our horses. It was frightening to realize this, and I felt helpless and vulnerable. How stupid of me to be on this quest at all, especially with my valuable horses, not to mention my beautiful wife. It was an invitation to disaster.

Just then four riders topped the rise and came into sight. They did not appear to be preparing to attack, but only curious. Do not misunderstand. . . . They were proud and haughty, and there was no question that they were in control of the situation. For one thing, they outnumbered us.

I was still sleepy from having just been roused, but was awakening rapidly. These warriors were well mounted and well armed. Their heads were shaved around the back and sides, and the remaining clump of long hair twisted and plastered with grease and paint into a horn-shaped ornament, which appeared to grow out of the top of their heads. It took me only a moment to realize that these were Pawnees. It was quite plain why they are called Horn People, and why their hand sign describes it.

Otter had scrambled out of bed and into her clothes. I raised a hand in greeting, using hand signs because I knew no Pawnee talk.

"*Ah-koh!* You are welcome to our camp!"

There was really little that I could do except welcome the visitors. They rode in rather insolently, looking over our horses and our packs, and, of course, Otter Woman. They did not bother to answer my hand signs for a little while. Finally, one of the riders turned to me.

"You are a trader?"

I acknowledged with a nod.

"You do not have much."

"That is true," I admitted. "It is the reason for our presence here."

Quickly, I identified myself, my nation, and my band, and told of our losses from the Big Whirlwind the previous season. He seemed interested.

"We heard of this," he signed.

I was beginning to think that *everyone* had heard. Well, yes, it was a very startling story. We found that it was a very useful thing, later. We could start to tell our Big Whirlwind adventure, and people would forget everything else. Some probably did not believe it, the way Big Whirlwind picked up the herd of buffalo, but even those thought that it was a great story. But I am getting ahead of myself.

These Pawnees were fascinated by the Whirlwind story. They wanted to hear more, and soon we were almost friends. In spite of what we had heard, it was as our trader friend had said. I could see that though their ways are far different, it would be possible to travel and trade in their territory.

These four, we learned, were young men on a hunting party. It was a bit early for the planting of their corn, and they were tired of the forced inactivity of the winter. So why not a hunt? We got the impression that it did not really matter whether they found game. In a way, they were doing as *we* were, following the restless urge to travel as the geese do, or like the buffalo.

They told us much about the country ahead and were quite helpful. We were also warned about the dangers farther north. Otter and I found it amusing, to be warned by Pawnees of the dangers of traveling into the country of "Cut-Throats." That, of course, is the hand sign for the Lakotas.

The horses? Yes, they were interested in the horses, but made no great comment. It seemed to me that they were more interested in my stallion than in the mare and foal. I have said little about him, but he was a great horse himself. One of the finest of buffalo runners . . . but no matter. What I am trying to say is that their interest was in horses in general. They did not seem to concentrate on the medicine-hat markings of the colt. They commented on the mare, but only in passing. Of course, we had intentionally kept her looking a little rough to conceal her real quality. Mane and tail uncombed, muddy . . . Otter had actually gathered a few burrs to place artistically in the mare's mane and tail. Despite this, these men saw that our horses were of quality, and commented on it.

"Of course," I told them in signs. "Are we not called the Elk-dog People?"

We joked about it.

Yes, they admired the foal, though not overly so. We took this to mean a comment on his quality, but nothing more. They did not know of his medicine, apparently. That in itself told us much. That part of this foal's importance was to be found farther to the north.

The entire incident also encouraged us greatly. Again, we found a ready acceptance for our story of deciding to trade to the north for the season because of hard times. Neither the Arapaho trader nor these Pawnees even questioned it. They were ready to accept that we were what we seemed, a young couple with three horses, a young foal, and no children yet.

We showed the Pawnees some of our flint knives and points, and they nodded politely but were basically uninterested. They were quite well armed. *All* had steel knives, and at least two carried small throwing axes. The Pawnees, you know, were trading with the French sooner than our people did. It was a matter of where we lived.

So, as I said, Otter and I felt that this was a good meeting. We learned much about how to talk with strangers of tribes other than our own. We gained some confidence. You might say that we were accepted as traders, though actually we had not yet done any trading at all. But we were feeling much more secure when we parted with the Pawnees that morning.

The Platte . . . You know a little of the French tongue, no? They call the river by that name. I am told that it means "broad" or "level," and if that is true, their name for the river is good. *Aiee*, it is *flat*! Wide and shallow and sandy. It is much like some of the rivers to the west of our Sacred Hills.

There are many places along this river that have almost no trees except a brushy fringe of willows. But there are other areas where there will be big cottonwood trees, many of them together. It looks like a forest along the river in such an area.

I tell you of that because we saw at one of those groves of cottonwoods an interesting sight. There was a village of herons. You know the big blue herons that we see in our own country? Usually only a pair or two, building their lodges in a tree along one of our streams. Fishing, sometimes, at a quiet pool. Yes, that is the one. . . . Their lodge is built of sticks and looks much like that of an eagle.

Well, as I have told you, there are few trees in some places along the Platte. But where the groves of big cottonwoods grow, these birds nest. We saw one place where there were maybe a hundred lodges. Yes, it is true! Ask Otter, if you doubt! It was as if all of the tribe of herons had gathered for their Sun Dance. Yes, of course they do not move their lodges as we do. But it was a strange thing, one we had never seen. We wondered greatly at such a gathering. Though we knew better, it was amusing to think of it as a Big Council such as that of the People. The noise and excitement and confusion, certainly, made us think of our Sun Dance and Big Council.

What? No, we were not thinking of this as a sign of any kind. It was not an incident that we witnessed. I am sure that the Village of Herons has been there for many generations. It will be, for many more. It is there, I am made to think, because there are few places for many days' travel where there are sticks to build their lodges. So they build where the sticks are.

All of this really has nothing to do with our quest, of course. I only tell of it because we found an interest in it. We saw many strange things on that quest. The Village of Herons was only one of the first.

We moved on to the north, through open grassland. I was reminded, in that area, of the region where the Tallgrass hills, our Sacred Hills, change to the shorter grassland to the west of us. Much of the country we were crossing appeared drier. The grass was mostly short buffalo grass, such as we know. The land was flat or gently rolling, and its spirit was good.

When we stopped to camp, we would kindle our fire and offer a pinch of tobacco to those spirits or any other who might chance to be there.

We did begin to wonder about wood for our fires. There are really very few trees for sticks. We burned buffalo dung, of course, but what if we came to an area where there had been no buffalo last season? They are not everywhere. This did not become a problem but was only something that we noticed. That was how we got the idea of why the herons gathered to build their lodges at the one place. That was where the *sticks* are.

We moved on. For several sleeps we saw no other people at all. That is a wide country, my friends! Our food supply was becoming tiresome. You know how it is in late winter, when the dried meat becomes tasteless and we long for fresh hump ribs? Even the pemmican does not lend the variety we crave. Remember, this was still early in the spring.

I was hoping for a chance to shoot a buffalo, but we did not see any yet. They were migrating north, of course, but at that season the herds were far behind us, and moving no faster than we were. I still hoped to find a lone animal or a small band that might have wintered there, as a few will in our area sometimes. But we saw none.

Then one morning we saw a small band of antelope. I recalled that I had heard much of their curiosity. They will come to investigate, it is said, something that they do not understand.

We stopped in a low spot, and Otter kept the horses there. I crawled out on the prairie toward the little band of antelope, keeping as low as I could.

When I thought that I was close enough, I took the ramrod out of my gun and stuck it upright in the sand. Then I took the brightly decorated buckskin case from the gun and hung it over the tip of the rod. Both ends hung down at odd and unnatural angles.

I readied the musket and waited. It was not long before the animals noticed the strange object, the fringe fluttering just a little in the breeze. They pranced and snorted, came closer and retreated again.

Finally one of the young bucks came close enough that I thought the ball from my thunderstick could reach him.

Carefully, I drew back the flint, sighted down the barrel, and squeezed off the trigger.

You know how, when the powder flashes in the pan, there is a moment when you can see nothing? The thick white smoke from the priming powder blocks out your vision. And there is a space there, between the flash and the boom, only a heartbeat's time, when you do not know. Sometimes you can tell, of course. Sometimes it is like the release of an arrow from a bow. There are some shots that you know will fly true. Some shots from the gun are like that, too.

This one was not. It seemed a long time before the boom of the gun, and I was in doubt. I raised my head and the breeze cleared the smoke away and *yes*! The buck lay kicking while the others, white rumps flashing, bounded away.

That night we ate until we were so full that our bellies hurt. Fresh meat and fresh liver. We had bites of the raw liver while our meat broiled, as is the custom of the People at the first kill in the spring.

Aiee, it was good! What? Well, no, not as good as buffalo. Antelope is strong and not as sweet as the flesh of buffalo. But I tell you this so that you realize. We were in *need* of fresh meat, and this antelope kill was welcome. So we made the apology:

> We are sorry to kill you,
> my brothers,
> But upon your flesh our
> lives depend. . . .

And the rest . . . We gave thanks and we enjoyed our good lives that evening.

8

The country through which we traveled now was mostly open prairie. I had the impression that we were just to the west of the place where, as in our own country, trees give way to grass. It is not a line, of course. Trees push farther to the west along the streams. Especially the big rivers. When we traveled away from the Platte, then, there is no big river for some distance. So there are big areas of tallgrass prairie.

I tell you this to give you the background for what happened to us there. In our own country it was now past the time when the People burn the grass. The Moon of Greening. Our holy men announce the time, and it is a springtime ritual. The return of the grass brings the return of the buffalo. They move into areas where the burn has cleaned out the old grass. The new growth is thick and lush.

As the apprentice to Singing Wolf, I had learned this skill . . . how to decide the time to burn, that is. It depends on observing when the new shoots of certain plants start to grow. Too early, the earth is left bare and the grass comes poorly. Too late, the new growth is damaged.

Then, too, there is a certain danger in the burn. The day must be calm, because in a wind, the fire takes on a spirit of its own. We can all remember accidents during the season of burning. The wind rises unexpectedly, and the fire changes direction. A living thing, it races through the grassland, faster than a man on horseback. And we have seen the flames leap over a stream that would be many paces across.

Now, I had noticed as we traveled that the new growth was becoming appropriate for burning. The People had not yet burned when we left, but I was certain that they had by this time. And spring was coming here, too, following along behind us as we moved. Even so, I did not entirely realize the situation until one morning as we prepared to break camp.

The days had been calm and warm, fine weather for travel. Now, somehow, there was a sense of change in the air. As the morning warmed, a breeze began to stir. Now, this was not a stiff wind, merely a stirring of the air from the south. But by midmorning we were definitely aware of its stronger flow. A weather change must be in the making.

We camped early that evening, to give us time to prepare what shelter we could in case of rain. Since the weather was warm, we would not need much shelter. We had been wet before, and would be again. A small streambed with a few willows over which we could drape robes . . .

To be perfectly truthful, my main concern was whether this area would be subject to the flash flooding that we see in our own country. I did not know. But, as we went to bed, I took a long look around, to make sure that we could move quickly if we needed. The stars were shining, and I saw no real threat. I could not understand, though, why I felt a certain sense of uneasiness. I could not identify it.

I slept restlessly for a little while and then awoke, feeling strongly that I had overlooked something. Otter Woman lay beside me, breathing softly . . . *aiee*, her face was beautiful in the light of the new quarter moon that was setting. But I rose anyway, to prowl the area. The horses seemed restless.

I circled the camp, noticing that the wind had risen slightly and was whipping sparks from the dying fire. In fact, I could faintly smell the smoke from where I stood, some thirty paces away. *Wait!* That could not be! I was *upwind* from the fire. I turned and looked around the horizon. *Ah!* There on earth's rim was a reddish glow. Not the red of a sunset, nor was it the yellowish color of the false dawn when it begins to grow lighter in the east to announce Sun Boy's return.

I was confused for a moment and turned to verify my direction by the Real-star. Yes . . . the line of sight established by the first two of the Seven Hunters pointed straight to their lodge at the Real-star. *North* . . . The red glow was *behind* me, above earth's south rim. I must have been very slow to admit that which must be quite plain to you as I tell it now.

Fire.

The wind was quickening and the glow in the distant sky was becoming brighter as I watched. Someone to the south had carried out the spring ritual. Or maybe it was a lightning strike or an accident. It did not matter now. The line of fire would burn across the entire prairie, creeping in calm weather, racing and roaring when the wind fanned it. It might run for many days, even at its fastest gait, never stopping until it reached a river too big to leap across. I realized that we had not crossed a stream of any size for several days, and the wind was still rising. The inescapable facts sent a chill creeping up my back. We were in trouble.

"What is it? Pup, where are you?" Otter asked, scrambling sleepily out of the robes.

"Over here," I called. She hurried to join me.

"*Aiee!*" she said softly. "It is not good."

I almost laughed, even at the time. Was there ever a time when that idea was more true? Maybe, when I think of it. Certainly, later I was to think so.

I put an arm around Otter's shoulders, and she, one around my waist. We watched, fascinated. It was only a few moments before we could see points of light along the skyline. Flickering, sparkling tongues of fire, writhing like a living thing. Now, you realize, of course, that this fire was a day's travel away. More than that, maybe. But it was moving toward us. At the speed it could travel in a stiff wind, such a fire could easily reach us by daylight.

Even more frightening was the *width* of the fiery front as it came over the distant prairie. It seemed to cover such a span that we could not even consider removing ourselves from its path. It was too wide. I knew that it was an impossible escape, anyway. The fire would be spreading not only to the north, toward us, but to the sides, also.

We must keep calm, now. . . . Dense smoke now obscured the distant flames so that we could not see their progress. This lent yet another worry.

"We must catch the horses," I told Otter. "The colt, too."

We had let the colt run loose as we traveled, because he would stay with his mother. Now it would be necessary to maintain control of all the animals. Horses often panic in a fire. Fortunately, Otter had handled and played with the foal all of his life. We had trained him to a rope around his neck and head. He had, in fact, proved very intelligent about the rope. After one hard fall from fighting it, he seemed to understand. It is more comfortable *not* to fight the rope. Some colts are very slow to learn this. Ah, you have owned such a horse, my friend Bull?

But this was important. We quickly caught the horses and Otter held them while I carried out our plan. The only possible plan, actually. I still remember the words of my grandfather when I was a child.

"If you are ever caught in front of a wildfire, there is only one thing to do: Light another fire, step into the burned area, and walk behind the advance of your own fire."

I took a brand from our campfire and stepped a few paces downwind so as not to alarm the horses. There I thrust my fire into a clump of last year's dead growth. In the space of a heartbeat it burst into flame and jumped to another clump downwind. It was a bit frightening to see the flames race before the wind.

In a short while there was a blackened area large enough to enter. It required some coaxing to get the horses to step over the low strip of fire on the upwind side. It was spreading slowly southward while the front that was fanned by the wind raced to the north. We located an open patch where there was mainly buffalo grass. It, being short, would not burn so fiercely. The horses were persuaded to step across that low line of fire. After the pack horse tried it, the others followed, seeing no harm to him.

It was a strange experience, in that blackened world. Now there was fire on every side of us. The ground was hot under our feet. Some clumps of grass still smoked, and fragments of old buffalo chips glowed red here and there. I had expected the smoke to be a problem. Well, it was smoky. But not a heavy, choking smoke. The smoke that was whipped past us by the south wind was thin. It came from the slow-burning line of fire moving *against* the wind. The roaring, dangerous fire was the leading edge of the wind-driven front. We could see such a front as the main fire raced over the hills toward us from the south. And to the north of us, as we followed the front of our own fire, we could see it growing and roaring as it, too, became a monstrous thing. And in our small but growing burned area we seemed safe. It was not pleasant, no. It was warm underfoot, the smoke made our eyes water, the smell was strong. But we were alive, and we had all of our packs and our horses. Our time of peril was past.

We reached the top of a little rise, maybe a bow shot from where we lit the backfire, and turned to watch. Thick yellow smoke poured in a blanket ahead of the advancing line of the main fire. And, my friends, the front was *wide*. Irregular, rather than straight, but *aiee*, it seemed to stretch from earth's rim on the east to that on the west.

Flame leaped up through or behind the blanket of smoke as the fire reached pockets of thick, dry grass. The loud crackle of exploding stems of the big plume-grass could be heard now.

We saw that the advancing front would meet the edge of our backfire soon, and we turned to watch.

Now, I have described that wildfire as a living thing. It was not until now that this description really became meaningful. A bow shot away, the south edge of our fire burned in a line across the prairie. It was of about the same width, too, but longer to the north, where the wind fanned it on. A long oval shape, you see. The wildfire approached that calm, slow fire of ours and its very approach seemed to fan our backfire into a fury. The two living things met with a crash, like two great stallions fighting. The joined flames rose in furious combat for a towering moment and then fell back, their energy exhausted.

But now the main fire was racing past us on both sides. We had seen a number of creatures in retreat as the fire advanced. Rabbits, a fox, a badger, a coyote pup. A trio of grouse flew overhead. We knew that some of these creatures would perish this morning. Others, by their cleverness or luck, would live to raise a brood this season. It is the way of things.

Now we saw some of these animals entering our burned area from the sides, as the fire raced past. I felt glad. Maybe in helping ourselves, we had helped some of them, too.

Then a very strange thing happened. Through the blanket of dense yellow smoke that was billowing past us on the west side of our burned area, I saw a horse. It was running in terror, trying to reach the safety of our burned-out backfire. It was close. . . . Flames were licking around the animal's legs as it leaped over the margin of our fire and into the safe area. It was only then that I saw a rider clinging to the horse's withers. The rider reined the horse around and looked back.

Then out of the smoke and flame came a *second* rider. This one was in trouble. *More* trouble. His horse was wild with fear and pain, and was fighting the rein, tossing its head. It now leaped into the safe area and, still fighting, stepped into a soft area or a gopher hole or something of the sort. It tripped and fell heavily, and the rider was thrown clear. He struck the ground hard and lay very still. The other rider rushed toward him.

We, too, rushed forward to catch the loose horses or to be of what help we could. The fallen rider was moving a little, but slowly and painfully.

As we approached, the smaller rider, the one who had not been injured, noticed us for the first time. In an instant that one had assumed a fighting crouch, drawn a belt knife, and was threatening us, in defense of the man on the ground. I was astonished at that, but even more so at the fact that it was a woman. A young and beautiful woman!

"Do not come closer," she warned in hand signs.

The way in which she held the knife spoke of experience. I had no intention of going any closer.

9

What a strange situation! Here were four of us, our lives in danger from the fire. One was injured, but the second was preventing our assisting him.

"Wait!" I signed quickly. "We mean no harm!"

The young woman was not impressed.

"Stay back!" she warned again.

She moved now to a spot where she could see to the injuries of her companion and, at the same time, watch us. The man on the ground, covered with the black ash of the burned grass, seemed to be badly injured. Some broken ribs, maybe, though he moved all his legs and arms well. His breathing was difficult.

"Let me try," Otter said to me.

She stepped forward slowly, under the watchful eye of the stranger girl, and began to sign.

"Can I help?" she asked.

The threat did not seem so great from another woman, maybe. The girl seemed to relax a little.

"Your husband?" asked Otter.

The young woman nodded, still suspicious. "Who are you?" she signed.

"We are Elk-dog People," Otter answered. "From the south."

"Not Pawnee? Crow?"

"No. Elk-dog." Otter repeated the sign "man-on-a-horse."

"We are Lakota."

The cut-throat hand sign was plain, but a little unsettling. Otter nodded, trying to act as if she met cut-throats every day.

"It is good," she signed. "It is better, even, that we are all alive."

The other woman still looked suspicious.

"Are we supposed to be enemies?" she asked.

It was a strange question at the time. We had just shared a tragedy, a nearly fatal one for them.

Now the fallen man managed to sit up, though in great pain.

"No, no," he signed. Then he spoke to his wife, in words we did not know. She turned to us and signed.

"My man says that he knows your people. His people are friends with yours."

"His people are not Lakota?" I asked.

"They are now," she signed proudly, almost haughtily. "He came to us to marry me."

"Who were his people, then?" Otter asked.

"Arapaho . . . Trader People," the girl signed. "They are friends to all, maybe."

This last part I took to be a bit sarcastic. Lakotas, we found, are very proud of warrior status. So are others of the northern tribes. But I will go on.

"Yes," I told her, "that is true. We trade, with Arapahos. They live to the west of us. Northwest, a little."

"Do you know their tongue?"

"No. But let us try to help your husband."

She was still reluctant but was calming a little. We had to admire her. She had been ready to fight and die, even, in the defense of her injured husband. Yet she was an intelligent woman, and it was apparent that she must have help. We were offering it. It helped, probably, that her husband knew our people, and in a favorable way. As it turned out, he actually knew a little of our tongue, from contact with our Mountain band. We even had a mutual friend or two. But I get ahead of my story again. . . .

We looked around the burned area where we stood, to find a place to spread a robe. The grass burns very quickly, of course, and cools again. Oh, there will be places where heavy growth, brush, a dead tree, maybe, will smolder for a day or two. But places where the grass was short, like buffalo grass . . . that will be cool again in a short while.

We found such a place, and Otter spread one of our buffalo robes for the man to lie on. We helped him to it and eased him down on the soft fur. It had caused him much pain, I know. I had felt the click or crackle of broken ribs as I assisted him to lie down. But he did not make a sound.

I felt of his arms and legs, and as I had thought, there was no injury there. His belly, too, seemed soft, and I thought that he was not bleeding inside. His biggest problem, of course, was to draw his air in and out. He could take only shallow breaths, and when he did, there was the sound of bone on bone.

I drew out my knife to cut away his leggings to use for a binder. There was an exclamation from the woman. She had drawn her own knife again and was threatening me. *Aiee*, she was like a buffalo cow with a newborn calf!

With the help of her husband we convinced her, at least a little, and I cut the leggings. They were scorched and burned but had protected his legs. There were a few blisters around his calves, but his moccasins were of a style that came up over his ankles a little way, and that had protected him some.

We helped him sit up, and the two women supported him by his arms while I wrapped the strips of buckskin leggings tightly around his chest. It must have been very painful, but once we had finished and tied it securely, the bandage helped him greatly. They eased him back to the robe.

Now the woman was apologetic for her suspicions. I waved her aside and told her in signs that it was nothing. But we both admired her greatly, that she had shown this loyalty in her husband's defense.

Now what? We had a need to look at our situation. Otter and I had lost little. Our horses were all safe, and were calming well after the excitement, becoming acquainted with the strangers' horses. Our packs were intact. We had food. Even a little of the antelope meat that we had brought with us.

The strangers, however, had lost nearly everything. They had wakened with the fire roaring down on them. There was time only to catch horses and try to outride the fire. Their best horse, we learned later, had broken away and fled in terror. It was a fine stallion, ridden by Lone Walker. . . . That was his name. . . . I did not tell of that yet, did I?

We were using several tongues, besides signs. Arapaho, Lakota, and our own. . . . Names translate oddly sometimes. This man was called by such different names as Walks by Himself, Walks Alone, Solitary Walker. . . . You know how it becomes confusing.

Anyway, his horse was gone. The animal that he rode into our lives was one of their pack horses. A stumble-footed, dim-witted beast, but the only one he could catch. The horse ridden by his wife, Plum Flower, was a better mount.

They had been forced to abandon their packs, sleeping robes, everything, to escape with their lives. They had been very fortunate to accomplish that. If it had not been that they had seen our backfire, *aiee!*

What? Oh, no, we never saw their other horses again. They may have survived, but who knows?

Otter took out some pemmican and shared it with the others. My heart was heavy for all they had lost. I had been wishing that there was something we could do for them. We had very little ourselves and were in unfamiliar country. We had used a good robe, for Walker to lie on. It would be difficult to take it back now. Yet we needed to move on. How far could we go to help these people?

Yet there was something about the couple that made my heart go out to them. Maybe they were much like ourselves. Young, no children . . . away from our People . . . and there was something to admire about them. There had been no word of complaint from either. Plum Flower had shown great strength of spirit when she had tried to defend her man. I did not see how we could abandon such people. After all, it could have been the other way. *We* could have been the ones who lost everything.

In the afternoon the entire landscape still smoked, blackened and desolate. The smell burned in our noses, and I was thirsty. We had a waterskin, and I saw a strip of green some distance away. I took Otter aside.

"We need water," I told her. "I will take the waterskin and bring some from there." I pointed. "Will you be all right?"

"Of course! But, Pup, we must talk of this. We have very little to share, you know."

I had been afraid of that. Otter was such an efficient person, always planning, saving what we have for best use. She would be reluctant to risk what little we had.

"We will talk of it later," I told her.

I caught my horse and set out for the distant line of trees, thinking as I went. Already the horses were hungry, and there was nothing to eat. I had seen them nosing among the smoking tufts. Water, too. They could go for a day or two, at most.

Maybe I could lead one or two to the stream tonight, a couple more in the morning. Maybe I could cut enough cottonwood branches to feed six horses. The People often wintered their horses on little more forage than that. Maybe I could cut enough to help Lone Walker and Plum Flower for a while after we parted.

I approached the thin strip of timber and saw that the water was good. Some ash had settled on the surface and now ringed the edges of the pools, but the water was clear. Minnows swam among the pebbles. I got down and drank deeply. Then I rose to look around, while my horse continued to gulp the cool water.

There was actually a grassy clearing here, sheltered in the trees. Its grasses were of a different kind and had no dry stems to burn in the spring, so this small area had been spared from the fire. This was probably why the little strip of trees had managed to survive the burnings through the years, too.

But I was thinking. . . . If we could find a way to bring the injured man here, the couple would be in a much better position to travel on when we left them. I looked at the small trees along the stream. It appeared to me that there were a few cottonwood saplings that might be useful. Two poles would form a makeshift travois, the trimmings, the cross-platform, and the horses could eat the leaves and twigs.

Meanwhile, I would bring the horses here to water and to graze a little.

I felt good as I headed back. Next I would ride our roan mare and lead the pack horse. The colt would follow. Then the horses of Walker and Plum Flower. Maybe I could care for them all before night. And I would talk with Otter about building a travois. I was still in doubt about how she would react to helping this couple when we had so little ourselves.

I handed her the waterskin and explained that I would take the horses to water. She took a sip and handed the skin to Plum Flower.

"I will go with you," she told me. "We can take all the animals at once."

I looked to the others and signed our intention. The two looked at each other and then both nodded. We began to gather the horses and attach lead ropes. I was wondering how to explain to Otter the idea that I had in mind.

I need not have worried. We were hardly out of earshot when Otter began to talk rapidly.

"Pup, we cannot leave these people. They cannot travel, they have no food, no weapons."

I had not expected this outburst. I knew that my wife was a kind and sympathetic person, but to have her arguing my thoughts caught me off guard. While I was still trying to think of something to say, she went on.

"We must at least help them to a place that the husband can start to recover. Maybe hunt for some meat . . ."

I nodded, as if I were considering the matter.

"Maybe we can think of something," I told her.

10

I was delighted when Pipe Bearer showed me the grassy clearing and the stream in the midst of a blackened world. I had been afraid that he would insist on moving on.

We watered the horses while he told me about his idea for the pole-drag. Then he started to cut the two cottonwood saplings while I went back to tell the others what we had in mind. By this time we were gaining trust in each other, and they readily agreed.

By evening we had transported Lone Walker to the stream, picketed the horses, and settled in. Walker was pale and exhausted, but in a much better setting than before. *Aiee*, how the jolting of the travois must have tortured his ribs. It hurts to think of it!

Now, about this couple . . . I must take a little while to tell you of them, because they are important to our story. We were coming into the country of the Lakotas, you know, and I began to see how this could be of great advantage to us. If we were in the company of Lakotas, it would remove much of the danger to us as strangers. We had talked in hand signs, and Lone Walker had a fair knowledge of our tongue, but it would be good to learn a few words in the Lakota language. Especially since we were pretending to be traders.

All of this was not something that we talked about, or even thought out at the time. We had just survived the fire . . . *aiee*, that was a fearsome experience! We were not ready to plan beyond that day, yet.

But without trying, we began to learn more of each other. We already knew that Lone Walker was a brave and courageous man. He did not complain about his discomfort. He was concerned about his wife, Plum Flower, but he need not have been. She was a strong woman and had come through the ordeal uninjured and in good shape. Both were concerned about their horses. As it happened, both horses had been scorched by the blaze. I still have in my mind the picture of Walker jumping his horse through the fire into our blackened area of safety. There were blue flames licking along the sides of its tail and streaming out behind. When it fell and rolled, those flames were extinguished. That animal was burned around the fetlocks, too. Plum Flower's mare not so severely.

Apparently the fall did not injure Lone Walker's horse much. I would not have been surprised at a broken leg. It did limp badly for a while.

But back to Plum Flower and Lone Walker. They had lost everything. Packs, robes, blankets, saddles, two horses, their supplies. It had been a very narrow escape for them.

We learned, over the next while, that they had been married only a little longer than Pup and I. They, too, had no children yet. Walker, with his trading tradition, had come to the Lakotas with his father as a trader. He had seen this lovely young woman and they had fallen in love. The following season he came back to court her.

Now he still had his tradition in trading, that of his people. They decided that though he would become Lakota, they would continue with some travel and trade for a season or two, or until their lodge was joined by a child.

"Yes, it is much the same with us," my husband told them.

This, of course, drew us closer.

They had been on the way to rejoin Plum Flower's Lakota people. They had wintered elsewhere, with his family, maybe. I do not remember. They had been caught by the fire, as we nearly had.

Very quickly, we found ourselves thinking of the four of us as a group, a party brought together by tragedy. Under such circumstances, even enemies have been known to help each other to survive. And here, after Plum Flower's threatening action in the heat of crisis . . . well, she was greatly troubled, you know. After that she seemed to present no great threat. She did not appear to be an enemy, only a woman in an emergency. She was only protecting her man. I might have done the same. Or I might not. Ah, do not look so hurt, Pup. Of course I would . . . I was only teasing you.

But now we must look over what we had, and what we would need. At first I am sure that Pup and I had thought in terms of dividing our supplies with the others and moving on. That did not last long, as I have said. We could not share our weapons, of course. For several reasons it appeared that it would be best to wait until Lone Walker could travel, and then move on together to the camp of Plum Flower's people. She knew where they had wintered, and she said it was no more than four or five sleeps. Probably more, I thought, with a badly injured man.

Plum Flower and I looked over the supplies. There was still a supply of dried meat. Enough, probably, for ten days for Pup and me, if we were careful. For the four of us, maybe half that time. We had a small amount of pemmican, stored in gut pouches. It was not the best quality. The fat causes it to become rancid, you know, as the weather warms. Dry meat is much better for traveling.

Even with the waning quality of the pemmican, I was thinking that we should give it to Walker, mostly. The mixture, meat, fat, and the nuts and dried berries would be better for his needs as his body healed.

Which brought our thoughts again to *How long?* We could tell better in a day or two, maybe. As my husband said in a half-joke aside to me, if worst came to worst we could eat the injured horse, no? Well, we have done worse.

Our biggest problem, our greatest need, was for robes. Lone Walker lay on one of our sleeping robes. We had another, and an old blanket. There were a couple of well-worn buffalo skins that we used for packs, and they might be used for shelter in an emergency. Well, we could take stock again in a day or two.

That night we sat in our little island of green and watched the red glow against the sky to the north. A little while after dark, Pipe Bearer walked to the top of the rise and looked toward the retreating fire. He came back and told us of the writhing, fiery snake as it crawled across the hills nearly a day's travel away. The wind had died with the sun, and the line of fire had slowed. Still, there was nothing to do but wait.

We were all exhausted that first night. We fell into our robes without any preparation except the ritual campfire. I am made to think that all of us were asleep almost at once.

It was along toward morning that the rain came. I was wakened by a distant drum of thunder and sat up to look around. Our fire was low, but the wind was rising again, fanning small bright coals among the ashes. At the same time I noticed fat drops beginning to patter around us, plopping into the grass or into the hot ashes with a hiss.

The others were rousing too, and we began to hurry around, trying to create some makeshift shelter.

That was an almost useless effort. In a few heartbeats we were all soaked, our teeth chattering with the chill.

Now, in all of the confusion, I noticed the cool efficiency of our new companion, Plum Flower. Her first action was to throw a fold of the buffalo robe over her husband. With that, he would be warm and dry. With a soaking chill, he would be only too likely to fill his lungs with the fluid that steals life away.

Her next action I did not notice until a little later. A simple thing, but *I* did not think of it until it would have been too late. When it did occur to me to look to saving the fire, the Lakota woman had already attended to what was needed. . . . She had thrown a pack cover over our little pile of dry sticks to keep them dry. At the same time, she had propped a couple of large buffalo chips on the upwind side of the dying coals. This protected them from the patter of the rain, preserving the life of the fire, as well as protecting our fuel supply. Can you imagine how it would have been in the chill darkness in a steady rain, trying to start a *new* fire? A fire that we needed badly . . .

Now we huddled over the fire's remains, shivering under the robes around our shoulders. Except for Lone Walker, of course. He had wrapped himself against the wet rain and was faring well. The others of our sodden little party managed to hold robes to protect the still living coals from the rain as well as the wind that might have scattered them.

The few small, dry sticks on that wet and chilly morning might have made the difference of life and death to Lone Walker. We began to feed them carefully to the glowing coals. *Aiee*, how wonderful the light of the new flames. Even more, the comforting warmth as the fire grew.

As it began to grow light, the rain slowed a little. Pipe Bearer cut some short poles from a willow to build the frame for a lean-to next to the fire. A couple of robes thrown over it . . .

We dragged the robe in which Lone Walker was wrapped into the shelter. He wanted to get up, but we told him not yet.

The four of us huddled together in the lean-to, sharing the warmth of the fire and of our own bodies. Gradually, we stopped shivering.

By the time the sun rose, unseen behind the gray of the sky, we were fairly comfortable. It is easy to forget, in all the comfort of a well-managed lodge, how miserable we might be without it. We were all still completely exhausted, having followed a harrowing day with a restless and miserable night.

Pipe Bearer got up to see about the horses. They were doing well, he told us. They would be highly unlikely to stray far.

There was nothing for them to eat on the prairie, except in the little islands of green along the creek where we were. The rest was black and water-soaked. The smell of the wet ashes was strong, and our faces and clothing, our hair—*everything*—was smudged with black.

But we were alive. Walker was extremely stiff and sore, much more than when he was first injured. An injury does that, you know. One stiffens the next day. I am still convinced that if Walker had been soaked and chilled like the rest of us that morning, he would never have left that first camp. He would have died there, coughing as his lungs filled.

The rain stopped, the clouds cleared, and by noon the sun was warming the prairie. *Now* was the time for Lone Walker to begin to loosen his stiffness. The warm rays from Sun Boy's torch would help to heal him. Plum Flower helped her husband up, refusing Pipe Bearer's offer of assistance. That was her way: Do for yourself all you can, before you accept help. She was a proud woman.

Walker stood, smiling thinly through his pain and leaning on his wife. Slowly, a step at a time, she helped him a few steps downstream to empty his bladder. Walker came back moving more easily and looking much relieved.

They were nearly back to our makeshift shelter when Lone Walker suddenly stopped with a gasp. He was looking upstream a few paces. We turned and saw only the horses, peacefully grazing or browsing the low bushes.

"*Aiee!*" Walker said, as if to himself. Then he turned to my husband. "I had not noticed," he said in our tongue. "A medicine-hat foal!"

You may think that it was unusual for one as skilled with horses as Lone Walker *not* to have noticed. But think on it. The fire, their escape, his injury, then Pipe Bearer took the horses away. The pain of moving . . . The horses were browsing among the trees upstream at that time. Then darkness, the storm. It was the first time that things were calm in Walker's life for a whole day.

"Medicine hat?" said Pipe Bearer. "You know of horses like this?"

"Of course."

"They are Lakota?"

"Sometimes. People farther west prize them."

My husband was excited. Here was someone who could tell us the significance of this animal.

"Tell me," he said, trying to seem only mildly interested. "What do you know of this medicine hat?"

Now I am going to let Pipe Bearer continue the story for a while. See, he is excited all over again at the memory. You see, for Pup and me, this was a big step on our quest.

11

It is as Otter has just told you. This was an exciting time. By accident (though are there *really* any accidents?) we had found a man who knew of these special medicine horses. Is it not strange how the spirits do their work?

"You know of this horse?" I asked. It must have been plain that I was surprised. Also, that I knew very little about it. Even so, Lone Walker told me all that he knew. At least I was made to think so, and we trusted him. There was much that *he* did not know, which we learned later.

The medicine hat horse is highly honored, Walker said, to the north and west. The reason is apparent. It wears the fur cap of the holy man. The one to whose mare this special foal is born is very fortunate, for it is a sign that he is favored by the spirits. Good things will happen for him.

"But is it not likely that someone would steal him, then?" I asked.

"Maybe. But think about it. To steal another's medicine would be foolish, no? It is a personal thing. Maybe even dangerous to one who would try to steal it."

Yes, I agreed that among all of the tribes and nations that we know, it would be very foolish to tamper with the spirit-gifts that have been bestowed on someone else. It could even be fatal.

"But I do not understand, my friend," Walker went on. "You are on a quest of some sort? Forgive me if I ask too much."

I assured him that I was not offended. He had freely told us what he knew. I could do no less, and I felt that even with my vision, I had not been given things that must be kept hidden. So I felt that I could confide at least some of it.

Now it may seem strange as I tell it, that I should be so quickly confiding in a stranger whom I had just met. But by this time I was no longer thinking of Lone Walker as a stranger. Our spirits had come together quickly, as if we had known each other before. Sometimes it is so. We meet someone and already know things about him . . . or her . . . No, let me not get too far from my story, here. I will only say that from that time, Lone Walker seemed like a brother to me.

I told them a little of my dream-vision, and of how I was puzzled and restless. I felt called to go and do something but did not know what. I spoke of consulting with my grandfather, the holy man, and told of my own apprenticeship.

"You are a holy man?" my almost-brother asked in surprise.

Now it is not good to boast of such a thing, of course. Among many nations, a holy man must deny it when asked. I admitted that I had studied to assist my grandfather.

"I do a little medicine," I admitted. "Nothing much. But I have great respect for the wisdom and the gifts of my grandfather, Singing Wolf."

"Ah, I have heard that name!" Lone Walker said in surprise. "Your people of the Mountain band talk of him with great respect."

I knew that this was true. Our whole nation spoke well of Singing Wolf. So, you see, the bonds of our friendship with Lone Walker were already strengthening. I continued, telling him of the birth of the foal and how, with the shedding of the baby hair, the fur medicine hat was revealed. Walker sat, shaking his head in disbelief.

"And what made you start north?" he asked.

"I cannot say, Walker," I told him. "I was made to think I should do so."

I did not think it necessary to share the intimate details of my visit from my medicine animal. Yet I could see that he was greatly impressed.

"My friend," Lone Walker finally said thoughtfully, "I envy you this quest. I saw a medicine horse once, when I was a child. It was to the northwest of here, many sleeps. I was strongly drawn and have never forgotten it."

I was expecting to hear more of Walker's story, but that was it. He had simply been fascinated by the idea of the spirit-horse with the medicine hat since he had seen one as a child. Now his lifelong interest had been rekindled by the meeting with us and our foal.

"I am made to think that there must be some purpose here," Walker said solemnly.

It surely did seem so to me. That Otter and I should have come this far to find ourselves in company with Lone Walker and Plum Flower . . . the two of *them* from different nations, far apart . . . the fire *forcing* us together, to stay together long enough to learn of each other . . . I felt that there were strange forces at work.

We stayed in that place for several days. I do not remember how many, exactly. It was until Lone Walker was able to travel. He did heal rapidly, for he was a strong man, who also had a very strong spirit. In a day he was up, walking slowly, a little farther each day.

The weather remained open and clear after the storm, making it unnecessary to share the makeshift shelter. By the third day after the rain had cleansed the black ash from the burn, there were sprigs of green showing everywhere. By the fifth day the rolling hills were green. That was also the day that we ate the last of our food supply.

I mounted my horse and scouted the vicinity of the camp, making a big circle. I was pleased to see some animals and birds beginning to come back into the greening areas. It should not be difficult to make some kind of kill. It would be a few days yet before Lone Walker could travel.

I thought that possibly there would be antelope in the area. My mind was really set on a feast of the broiled hump ribs of buffalo, but that was a slim chance. By noon I was thinking of Walker's pack horse, and how it might taste. The idea became better and better. It wasn't much of a horse for using, anyway.

It was about that time that I heard a shot, from beyond the next rise somewhere. As you know, it is hard to tell direction of a sound on our rolling prairie. A gunshot, particularly, rolls and bounces and reverberates. You hear it three or four times, maybe.

I stopped my horse to think about this for a minute. I was sure that the sound had not come from the direction of the camp. There was only the one shot. At least I thought so. It must be someone else, hunting. If it had been a fight, there would be more shots. Unless, of course, someone killed another from ambush or as a murder. These were not pleasant thoughts in strange country. I decided that I must learn more. We were too vulnerable to remain in doubt.

I rode toward the crest of the low ridge, debating whether to ride forward until I could see, or to dismount and crawl. I decided to ride, mostly because there was no place to tie my horse. And, yes, of course, because I am a little bit lazy. And I had no desire to be on foot in case the horse decided to leave without me.

I readied my gun and checked the flint and the priming pan. I did not know what to expect, and I must be ready to protect myself.

I was nearly to the point where I could see the prairie beyond, when I heard running horses. At least I thought so. Not buffalo . . . the sound of their hooves is different, heavier. Yet this was heavier than deer or antelope, who make little sound as they run.

While I was still thinking about this, and wondering what, if anything, I should do, the animals topped the rise, coming straight toward me. *Elk!* A band of six or eight, running in fright. A massive bull, looking strangely like a horse without the antlers he would have at other seasons, thundered past me. An old cow veered away.

I was probably not thinking at my best at the time. Otherwise I would not have done so stupid a thing. Until I knew more about the situation, I should never have fired a shot. I knew quite well that someone was in the area. Friend or foe, I had no idea. Yet when a fat yearling bull almost ran over me . . . well, yes, I shot him. He nearly ran into my gun barrel, and what was I to do? Between the flash and the boom of the musket, I knew already that I had made a mistake. Now whoever had fired the other shot was aware of my presence, and I had no idea . . . Yes, you laugh now! It was not funny then, I tell you. And how stupid . . . *aiee!*

The young bull fell, almost beside me. My horse whirled, wanting to chase the other elk. He was the one I used for a buffalo horse, and he was accustomed to chasing a running animal. Now I had one more problem. I must reload, to be able to defend myself. And I could not reload on the back of a dancing, prancing buffalo horse who wanted to run away with me anyway. I desperately wanted to ride the short distance to the top of the slope so that I could see what might lie before me. I was not sure that I really wanted to see it. I had the thought that I would find out sooner than I liked. Regardless, I must reload.

I swung down and quickly tied my horse to a hind leg of the fallen elk. It was still kicking feebly, but I yanked the rope tight and began to reload my thunderstick. I was just ramming the patched ball home when the riders topped the rise and paused to sit looking at me.

There were three of them, young men on fine horses. They were maybe half a bow shot away. I waved an arm to let them know that I saw them and tried to appear casual as I dribbled powder into the priming pan and closed the frizzen, then lowered the flint to half cock. Now I was as prepared as I could be, under the circumstances.

I tried to appear casual as I propped the musket against the dead elk, now still. I turned to face the riders, my hands empty. That, to show confidence that I did not really feel. At least I hoped it would appear that way.

Now I had a moment to study them and try to plan what I would say and do. From the way they wore their hair, I thought that they were Lakota. Lone Walker wore the Lakota style, but he had not really been able to take proper care of it. . . . Did the hair of these men look like Walker's? I thought so, but what if I was wrong? They still sat at a little distance, and I could not see clearly. I had never seen many Lakotas. Only a couple at the French trading post, a few seasons back. What if I made a big show of being a friend of Lakotas, and these were Crows or Blackfeet, *enemies* of the Lakota?

There was nothing to do now but to play out my situation. It did not help much to notice that one of the men turned in his saddle and signaled to others who were not yet in sight. I was able to see that he signed "Only one."

As calmly as I could, I raised my right hand, palm forward, in the hand sign of peaceful greeting. I followed it quickly with other signs that seemed appropriate.

"Join me, friends! We have meat!"

They answered with laughter, but I did not think they were laughing at anything that I would have considered very funny. Now they rode down the slope, rather arrogantly, weapons ready. I had a fleeting thought that I might be able to fight them if I must. Kill the big one who seemed to be a leader, try to reload if I had time before they recovered, and use my hatchet at the end . . . It would have been fatal as well as stupid. Well, I *said* it was only a fleeting thought! *Aiee*, Bull, you would probably have tried it!

Anyway, they approached. I still thought that they looked like Lakota, but they also looked pretty grim. They drew up a few paces away and sat studying me. I did not know whether I wanted them to be Lakota or not.

"Welcome," I signed. I could see my musket, within arm's reach, but tried not to look at it. Any movement in that direction might be my last.

Their leader made the single hand sign for question . . . all inclusive, demanding that I answer anything that they might wonder about me. I did my best.

"I am a trader," I signed. Even as I did so, I realized that here was a fortunate coincidence. The trader sign is also that of the Arapaho sometimes. Most of the people of the plains recognize the special status of Arapaho as traders. Well, Lone Walker was Arapaho, as I have said. So whether these young warriors were Lakota or one of their enemies, the trader sign might be a very fortunate identification to use.

That idea was quickly shattered.

"You lie," the big one signed. "You are no trader. You ride a war horse and have no packs."

12

It was, naturally, a tense moment. My heart was pounding, my hands sweating. I tried not to let it show.

"Even a trader does not take his packs hunting," I signed. "My heart is good that you drove the elk toward me. You made a kill, too? I heard your shot."

They nodded, still not entirely convinced.

"Where is your camp?" one signed.

"Over there. Beside a stream. One of our party was injured in the fire. We have been unable to move on yet."

"Your party? How many?"

The inquiry was quick. I hesitated for a moment. There was no point in lying. They could easily see if I told truth, and it would be to our advantage to do so.

"Four," I signed. "My wife, another trader, and his wife."

Again I used the double-meaning sign for "Arapaho," this time quite truthfully.

"We have used all of our food," I went on. "What we did not lose in the fire. This kill will be welcome."

I was looking to their party, rather than ours. I was still alive, so my confidence was growing.

"You are Lakota?" I asked, though it bothered me some to make the cut-throat sign. After all, it is very little different to sign "Are you going to cut my throat?" Yes, it is amusing now. Then it was not.

It was a great relief when they nodded.

"Your *people* are Arapaho?" one of them signed.

"No. Elk-dog People. My wife, also. The other trader is Arapaho. His wife, Lakota. I do not know their band."

Even as I signed it, I had a moment of dread. What if these *were* enemies of Lakota and had been lying to test me?

"You lie!" signed the big one. "There is no trader like that in this region."

"Yes!" I protested. "It is as I say!"

There was a brief discussion among the three, and they turned back to me.

"How is the woman called?" the big leader signed.

I saw no point in being deceptive, and many reasons to speak truth.

"We call her Plum Flower," I signed.

The eyes of the other man opened wide and then squinted angrily.

"You lie, again!" he accused. "Plum Flower is my sister. She and her husband have no partners."

"Wait! It is as I say," I protested. "We only met them during the fire. Lone Walker was injured when his horse fell."

"We will see if you tell truth!"

He spoke to the others, and one turned away toward the crest of the rise, presumably to let others know what was happening. I tried to remain calm. I did not even know the size of the Lakota hunting party.

"Does it not seem good," I asked in signs, "to butcher out this elk before the day is over? Our camp needs it."

The big man almost smiled.

"Go ahead," he said. "You must speak truth. No one would make up this strange a lie. And it is true that Plum Flower's husband is Lone Walker. Is my sister safe?"

"Yes," I told him. "Quite well. She was ready to kill me when we met, to defend her husband."

Now the Lakotas laughed aloud.

"That is my sister," he agreed. "You *do* speak truth!"

The other man returned as I started to gut out the elk. He was leading a pack horse.

"There are five of us," the brother of Plum Flower explained. "An early hunt. You know the hunger for fresh meat in this season?"

"We know it well. How are you called?"

"Oh! I am Swimming Elk."

"Where is your camp?"

"One sleep north. We came south, hoping to meet buffalo. You have seen none?"

I shook my head. "Not yet. They will follow the fire, though. How far did it burn?"

"To the river. The grass greens well, no?"

We were now into a conversation about the weather and the game, and it was good. I finished the rough dressing of the elk and signed an invitation.

"You will camp with us tonight?"

Swimming Elk nodded. "It is good."

Now the others of Elk's party topped the rise with a second pack horse. It was loaded with haunches of meat, still wrapped in the hide. They had discarded the head and the bony parts to pack more efficiently.

"Your yearling is not too big," Elk suggested. "We can lift the whole thing and go now."

It was a good idea and would hasten our return to the camp. I knew that Otter and the others would be concerned. They would have heard the two shots, a little while apart, and would be unable to understand what had happened to me. I nodded, and it took only a short while for us to lift the carcass to the back of the pack horse. The gelding grunted under the load, but he was a sturdy animal. We were impressed by the horses of the Lakota. But more of that later.

It was a triumphant hunting party that approached our camp. As soon as we were close enough to see the area, I rode ahead with Swimming Elk. I could see the two women watching us and signing to each other, as they tried to identify the other rider.

We kicked our horses up and moved on at a canter. I could tell the instant that Plum Flower recognized her brother. She ran toward us, followed closely by Otter.

Swimming Elk looked over at me with a smile. "You spoke truth!" he signed.

Everyone was talking at once, and it was a happy time. Elk swung down, embraced his sister, and then walked on toward our camp. Lone Walker was on his feet, smiling. They exchanged greetings in Lakota tongue.

My arms were full of Otter Woman, who was full of a hundred questions.

"We heard your shots," she told me. "I was very worried, Pup. I was about to come looking for you!"

She was holding me as if she would never let go. I hope she never does!

"You did not make a kill, even in two shots?" she chided me. "*Aiee*, you must be growing old, Pup."

You see, the rest of the party had not yet come in sight around the shoulder of the hill.

"I am not dead yet, woman," I told her. "You think I am not a hunter, as well as bearer of the Pipe? Behold!"

I had seen the first of the other riders and turned now to wave an arm, to call her attention to the sight. Riders, pack horses, heavily laden with meat.

Otter laughed, of course. "You had no pack horse! Those are *their* kills!"

"*Aiee!* One is mine, one theirs. They camp with us tonight. Five of them, counting Plum Flower's brother."

"Yes. She told me who he is. This is good, Pup. Where is their camp?"

"One sleep north, Elk says."

It was an evening of feasting, reunion, and celebration. We were honored to be a part of it. The best cuts of the fat yearling were broiled almost continuously all evening, and we ate great amounts of fresh meat. Most of our talk was in hand signs, though Walker was very helpful in translation when it was needed.

Before the evening we were trading stories of Creation and of long-ago times, and it was good. How different now, our feeling toward Lakotas, the dreaded "cut-throats." It is difficult to think of killing a person with whom you have shared meat, no? The Lakotas were also very helpful in riding up and down the stream to gather fuel for all the cooking we were doing. We had depleted much of the supply that had been near at hand.

During the course of the evening Swimming Elk took me aside.

"I did not understand," he signed, "all you have done for my sister and Walker. They lost everything! You had only a little but used it to help them."

"It was nothing," I told him. "They would have helped us."

"They would, but many would not," he answered. "I will not forget, friend."

"It is good," I told him. "But you see how I needed that kill!"

"You *needed* it!" he laughed. "Let us eat some more!"

I was made to think that this was a great step forward on our quest. Oh, yes, let me not forget! Before dark there was much comment on the foal, the medicine hat colt. He seemed to relish the excitement and attention, and was willing to show off his gaits, trotting and loping around the camp as he became acquainted with the other horses. Most of the comments, unfortunately, were in their own tongue, but we could tell that they were admiring and favorable to the quality of the animal. This, of course, was a mixed feeling for us. It was good to have him admired but made us nervous. Would someone want to steal him? Later we began to realize that we need not worry about that with these people. We had been accepted by them, so we were considered to be part of their group. One does not steal horses from his own people, does he? No, they would be more likely to protect our property, as well as ourselves, from any mutual enemy.

And they did have enemies, though not in that area. We began quickly to learn of this very large nation, who control much of the north country. We exchanged Creation stories, as I have said. Both the Lakota and ourselves came from inside the earth. I wondered whether we knew each other below. . . . No, not seriously. It is a joke. But as we crawled out through the hollow cottonwood log, they climbed up the roots of a giant vine or tree. I was not sure. . . . The hand signs made it harder, you see. "Root" could be of any plant. But *big* roots . . . Whatever.

We began to recognize a few Lakota words, and to ask Lone Walker for aid in learning. He was very helpful, telling us much that was valuable later. There are three main branches of this nation, Walker said. All are called Sioux by the French. They call themselves Lakota in the area where we were. Farther east they are Dakota, and farther west, Nakota. Their tongue is only slightly different, and they understand each other well.

Now they also have many bands. Our Elk-dog People have five. Six, counting the New band. These have many. They are far-spread, and their bands are probably more important to them than the nation. They have several Sun Dances in different places.

Here is also a strange thing: Some of their worst enemies speak in similar tongues! Crow and Blackfeet have some of the same words. *Aiee*, I get ahead of my story. But I am made to think that at one time these enemies might have been only wide-separated bands of the same people. But no matter.

I started to speak of the horse, and how he got his name that first evening with the Lakotas. We kept hearing this word in their tongue, as they watched the colt or discussed him. I gathered that they were speaking favorably, because of their facial expressions as they said it.

Finally, out of curiosity, I asked Lone Walker what was the meaning of the repeated word that they were using. I mentioned that I took it to be good.

Walker laughed. "Two words, really," he told me. "One is 'good,' or 'wonderful,' as you guessed. The other means 'hat.' They are calling him The Hat, The Good Hat."

It does not translate well, but it is a good name in Lakota. Since we were learning their tongue, it seemed to make sense to use their phrase, so it became the colt's name: Good Hat.

13

My husband has told you of our meeting with the Lakotas. I will tell you more of them. First I was impressed by their appearance. I thought that it was only coincidence that those first men, the hunting party we met, were so tall. Their leader, Swimming Elk, was one of the tallest men I had ever seen. Pipe Bearer is tall. There are many among the People who grow tall, much taller than some of our neighbors. But the shortest of that hunting party was nearly as tall as my husband. And the brother of Plum Flower was at least a hand's span taller.

But they were also handsome. . . . Ah, I see that look, Pup! You know that they are. You also admired the beauty of their women. . . . Now, my friends, it has always been a saying among the People that we have the most beautiful of women. Our neighbors formerly tried to carry off our young girls to raise for wives. "Our women are prettier than theirs," we said. And it is largely true. Our women are tall, with long, pretty legs and handsome faces.

But we found this also to be true among the Lakotas. We had already noticed the remarkable beauty of our new friend, Plum Flower. And she was tall, too. A little taller than I. But the shape of her nose, her cheekbones, her chin . . . well, any woman would like to look like that! And when we reached the camp of the Lakotas, we found that this was the normal appearance of their people. The men tall, handsome, and dignified. The women, beautiful of face and figure, long-legged, and active. Their status is good, too, much like our own. They are *respected* by their men. Not like some of the tribes and nations we have known.

I understand that the women of our allies, the Head Splitters, were once treated with less respect than they are now. I am made to think that maybe they have changed some from their contact with the People. No matter. Back to the Lakotas.

We were received at their camp with great honor. We had traveled very slowly because of Lone Walker's condition. A couple of the men had gone on ahead with the pack horses and the meat, so that it could be used. We had smoked and dried some, and of course we had eaten all we could.

Walker had found that he was more comfortable walking part of the time. It did not pound his sore ribs as badly as the bumping gaits of a horse. Maybe Pipe Bearer mentioned that. . . .

Anyway, when we approached the camp, everyone there had already heard our story. We were welcomed with great respect because of our having helped Walker and Plum Flower. Add to that the fact that we had the medicine hat colt. *Aiee*, we were honored guests.

This was a big camp, by our standards. Not as big as our Sun Dance, when all our bands gather. No, not half as big . . . maybe a third. Yes, about that size. More than a hundred lodges. There is a limit to the size of a band, you know. There must be enough grass for horses and enough game to feed its people. I am made to think that they move more often than we do . . . the bigger bands like this one, I mean. They have to, to find grass and game. There also seemed to be more dogs than we have. I know, sometimes we have many dogs. They have even more. They eat them, as we do, when we have no game available. Some prefer the stew, too.

But I was trying to tell of their ways, so that you could visualize our experience.

Their lodges? Yes, much like ours. Big lodges, facing east, of course. The shape of the doorway, the smoke flaps, a little different. Not much. Any of us could set up and use one of their lodges, as they could ours.

We paid our visit to their band chief, as is the custom, and he welcomed us. He was an older man, as tall as Swimming Elk, very handsome and dignified. This man looked as a leader should look. He was very gracious, and spoke again of our help to Plum Flower and Walker. We were made to think that he was a relative of Plum Flower's family, but it is hard to tell. In a way, it is like our custom among the People. "Uncle" is used for any male older than ourselves, and any older woman is our "grandmother."

They also had some customs that we found strange, though some we have encountered elsewhere. A man may not speak to his wife's mother. For instance, the mother of Plum Flower could not carry on a conversation with Lone Walker. This, because in case of her husband's death, she would become part of Walker's family . . . his wife, though not his wife . . .

You can see how confusing that could become, when explained to us partly in hand signs and in tongues not familiar to us. But it was very strange to sit together and to have Lone Walker say to his wife, "Tell your mother this or that," when the woman is sitting across the fire from him. Then Plum Flower would repeat it, and her mother would answer, "Tell your husband so-and-so."

These were not things of great importance at all. Just talk of the weather and such things. Small talk, jokes . . . It must have been hard to pretend that one did not hear the joke until it was repeated. Yet we have customs that must seem strange to them, I am sure.

Some are much the same, though. Men sometimes have more than one wife, as the People do. A little more often than we do, maybe. I am made to think that this is the reason: They are engaged in war a little more than we, so more of their men are killed. That, of course, is the main reason for more than one wife. If a woman is widowed, there must be someone to hunt meat for her lodge and her children. As you know, the most usual arrangement among the People would be for her to move into her sister's lodge as a second wife. It is our way. Not required, but expected, maybe.

Yes, I know there are men who seem to be possessed with how many wives they can acquire. That is more common among our allies the Head Splitters. Did they not once have a chief called Many Wives? But that is another matter. What I was saying was that the Lakotas are greatly concerned with family, as we are. Like us, they take care of their own. Customs differ, but people are people, no? As we played the part of traders, we quickly learned that to be true.

During this time with the Lakotas, we were guests in the lodge of Plum Flower and Lone Walker. Yes, they had a lodge. It had been kept for them by relatives, and when we joined the band, we helped to set it up. Who owns the lodge? *Aiee!* I was never sure. As you know, in some nations the lodge is owned by the woman. In some, by the man. I was made to think that among the Lakotas it could be either one. The lodge, that of Plum Flower and Walker, it seemed that *both* did. That, because both her family and his had contributed skins and work to make the lodge cover. Gifts of poles, maybe, too. Both were strong families.

Pipe Bearer helped with the hunting while Walker was still recovering from his broken ribs. As he has told you, the two men had become close friends . . . "almost-brothers." And it was good.

I mentioned the horses of the Lakotas. My husband will probably tell you more about them, but my family has also a tradition of fine horses. And, I would tell you, these were fine animals. Well, mostly. Not all horses may be of good quality anywhere. But as a group, a band of these horses presented as fine a quality as you will see.

They steal horses, of course. An honorable contest, and not quite as dangerous as war. Lakotas steal from Crows, both steal from Blackfeet and Arapaho, all from Shoshone, and the other way around.

The colors of these horses were different. We saw no bays or browns, and none of dun color. Most were blue roans, with sometimes a red roan. A few were black, and many had white on their faces.

But let me not talk of these things. I know that Pipe Bearer can describe horses better than I. Here, Pup . . .

Well, Otter could tell of this. She is only being kind to me, no? She knows how I love to talk of horses.

Really, she has spoken well of the colors. Never did I see so many roans in one place. She mentioned the blacks, too. Sometimes there would be an animal, usually a black, with a patch of white on its ribs or shoulder. Not the paint-horse such as we see, or the kind with a spotted rump. Just a ragged white patch here and there.

And Otter mentioned white faces. Is that not odd? Our horses often have a spot of white between the eyes, or maybe a stripe running down to the nose. But here, many with the whole nose or face white, clear around the eyes and onto the jaws.

Another thing . . . we saw very few with white feet. You know, many horsemen do not like white feet. The hoof is soft, and the horse goes lame easily. I tell you now, very few of the horses of the Lakota have even one white foot. Their hooves are black and hard as iron. I had not expected to be so impressed.

I had opportunity to hunt with the Lakota men, and to see these horses at work. Again, I was made to see their toughness, their endurance.

The build of these horses is a little different. Good, broad foreheads with large, wide-set eyes, a tapering muzzle, small ears, and an *intelligent* look. They are of medium height, about right for running buffalo. Deep chest, short, straight back. The tail is set much lower than on our horses, and there is a slope to the hip. . . . Looking from the side, you can see that the slope drops off sharply from the top of the hip to the rump and tail. This makes the haunch heavy and powerful from the flank on back, you see. I will show you later, on an animal or two. *Aiee*, the wide muscle on some of their stallions! This gives them tremendous endurance.

But I get carried away and forget that I am telling a story, here. What? Better than our horses? Ah, I would be foolish to admit that, no? Look, Bull, it is like this: If I have the best horse alive, I still admire other fine horses, no? Some of them are better than some of ours, maybe. Some of ours better. What I am saying is that the horses of the Lakota are *different*. They are suited to their purposes and are excellent buffalo runners with great endurance. I was made to think that here was breeding stock that would mix well with our own, though. That is why we brought home a few.

Aiee! I have enough trouble with getting ahead of my story, Bull! Yes, I know you are a horseman. We will look at them in the morning, no?

What? Lone Walker's horse? Oh, yes, I meant to tell of that. Walker had been unable to catch his best mount when the fire had swept down on them. He rode an old pack horse to safety, as we said. His biggest regret, I think, even worse than his ribs, was the loss of his favorite stallion. One can grow new bone and skin, but it is hard to replace the one best horse that he owns in a lifetime.

We searched for it while we were in the area, Walker's friends and I. But we did not see any trace. No sign of dead horses, though. We followed the vultures but found only smaller animals, victims of the fire.

I was made to think that Lone Walker's stallion was wise enough and strong enough to save himself and their other two horses from the fire. But we never found them. That stallion probably has his own herd now.

14

We were still with the Lakotas, in the lodge of Lone Walker and Plum Flower, when it came time for their Sun Dance. Why did we stay? It is hard to explain. Yes, we felt the pressing need to continue the quest. But at first we felt the responsibility to Lone Walker, and to provide for Plum Flower as she cared for him. By this time she and Otter had become very close friends. Like sisters, as Walker and I were almost-brothers. It did not seem good to leave them until Walker was able to hunt a little.

Yes, I know. Someone else would have seen to their needs. They had friends, and Flower had relatives among the Lakota. But it was not the same. Just as our heart is better toward one with whom we have shared meat . . . There is a closeness, a tie that binds us to those who have struggled to survive and suffered together. This is a bond that might *never* be severed. . . . I hope that I am making myself understood.

Anyway, that made it easier to set aside our plans from day to day. *Yes, we will leave soon . . . not today, but soon.* That is how it was, and the Moon of Greening gave way to the Moon of Growing. Their seasons are a little behind ours in the spring, of course, being farther north.

But the time was coming for their Sun Dance. Walker and Plum Flower were beginning to urge us to stay for that event. We would miss our own, of course, either way.

Now, the Sun Dance is observed in many nations in the grassland. I am made to think that the purpose is mostly the same for all who hunt the buffalo. *Pte*, the Lakota call him. But when the earth wakens with the return of Sun's torch, the grass grows. This return brings the return of the buffalo, who eat the grass, to grow fat so that we can eat them. Our Sun Dance is to give thanks for this yearly event. We pray, act to fulfill vows we have made, and make new vows in supplication. It is our renewal of faith, of patriotism, of our health. . . . You are familiar with it, of course. Some nations do not have a Sun Dance. Head Splitters often attend ours, you know, having none of their own.

Now, I am mentioning all of this to tell you of a big difference in the customs there among the Lakotas. That is, in the vision-quest. Yes, ours is a quiet, private time of fasting. A young person goes away by himself (or herself, of course) and fasts and prays. Many times this leads to contact with that person's medicine creature, his guide. Sometimes not. It can happen before or after, too, you know.

Now, among the Lakota, the vision-quest is a *part* of the Sun Dance. A warrior, coming of age, goes through a ceremony to celebrate, and to ask for spiritual guidance. Thongs are fastened to his chest, by means of skewers in the skin. He is tied to a pole or a cottonwood tree by these thongs. He fasts, prays, and dances while he is tethered. How long? Three or four days. He tries to break the skin to free himself.

Aiee! I see the looks on your faces. No, you misunderstand, my friends. The cutting of the skin is not the important part. That is a small thing, no bigger than a fingertip on each side. You have all lost more skin than that, just falling off your horses. It is their way, and a part of the ceremony.

I had noticed something when I bound the broken ribs of my almost-brother, Lone Walker. On his chest were two small round scars, one on each side, above the nipples. They were the size of the end of my thumb, maybe. I wondered about them at the time. They looked much like a healed bullet wound, or the mark of an arrow. Now, when I saw their Sun Dance and their vision-quest ceremonies, I realized . . . Lone Walker carried those scars as a reminder of his own vision-quest. There is another ceremony, too. . . . No, I will tell of that, later.

And although the ceremony is public, the vision-quest is at the same time very private. The fasting, as we know, clarifies the senses and gives more intense exchanges with spirit-matters. It is often at this time for the Lakota that one's medicine animal speaks to him.

One of our new friends told me of his own experience. I say "new friends," though by that time, when they celebrated the Sun Dance, it had been some time . . . more than a moon, since we had joined the Lakotas. This man, No Tail Dog, was a friend of Walker's, and I had hunted with him while Walker's ribs healed. I had come to respect this man greatly but was not really prepared for him to share his vision-quest experience with me. I was greatly honored that he would do so.

It was the third day of his quest, he said. He was exhausted, because it is hard to sleep half standing, and he was unable to lie down because of the rope to his chest. He was leaning against the pull of the thongs, wondering if today might be the day he could break the skewers free. He tried to focus his eyes on the strips of skin to see if they might be stretching to the point that he might be able to put forth the extra effort. . . . There must be a freeing of the spirit after that confinement. I do not know. I was invited to participate, and that too was an honor to me, but I did not do so. I have had my vision-quest experience, in the way of the People. I talk to my medicine guide, though sometimes I feel that I may not listen when he tries to speak to my heart. . . .

But back to No Tail Dog. He told me that he was half sleeping, letting the thongs in his chest help to support him, and looked up at the rope that connected them to the pole.

There was a grasshopper sitting on that rope. *How curious*, thought No Tail Dog. It was an unlikely place for a grasshopper to sit, you see. It took him a little while to realize that there might be a reason. The creature had approached him despite the dust and sweat and the confusion of the dancers.

Then it came to him: This must be his medicine guide! As he realized this, there was a great feeling of joy, a lifting of the spirit, and it was good. I am sure that some of you know the feeling. It might come to us in different ways, and we cannot really describe it. But I am made to think that it does not matter how it comes to us. If we have that experience, it reaches our hearts, and we have greater understanding for others. For *their* experience, though it be different. So I was able to feel joy for No Tail Dog as he told me.

"Thank you, Grandfather," he whispered to his medicine grasshopper. "Thank you for coming."

The grasshopper then flew, with a showy clatter of red inner wings, and perched on the smoke pole of a lodge nearby. Dog took this as a sign, and to this day his lodge and his shield are decorated with his totem, a grasshopper.

Why do I tell you these things? *Aiee*, I wonder, myself! But what I am trying to do, maybe, is to tell of how we, Otter and I, came to feel so close to these people, and so quickly. We were accepted much more easily than we would expect. Our experience of survival from the fire with Walker and Flower made us kin with them and allowed us to be accepted by their people. In turn, we were made to understand their customs and their ways. We have met people whose ways I did not understand well at all. But these had a feeling of the spirit that we could feel, too, and we found it good. It helped us much, later.

The camp of these, the people of Walker and Plum Flower, was ready to move after the Sun Dance. They would travel to the north for the season. A few sleeps, maybe. We were made to think that their move to summer camp is much like ours.

We decided that this was the time for us to leave them and continue our quest. Lone Walker was doing well and would soon be able to hunt. Meanwhile, if they needed help, No Tail Dog and other friends and relatives would gladly help them. We felt that we should move westward or maybe northwest, toward the Crow, Blackfeet, and Shoshone.

"Walker," I told him, "I am made to think that we must continue our quest." I told him of the direction that we proposed to take.

He nodded in understanding.

"My heart is heavy, almost-brother," Walker said. "But you are right. You must do as you are called."

The women, too, were saddened over the parting. Plum Flower and Otter Woman had become like sisters, and we knew that parting would be hard for them. In fact, Lone Walker and I talked of it a little, and of how lonely it would be for Otter on the trail.

"Of course, she will have me," I boasted.

"That is true," Walker laughed. "And Flower has me. Maybe that is why they need each other, no?"

It was the next day when he approached me in a more serious mood.

"Almost-brother," he began, "Plum Flower and I have talked."

He paused and I had no idea what he was trying to say. I knew that both of the women were sad about the parting to come. I was sure that they had talked about it, as Walker and I had done. But I waited.

"We, Flower and I, are made to think that we should go with you," Lone Walker said bluntly. "You will need help with talking to these other people."

"But you . . . we have hand signs," I protested. "Walker, do not feel that you owe . . ."

He held up a hand to silence me. "No. We do owe you our lives, but that is not it, Pup."

They had begun to call me by Otter's pet name for me.

"This is for myself," Lone Walker went on. "Your vision, the colt . . . I must know more about the medicine horse! I will help you to find out. If you will allow me, of course."

I was deeply touched by this, and I had to swallow before I could speak.

"It is good," I told him. "I am honored, Walker." And I was quite sincere. My heart was full.

"When will you leave?" he asked.

"We had not decided. We have no preparation to make. When does your band break camp?"

"Two days. We can strike the lodge and let someone . . . Flower's brother, maybe, will take it for us. We will travel light, as you do."

So it was decided. I began to have more confidence in our quest very quickly. To be guided by someone who knows the country and the tongues of its people was a great help to us.

We began to prepare our packs and to see to our horses, that they were ready to go. We had spent much time with the colt, and he would now lead well with a halter around his head.

And, *aiee*, how he was growing! He had gained much favorable attention while we had been with the Lakotas. Much at first from his markings. But then at second look, it was apparent that here was, also, an animal of very superior quality. The long, flat muscle of his hind quarters was beginning to bulge with power. His constant activity caused growth in his using muscles. He was taller and heavier each time I looked at him, it seemed.

Now that it had been decided, that Walker and Flower would go with us, the women were busy with preparations. It occurred to me that both had been withdrawn for the past few days, talking quietly between them. Now they were chattering happily as they packed.

I wondered somehow if they had discussed between them the possibility of joining in this quest.

15

Pipe Bearer has told you of the Sun Dance of the Lakotas. He has told it well. It was exciting, even fascinating, to see the ceremonies of another nation in this way. As my husband says, we felt no urgency to continue on our quest yet. It was as if this was a time of preparation. We had not forgotten our purpose in being here, but it seemed only sensible to learn what we could of this north country while we had the chance.

During that time we were learning a great deal that would help us. We both were beginning to carry on conversation in the Lakota tongue. We were learning their customs. Pipe Bearer had hunted with Swimming Elk, No Tail Dog, and other men who were friends and relatives of Lone Walker and Plum Flower.

I had met some of the women. Plum Flower and I spent several afternoons visiting in the lodges of these. As among the People, women like to work together and gossip while they sew or decorate with quills or beads. It was a good way to learn the language, too.

Plum Flower had much to do, to replace the garments they had lost in the fire. I was pleased to help her in this. I had a little more experience with the new small glass beads of the

French traders. They were more skilled in the use of quills. So it was interesting to share our respective knowledge.

In the course of all this, we visited and worked in the lodges of several different women. Again, I found that some lodges are much more pleasant to be in than others. It seemed to depend much on how the wife or wives related to their men. And, as among the People, some marriages are better than others. Well, some husbands are better than others, no? And, yes, Pup, I will say it before you can . . . some wives, too. Seriously, we have always felt blessed. But that, too, is another story.

What I was trying to relate, before I was distracted here, was of the ways in which we saw these marriages. It was a help, maybe, *not* to know their language well. If we are around a family whose tongue is not ours, I am made to think that we can see their relationships more clearly. We are not distracted by their words, and can see more clearly the other things that often go unseen. The way they glance at each other, their little smiles and secret looks, a touch or a gesture. All of these things identify a happy lodge.

An unhappy lodge, of course, has a spirit that is uncomfortable. It is not good to be a guest in that lodge. But a happy lodge is a warm and welcome place. Its spirit is good and reaches out to enfold not only its family, but the visitor, who feels at home.

All these things came to mind in this, a situation where we had to go much by how it felt, rather than what was said. The women in the circle of Plum Flower's friends and relatives had their favorite lodges in which to gather. One of the best was a lodge with three wives. These women were sisters, and all looked much alike. All were round and a little fat and had smiling faces that crinkled the eyes nearly shut when they smiled. I could not easily tell them apart. I learned that there were ribald jokes that their husband could not, either, and that it was a game with them. I do not know about that. It only seemed to me that it was a lodge with a good spirit. As the saying goes, if the children are fat and the women happy, it is good.

It occurred to me later that I never did know how long that lodge had had the three wives. One was sit-by wife, the first in the lodge. Her bed was to the right of her husband's place, across from the doorway. The others, to his left. I do not recall ever hearing how and when the other women had lost their husbands and moved in with their sister.

That was a happy lodge in which to visit and work. Some lodges, it was apparent, the women preferred to avoid. One of these was the lodge of Plum Flower's sister. Some of the men of the Lakotas are haughty. Yes, some of our men are, too. That is true. I should not lump all the men of any group together. Yes, nor the women either. . . . *Aiee*, let me go on, no? I have stepped on my own tongue. I admit it. Where was I? Oh, yes. Flower's sister.

I do not think that she was really unhappy. Her marriage may have been good. She was a lovely and a loving person. But her husband, Bull's Horn, was so distant. . . . He had no close friends and always seemed to think himself superior. Maybe not . . . I do not know. But he was not much fun to be around. Anyway, the spirit of that lodge was strange, not warm and welcoming. I only use it for example of what I was saying. I became distracted.

During all of this time, Plum Flower and I were growing closer. We laughed at the same things, we shared little thoughts and secret ideas, as women do only with special friends. I was beginning to dread the time when Pup and I would move on. Flower and Walker had been very helpful in our learning of their language and customs. I began to feel that we would be lost without them as we traveled on.

Yes, I admit that Flower and I had mentioned to each other that it would be good to stay awhile. I am not certain when or how the idea came to us that they might join us in the trading venture that was really our quest. We did not discuss it in great detail, you understand. It was more like this: When

Lone Walker would mention his curiosity about the medicine horse, Flower would quietly agree. Then Pipe Bearer would wonder how well we could communicate without Walker's language skills. I would say, yes, that we would certainly miss that, and would mention it to Plum Flower.

That was how we went at it. I was probably dreading being a woman without female companionship more than I realized. And we were all young, and there was excitement to be had, you know. It might have been different if we, either of us, had had a child. But we did not yet. So the whole world was ahead of us, and we did not yet understand our mortality. Tragedy always happens to someone else, no? So, yes, Plum Flower and I quietly encouraged the idea that they might go with us on our journey. Maybe we did not realize to what extent we were influencing our husbands. Or maybe we did. . . . It is for men to wonder.

Aiee, Pup! You did not know *that*? It has always been so!

But let me go on. After Lone Walker spoke to my husband about going with us, it became a time of great excitement. Plans grew. We had only two days, you remember, before the band was to break camp. It was a busier time, now, to help provision a bigger party.

To make a better showing as traders, Lone Walker assembled an assortment of items that could pass as trade goods. He borrowed from friends and relatives and soon had two respectable packs. He and Pup selected horses, two for Walker and Plum Flower, and a pack horse for their goods. Our own horses were in good shape. They had gained weight on the new grass, while they had not been working.

The day came, and not long after daylight the first of the big lodges came down. I have always thought that moving day is a time of great excitement. Some dread the work of it, but the thought of new sights and sounds and smells, new experiences, always excites me. It did that time, too, among people of another nation, just as among our own. The confusion, excitement . . . Oh, yes, you know how such a move always excites the dogs? And think of a village that had maybe twice as many dogs as our own. It was a noisy morning, I can tell you!

We helped to take down the lodge and packed the cover for travel and storage. Swimming Elk and his family would keep it until Walker and Plum Flower rejoined the band. Walker went into detail about it. Elk and his family could feel free to use the lodge or let someone else use it if they wished. As you know, it is better for a lodge cover to be used than to be stored. There is less damage from mice, and the skins do not deteriorate so badly. The poles, of course, have a value of their own, beyond that of the lodge cover. They would be a nuisance to transport, but these were fairly new, and of good lodgepole pine. It was well worthwhile to look after them.

"But feel free to use them if you need them," Walker told Elk.

It would be only two or three moves before they would rejoin the band, but during that time Elk's family might as well use these poles for replacements if they needed to. It looked like a good plan.

We watched the long line of horses, people on foot, travois, and dogs begin to wind its way to the northeast. It could have been a column of our own People on the move. They had "wolves" out in front and on the flanks, as we would. Young men drove the hundreds of animals in the horse herd, on the downwind side of the column. In narrow places they would bring up the rear.

We were ready to go, too. We would travel to the northwest. This was a time of excitement. We did not really know what we sought, only that it was important. We all felt it. The four of us looked at each other for a moment, and we all laughed, and it was good.

We mounted, and Lone Walker led the way. He was a little slow, we noticed. It must have been uncomfortable for him those first few days. It had been apparent that though his ribs were well healed, he was stiff and weak from the forced inactivity. He had mentioned it while we were doing the heavy work of taking down the lodge. But he never complained, and in a few days he seemed as strong as anyone.

We traveled well that first day, though it is always the hardest. The traveler must always learn the ways of the various pack animals, as well as those that are ridden. In this case, we were also in strange country, and the four of us had never traveled together before, except right after the fire, when Walker had been badly injured.

We did have the advantage of having lived together, though. We knew each other's ways. Even so, we were tired when evening came, and we made our camp.

There was something important about that first camp, and I think that we all felt it. My husband kindled the fire and offered a pinch of tobacco to the spirits of the area. Lone Walker added a pinch of sage. They place great importance on the use of sage in that region. Did I mention that? We came to use it, too. It is like the use of tobacco, to establish a contact with the spirits who live in a place. Or, yes, some use a few cedar leaves, in other areas.

I am made to think that it is all much the same, that first fire in a new place. It is like one's visit to the chief of a village or camp. When a stranger arrives, he pays his respects to the leader, no? And the first fire in a new camp is for the same purpose, to pay respects to whatever spirits live there. *I am here*, we declare by our offering of tobacco and sage or cedar or sweetgrass. *Here I will camp, with your permission.* It is only right to do this, to recognize and honor the spirits of a place.

In our travels we have seen this custom, that of the first fire in a new place, carried out by many different peoples. Always, I think back to that night, the four of us, friends starting out on a new quest. It was the first night of that part of our lives that we would spend together. The first without a crisis, anyway.

The sunset that night was beautiful. Sun Boy chose his paints well. There was a gentle breeze from the south . . . from *our* homeland in the Sacred Hills.

We watched the stars appear one by one, and marveled once again. There was a new moon, and the evening star near it seemed to be a good sign for the success of our quest.

And it was good.

16

It was as Otter Woman has said. We traveled northwestward, across rolling prairie that was not unlike our own country. A bit drier, maybe. There were fewer villages of growers than we would see farther south. I was made to think that this was because of the dry climate. It was better for grass than for corn and beans and pumpkins, maybe. For whatever reason, we did not encounter many people, and those only along the streams.

Trails, too, were not so plain as in other areas where we have been. The sky is wide, and so is the earth. There was game . . . we could kill a buffalo or elk when we needed meat. Oh, yes, the buffalo came back!

There were a few days when our main problem was to avoid them. The creatures would stand and look at us, and move out of the way when we approached. But there was a day or two when the prairie was black with buffalo as far as we could see. In all directions, too. That made us uneasy. What if they had all started to run? We were careful to move slowly. Actually, our greatest danger was not the chance of a stampede, probably. It was our need of grass for the horses, and water for us all. These great numbers of buffalo ate all the grass. And what water they did not drink from the smaller streams was not usable. It was trampled into muddy soup and fouled with their dung and urine. There was a time when this became a real threat to our survival. We saw no point in trying to travel, so we camped in a bend of the biggest stream we could find. We prayed a lot. There were a few cottonwoods and willows, and enough dead sticks to keep a fire going. The smoke helped to keep the buffalo from crowding us. Our horses browsed the cottonwoods. The water was foul, though. We tried straining it through a blanket, but the taste was bad, even without the dung.

Lone Walker then suggested that we dig a hole a little way from the water's edge. I remembered then that in the western part of our own country, that is done to *find* water in a dry, sandy riverbed. Do not the Head Splitters have a saying that in the dry season their rivers run upside down?

We chose a sandy spot near the water and started to dig with our hands, taking turns. Plum Flower found the bleached shoulder blade of a long-dead buffalo, and it was a good tool for scooping out the sand. It was not long until we could see water seeping into our hole. We deepened it a little more and cleaned it out, and then waited for it to fill. It was slow, of course, but in that way we managed to have enough water for ourselves and the horses.

Three days, I think, we stayed there. One morning we woke to find the buffalo gone. We could see scattered remnants of the herds to the north, a day's travel away. We waited another day, hoping that the stream would start to clear. It did, but very slowly.

Aiee, that was an experience we could have done without! As important as buffalo are to our people, there comes a time when one becomes sick of them. For days my nose and lungs were full of the smell of buffalo. I would take a deep breath of clean, fresh air, and when I breathed it back out, it smelled and *tasted* like buffalo and their dung.

What? Oh, yes, the colors! Otter Woman asks me to tell you of the colors of these buffalo. You could tell them, Otter. Well,

I will, then. It is nothing, only a curious thing that we noticed. There is a wider range of color in that northern herd. I had heard this before but had not seen it.

In our country the buffalo are mostly brown. Dark, nearly black, with a few somewhat lighter. We are not talking of the sacred white animal, which is seen only rarely, of course. Only the slight variation with which we are familiar. Newborn calves are lighter, yellowish or red, and become darker as they mature. There are still some individuals that we see, a bit lighter brown.

But in the northern herd there are many animals that are much lighter. Some as light as our brother the coyote, even. We saw one or two that were an odd blue-gray mouse color. No white ones . . . they would be spirit-animals, of course.

After that adventure with the great northern buffalo herd, we moved on and traveled well. The grass recovered quickly in a few days. The good weather held.

As we traveled northwestward, I began to see a change. Not only was it drier country, but there was something else. . . . It took me a while to realize what it was. The streams that we encountered all seemed to run *north*. In our country they run eastward or to the south. I thought maybe I was turned around in my sense of direction, so I said nothing at first. I looked at the plants that follow the sun. I watched its path during the day.

When the stars came out, I verified what I thought. Yes, the Real-star was where I expected. Then I was right . . . the streams here *were* running in the opposite direction from those in the Sacred Hills. I mentioned this to Lone Walker that evening around the fire.

"Yes," he said, "they run north in this area. All run into a river that runs east and joins others. We will see it in a day or two."

That began to make more sense to me. The main rivers in the country of the People do run eastward. The River of the

Kenzas, and below it, the Ar-kenzas River. The river now called the Platte by the French . . . Yes, all run to the east. And now we learned that, yes, they run eastward in the country of the Lakotas, too. One other thing we learned. The river may be called different names by different tribes or nations or towns. That became quite confusing sometimes.

We should come to a river, Walker said, that was called by the name of the people who lived there. He often used hand signs to make clear that in which we encountered a language problem. Yes, we still had some of that. But when he spoke of this river, he used the hand sign for the "finger-cutters," the Cheyennes. They cut a finger to mourn the death of a loved one, you know. Just as some cut their hair or gash their forearms. I had thought that we were too far north. Our Red Rocks band often has contact with the Cheyennes, and that is much farther south. Walker, with the trading and travel experience of his people, explained that there are Northern Cheyennes and Southern Cheyennes. It was very convenient to have a man with his knowledge to explain some of these things.

But now we were approaching country that was strange to our companions, too. It would be good, Walker thought, to encounter some people, and to inquire about what lay ahead. We watched carefully for any signs of others. The country was becoming more forbidding, the grass thinner, and, consequently, there was little game. Somewhere in this region was an area that Walker called the Bad Place, but he did not know exactly where. We asked about why it was bad, and Walker shrugged.

"No water, nothing grows, no game, nothing. Its spirit is bad, too. An evil place."

Well, there are places like that, of course. Some places are bad because of the bad things that have taken place there. Others have had a bad spirit since Creation, maybe. Just as the spirit of some places is good. There may be bad places, as well as sacred places, no? I will tell more of that later. But for now . . .

We did find a band of Cheyennes, camped on one of the north-flowing creeks. They were glad to see us, and we traded a little. You have to understand, now, that as traders from a different area we were not in any great danger. We could even walk into a camp of people who were enemies of the Lakota. After all, of the four of us, only Plum Flower was Lakota. Though Walker was following his wife's customs, he could claim to be Arapaho. Otter and I were Elk-dog People, unknown in this area, so we had no enemies. If we entered a camp *friendly* to Lakota, we would lean heavily on that identity. There was little real danger, or so we thought. Most people will give a stranger a chance to introduce himself before killing him. . . . Ah, that did not come out as I intended! But you know.

The Cheyennes were friendly. They were preparing to move southward in a day or two, because game was scarce. We traded a little, and told stories that night, and asked about the country. They gave us good information about the Bad Place and its location. It is bigger, they said, than we had been led to believe. To go all the way around it would take several sleeps. To try to cross it, very dangerous. Impossible, maybe.

They suggested that we go straight west two or three sleeps, then turn north. There was good country, good hunting there, they told us. They mentioned several times an area of pine forests that sounded like a mountainous region. We asked about it and were confused by their answers. Not really the mountains, they said. There was more prairie to the west, and *then* mountains. *These, then, are hills?* we asked. *Well, yes, but like mountains . . . Aiee*, we did not know what to think. We saw these hills later. Yes, they are like the mountains. Rough, rugged, but not so tall . . . thick forest.

The Cheyennes warned us again about the Bad Place, but we thought that though they seemed afraid of it, they were fascinated by it. That, of course, made us curious.

"Maybe," said Walker, "we should go close enough to take a quick look."

It was tempting. Here was an exciting, possibly dangerous, curiosity. As I have said, we were young and curious, and had few responsibilities. And the Cheyennes had actually seemed to suggest that this was something that one should see. I am made to think that they are much like ourselves. At least in this way. They had assured us that we would be able to see the dangerous country clearly.

"We would not blunder into it without knowing?" we asked.

The Cheyennes laughed. "No, no! You will *know* the Bad Place."

The problem, you see, is to know it is there, and how to travel *around* it rather than trying to go *through*.

So after discussion around our own fire after we left the finger-cutters, we finally decided. We would skirt around the edge of the Bad country on its south edge, and then turn northward along its western edge. That would take us into the small mountains they told of.

Now, it may seem strange to you that we were planning to see all these things that might tend to interfere with our quest. But think on it. . . . All of these places are powerful places of the spirit. Our quest wás a spirit-quest. It was not hard to convince ourselves that we *must* see these places of the spirit to learn whether we were meant to take our quest there.

So, as our Cheyenne friends had suggested, we followed one of the streams north to the river, crossed it, and headed toward the Bad Place to see whether it had meaning for our quest.

17

The "Bad Place" truly was. Our curiosity took us along the south edge of it, and it was as the Cheyennes had told us . . . Bad.

My friends, there are places in our own country where very little grass can grow. There are a few plants that do, though. You remember the saying of the People about such an area. "Everything that grows there carries a weapon." Cactus, thorny plants, Real-snakes . . . (At least they rattle a warning.) Scorpions that sting, hairy spiders . . . It is not the sort of place that we enjoy. We cross it to get where we are going. After a rain there are even flowers that bloom for a little while, but we do not find its spirit good.

Let me tell you now, though. Compared to the Bad Place, that dry desert that we know is like the breath of spring. The Bad Place is so parched that *nothing* grows there. We saw places where as far as the eye could see, not one blade of grass, not one cactus, even. Just piles of sandy clay. It is all the same color, each little hill exactly the same as the hundreds of others, as far as we could see. Not even a buzzard circled over it to look for dead or dying. They know. There is nothing there to die, for there was nothing alive to begin with. We could see across it the distance of a day's travel, and it was the same, on beyond that. Anyone would be a fool to try to cross it.

And its spirit is bad. It made us uneasy even to camp near the edge of it. My mind played tricks on me, maybe. I had the idea that one who rode out into that maze of hillocks, all the same, would never come out, but would disappear, and would ride forever in that dry-baked miserable sameness. Otter Woman felt the same, and so did our friends. Neither of them had been here before but had heard its story.

Well, it was worth seeing, if only to make us appreciate the rest of the world. We rode westward, skirting between the Bad Place and the river. As you can imagine, we camped each night nearer the river than the rough and threatening country.

Of course, we had to keep the bad part within sight most of the time, or we would not know when to turn north again. Several times we thought we had reached the end of it and would start north, only to find that it was not true. Just a curve in the outline of its edge. A time or two we had to backtrack out of the dead end we had ridden into.

It was in one of those pockets that we made a discovery that frightened us all. We had just realized that we must backtrack, and were turning our horses, when Plum Flower gasped. We all looked around quickly. In a setting as threatening as this, when anybody gasps, one looks. It makes the hair stand on our necks, for we fear the unknown.

Now, we were between two of the little hills that I mentioned, and our way was narrow. The thing that had caused Flower's reaction did not look like much when I first glanced around. It was only a rock, thrusting out of the dull gray-brown clay of the slope. I did not see anything so startling about it. It was whitish, and we had seen many rocks. It was sticking out of a slope like a thousand other hillsides we had seen that day. I turned my horse in that direction, thinking that maybe there was a snake or a scorpion or some small creature that I did not even know. Plum Flower was not inclined to be squeamish or to overreact.

It took me a moment to realize what I saw. I sat staring at the rounded end of the stone, unable to put things in their proper place. I was looking at the end of a *bone.* I could see the shaft of it, where it protruded out of the clay. At the outer end it was larger and rounded. It seemed to be a leg bone, but the size . . . *aiee!* The shaft was so big . . . when I dismounted and approached it, I saw that I could not have reached around it with my two hands! I did not try it, though. My skin felt a chill, though the day was hot. I could think of only one thing. I did not know how long that bone might be, but I could see its thickness. *How big a creature could it have been?*

I tried to think of the size of a leg bone of the biggest buffalo bull I had ever seen. This bone would dwarf it by comparison. The beast must have been three or four times as big as a buffalo!

Of course, I was also wondering whether it ate grass or meat, and if there was any of its kind still around. It was a very uncomfortable feeling.

"Look!" said Otter suddenly. "Another one!"

It was true. Once we had realized what we were seeing, there were other bones, big and little, all around us. I saw a rib as long as I am tall, more leg bones, and a joint of backbone that would have been too heavy to lift.

We realized, of course, that these were old bones. The kind that have turned to stone. In our own country we find the bones of great fishes in the white chalk beds, you know. But old or not, the spirit of the place became even more uncomfortable. Do the spirits of such creatures last forever? And how do they feel about the intrusion of mere people?

We looked to Plum Flower, for this was her country. Or nearer so than any of the rest of us, anyway. It did not help that she looked pale and shaken.

"You know of this?" her husband asked her.

Plum Flower nodded. "Let us go now," she said softly. "I will tell you later."

Even the horses were eager to leave the area. Yes, maybe they felt *our* concern and our fears. Or maybe they too felt the bad spirit of the place.

Did you ever notice that some horses, like some people, feel such things more strongly? They see things that we do not, and that other horses do not. I think so, anyway. Maybe they too are given gifts of the spirit sometimes. Why not? Of course, I was thinking in terms of the medicine hat horse anyway.

It did seem that the colt, Good Hat, was especially impressed by the giant bones. He would stare at them, ears up, every muscle tense as he sniffed, trying to tell what was happening. Then he would jump and wheel away to run. It was as if he knew and saw things we did not.

We left quickly, glad to be out of there.

We camped early that night. As soon as we found a place on the river that seemed far enough from the threat of the monsters who had left their bones in the Bad Place.

I had begun to wonder whether every one of those hundreds and thousands of little hills of sandy clay was a burial mound for the giant beasts. Or were they giants who stood upright on two legs, men three or four times the size of ordinary men? We had seen no skulls, and not enough bones to tell what sort of creatures they might have been. More important, were there any that still *lived* of this strange race? It was not a comfortable feeling, I can tell you, as the darkness fell. In this strange, forbidding country with its threatening spirit, *aiee!* I wondered why we had come this way. Surely, it had little to do with our quest. It seemed that a threat hung over our camp. We offered the traditional pinch of tobacco in the newly kindled fire, making it a large pinch.

Oh, yes. I had also offered tobacco at the place we found the bones. We did not stop to burn it—I just tossed it over the bones. I do not know . . . it seemed like a good idea at the time. It may not be that the spirits of ancient giants are pleased by the gift of tobacco in their honor, but it was worth a try. But back to that uneasy campfire on the river in that strange place.

Little was said until we had the fire going. Somehow a fire reassures us. It is not only an announcement of our presence, maybe. It is also a reassurance to ourselves: *Yes, I am still here. I can tell, because I have just made a fire, and here I sit.*

Maybe no one else feels that satisfaction and assurance. Well, I see some nodding of heads, so I know you understand. What I was trying to tell is how we felt that night. There was never before so important a fire, since the People crawled through the log into the world.

We ate a little, dried meat that we carried, and finally, when we had settled in, Plum Flower began to talk.

"I am not a storyteller," she apologized. "I had almost forgotten about these bones."

"You have seen them before?" asked Otter Woman.

"No, no. But I have heard their story. A very old story . . . back to Creation, maybe before."

"Before?"

"Maybe. I do not remember. A storyteller would be required to remember and to retell it perfectly. In the nation of my husband, you know, the storyteller must practice until he tells it *perfectly*. If he does not, the stars will go out."

"*Aiee!*" said Otter.

"That is why I explained," Flower went on. "I am not a storyteller, and I take no blame for what may happen if I tell it wrong."

We all nodded in understanding.

"So I will do my best, but I can do no more than that," she stated. "Back then, at Creation, there was only one language. All humans and animals spoke it. Many of our stories come from that time, no?"

We all nodded but said nothing.

"Well, at that time, or maybe *before* we came from inside the earth, there was a race of evil giant creatures. Great lizards and monsters of all sorts. They were evil and they fought and killed each other."

"Did they eat *people*?" blurted Otter.

I wanted to know, too, but I would have waited. Maybe the story would tell. But Otter gets to the point quickly, no?

"That is what I am not sure," Plum Flower admitted. "Maybe so. It has been a long time since I heard this story, or even thought about it. I was as surprised as you when we found the bones, Otter."

"Forgive me," Otter said. "Please go on."

"Well, anyway," Flower continued, "they were evil. *Very* evil. So bad that the Great Father feared they would spoil the rest of Creation. Or maybe that they would eat all the people, Otter. Maybe that was the reason He decided to destroy them all. So He caused fire to rain down from the sky. It must have been a terrible time, because the effect was so powerful that the great beasts were not only killed but driven deep into the ground. None have been seen since."

Now, my friends, that was *my* favorite part of the story, that none have been seen since. I had wondered about that, and it was reassuring to learn that I need not worry. Well, maybe I still worried a little bit. The night was dark, and out there still lay those bones. None of these creatures had been *seen*, or so Plum Flower said. Did that mean that there *were* none? We had seen none of the bones before, either, but *they* were real. I still felt uneasy about it, until we were far from that place.

"What happened then?" inquired Lone Walker.

"After the fire from the sky killed them?" asked Flower. "I am not sure, Walker. Since I cannot remember more, I am made to think that then it became possible for the people to raise families and spread over the earth. The animals, too. The giant creatures are not in any more of our stories. So their destruction must have been complete, no?"

"And you must have told it well, Flower," said Walker with a loving smile. "See, the stars are still up there."

So we assumed that the story, as told by Plum Flower, was true. Besides, if there had been danger, would not the Cheyennes have mentioned it?

We all felt better as the fire burned low and we sought our sleeping robes. Not good, but better.

18

Well, I have told that part, about the giant bones. *Aiee*, I think about that night. It was better in the morning, as the light of day drove away our fears. But, friends, you would have had to be there to realize how it was.

In another day's travel we were plainly to the point where we would leave the evil behind as we changed our direction northward. Travel was much easier, too. The land was level and rolling, there was more grass . . . not the lush grasses of the Sacred Hills, but enough. . . . We saw elk and antelope and scattered buffalo. Enough to furnish us meat as we traveled.

One day we saw smoke in the distance. We were still jumpy about smoke, maybe, though there was no danger from fire at this season. Still, smoke meant people, and we needed to know more about them. We stopped on a low rise and studied the distant smudge against the sky. The morning was calm and still, and the smoke seemed to hang heavily in that one area, rising slowly as the day warmed. There seemed to be a camp or village there to the north, a half day's travel away. It would be nearly in the direction we were traveling.

Now, our purpose was to learn about the horse. We were to appear as traders. The only thing to do was to head directly toward the distant smoke as if that was what we sought. In a way, it *was* what we sought. We started on.

It was not long until one of us noticed another smudge of smoke to the northwest. This was far different in appearance, though. The first was plainly the gray smear of a camp and cooking fires, which always tends to hover over a large group of people. This new smoke was a clean white puff, round and fluffy, like a small cloud against the clear blue of the summer sky. We watched as it grew a little and then simply floated on upward. Another puff rose from the same place, and then another . . . four in all, evenly spaced, the same size and shape. It was a strange, yes, a worrisome thing. We were uneasy about it. For one thing, how could a fire start and stop like that? There must be powerful medicine at work.

"I know!" said Plum Flower suddenly. "It is a signal. My people sometimes do that."

"She is right," Walker agreed. "Maybe they are telling about *us*."

That was not a comfortable thought, that we were being watched, and that those who watched us were telling others a day's travel away about it. It gave me a sort of helpless feeling, as if I had no control over what might happen.

"But *how*?" I asked. "How do they do it?" This was unfamiliar to us.

Plum Flower explained. The smoke signal needs a calm, warm day. They build a small fire with dry wood that will *not* smoke. Then smother it with grass, and two people hold the corners of a robe or blanket to smother it more. Then they can lift the blanket to let out a puff of smoke, put it back on . . .

"Maybe," Walker suggested, "they are signaling four . . . four of us?"

"Maybe," agreed Flower. "But four . . . ah, who knows? Four directions, the four colors . . . this could even be a prayer ceremony, no?"

We never did find out, though it seemed that probably it did have to do with us. When we reached the camp of these people, they were not surprised.

This smoke signal is an interesting thing, though. I have wondered why no one has used it in our country. I am made to think that it is because of the wind. There are some days in our Sacred Hills when the smoke signals could be used. Yes, we tried it once. It would take some practice. But most days in our country have a south breeze. Is not the Kenzas' name for themselves South Wind People?

From watching the way in which these people used the smoke, though, I was made to think that it is a thing the young men like to play with. On a good day, they enjoy it. At times it is important, but usually only an amusement. At least, so it seemed to us. If we ever tried to depend on it, it might be on a windy day and would fail.

We talked of this some as we traveled toward the smudge of smoke in the distance, where we expected to find a camp or village. We did, of course. We could see the pointed tops of the lodges when we also noticed a group of riders coming out to meet us. There were five or six young men who were well armed and effective looking. This was not an official delegation to welcome us, and no real authority was evident. Mostly curiosity. Our own young men might do something of the sort, if they had nothing better to do. Probably some of their friends had sent the smoke signal.

We also suspected that in that country there was more fighting and skirmishing than we have at home. That is a wide area, with more nations living there and hunting across it. More space, but many different hunter nations. They fight, form friendships, disagree, and join to fight someone else. We were impressed at how complicated the rules for these skirmishes can become. It is possible to count honors . . . count coup, they now call it there. . . . To count several coup on the same enemy without even killing him. Well, think about it. It is more dangerous to strike an enemy *without* killing him, because he may strike back. So it takes more bravery, no?

These complicated rules lead to a way in which they decorate the eagle feathers that they wear or tie on their weapons. They cut or trim the feather sometimes, notching it or stripping a part of one side. Paint is used, too, usually black on the white part of the feather. Spots, stripes . . . We never did completely learn the meanings involved.

Sometimes it seemed to us that their war was more of a game. A truly bloody game, to be sure. But we know of times when after a battle, they would sit down together to trade horses or weapons. If the two groups who fight are long-time blood enemies, of course, it is more serious. Then they try to kill all they can. But forgive me, my friends, I am rambling. There is so much to tell.

These people, the ones in the camp whose smoke we saw, were Lakotas. Did I mention that? Yes . . . Well, they were a different band of Lakota, not in frequent contact with Plum Flowers's people. *Aiee*, they are a widespread nation. These spoke with a slightly different accent. So we did as I mentioned before. We said only that we were traders. I from the south, Elk-dog People. Walker from the Arapaho, Trader People. And that these were our wives.

It was obvious that Flower was Lakota, of course, from her hair and dress. And as I have said, Walker had taken on their dress and their ways. But anyone, even enemies of the Lakota, could understand and respect this situation. A trader, having taken a Lakota wife, will wear garments made by her. This seemed to present no problem to them. They thought nothing of a trader dressed as one of their own, and using some of their tongue. And as for Otter and me, they did not know our people anyway. Mostly they were interested in us, and curious about us.

And, of course, there was Good Hat, the colt. He created quite a sensation. Again we tried to act as if he was not unusual, or that we did not *know* that he was. That would gather more information.

Walker understood their tongue, but again pretended to know less than he really did. That was a useful tool for us. If Walker kept a blank look on his face, others would talk freely, as if we were not even there. In this way we learned much. Not just there . . . it was useful in several other situations, too. Walker was very capable with languages. Some people are, others will never be comfortable with a tongue not native to them. I do not do very well with it myself. Otter is better than I. But at that time we had Lone Walker. And, *aiee*, it seemed that he could learn a new tongue in half a day. Not really, but almost.

But about these different Lakotas. As with all the nations that live in skin lodges, many of their ways were familiar to us. The east-facing doorway, the smoke flaps . . . Walker told us that some of their words were pronounced differently, but they seemed closely related. We felt quite at home.

We traded with them, and traded stories around the fires in the evenings. I wanted to learn the ways of these people, because I thought that they might help me learn more of the horse that wears the medicine hat. Many times when we look at the ways of others, we see things that are important to them, but it is not clear to us *why*. This was much that way, about the horse. I wondered if we would *ever* learn.

But we enjoyed telling our stories and hearing theirs. We told them of our experience at the Bad Place, and they thought it quite funny. I can see now that it *was* amusing, but it was not at the time. We did hear the story of the evil giant creatures from their storyteller. It was much as Plum Flower had related it, and we were pleased for her that she had told it well.

"Of course," she said when we mentioned it. "Are not the stars still up there?"

She was pleased, of course, but made a joke of it. We were beginning to know that here was a very capable woman, as well as beautiful.

Where was I? Oh, yes, the story fires . . . We had heard many of their stories while we were with Plum Flower's people. Still, it was interesting to hear them from another storyteller. There are always slight variations.

We told them of our Creation story, and how the People crawled through the hollow log into the world. This was mostly in hand signs, with Walker translating. Even so, I was able to use the joke that we sometimes play on the listener.

When we tell of the Trickster, the Old Man of the Shadows, and how he sat astride the log, you know? Each time he struck the log with his drum stick, another of the People popped out. Then the storyteller leaves a long pause, and usually someone asks, "Are they still coming through?" Sometimes, if the question does not come, the storyteller has someone ready to ask it.

We could not very well do that in this situation, but it was a good audience. I managed, with Lone Walker's help, to capture the imagination of the listeners. I could see in their eyes that the story was real to them, so I took the long pause. I was nearly ready to think that it would not work, when a young man spoke. I knew, of course, what the question would be.

"Are they still coming through?"

"No," I told him sadly. "Fat Woman got stuck in the log, and none have been able to come through since that time. That is why we have always been a small nation."

This was especially effective in the country of the Lakotas, because they are so many and so widespread. And, of course, because their story is similar to ours. They came from inside the earth, too. They could see the similarities.

"Ah!" said an old man. "Without your Fat Woman, you might be as many as the Lakotas!"

It was one of those times when you would have to be there to understand how it was. But it was a pleasant, happy time.

We felt at home with these people, and we stayed for a few days. We were told much of what lay ahead of us, too. The mountains to the north of us that were not really mountains . . . the tribes and nations we might meet . . . all enemies of the Lakota, of course.

We did not learn much about the horse, except more of what we knew. The medicine hat was of great importance.

19

I agree with most of what my husband has just told you. Our time with the Lakotas there was good. And, yes, I had never heard the story of Fat Woman and the log work so well. It was truly perfect.

I was bothered a little by one of the customs we saw there, I must tell you. You know how we sometimes decorate the tips of our lodge poles with streamers or tufts of horsehair? It is the same with them, but in that camp I was startled that many of these decorations were scalps. Pipe Bearer has told you of the warlike nature of the people in the north country. Of course, there are warlike people everywhere. Our allies, the Head Splitters, are more so than ourselves. The Snakes, to the south of us . . . Shaved-heads, with whom we have fought. And, yes, we ourselves have taken pride in our valor in battle. Our songs and dances tell of past victories.

But these displays gave me an odd feeling. Pup and I had been married for only about a year, you know. The People were at peace, and had been since we were born. It gave me a strange sadness to see the lodges with maybe ten or fifteen scalps fluttering from the poles. I could not help but think of the fact that there had been mourning in that many lodges for those warriors. Maybe not all warriors, either. The scalp of a woman is no different to some.

I mentioned my feelings to Plum Flower, and she smiled.

"Yes, but it is our way. It shows our pride in our men, who did *not* lose their scalps."

I reminded her that I did not recall such decorations in the camp of her own band.

"That is true," she agreed. "A few, maybe. But we have fewer enemies there. Pawnees, occasionally. These Lakotas, though, have other enemies. Everyone is their enemy. Cheyenne, Crow . . . I can see how you feel, Otter, but look . . . this tells everyone of the bravery of the warrior who lives there."

I could see that. I did not understand why it concerned me at all. I kept thinking about the fact that under other circumstances one of those fluttering scalps could be that of *my* husband. My eyes would fill with tears, and my stomach was sick.

"What if one of those belonged to Walker?" I blurted.

I was sorry that I had said it, because it was a cruel thing. I had no right to criticize the customs of her people. But I was tired, and my stomach did not feel right, and I was grumpy.

Plum Flower stared at me for a moment. It was the first time that we had exchanged cross words. She touched my hand.

"I do understand," Flower said. "It is not the way of your people."

I shed some more tears, even while I was laughing at myself for the way I had spoken. Plum Flower was laughing too, and I knew that it was good between us.

I felt better when I realized that I had not destroyed our friendship. In fact, Flower helped a great deal.

"Sometimes I feel that way, too," she whispered to me.

We dropped that discussion and spoke no more of the custom of scalps on lodge poles.

We did not stay long in that camp. We were anxious to move on. My husband was beginning to feel an urgency, I think. It was already apparent that we would not be able to return to the People before Cold Maker roared down across the plains with his snows and icy winds. We would have to winter somewhere in this country.

We had not realized how large an area was involved. We talk of other nations or tribes or clans and do not stop to think of distances. But we were just beginning to understand that one could spend a whole season just traveling from one side of the Lakota nation to the other. It was now the Red Moon, the hottest of the summer, and we had not even reached the nations who would be able to tell us about the horse with the medicine hat.

I spoke of this to Pup and the others, and we talked of it one evening around our fire.

"It is no problem," Lone Walker insisted. We will winter with someone wherever we are."

It is so with traders, we found, and Walker's people are the "trader people." Walker saw no reason at all to be concerned about it. It is their way. Plum Flower added a word of agreement and encouragement.

"My people are widespread," she pointed out. "We can find a winter camp of Lakotas and join them, wherever we are."

That was largely true, we found. Plum Flower had a better understanding of just how widespread her people are than we did. Even so, she had never been this far west before.

After talking of this, we agreed that we must wait and see. There was no way to tell how long the quest might take. It was the quest of Pipe Bearer, and only he would know when it was over.

We had been told of the country to the north of that place, and of its good spirit. Mountains, yet not really mountains. I could not understand what that meant. Of course, I had never seen mountains, and neither had my husband. Both of our companions had, however, and tried to explain.

"In the part where my people live," Lone Walker explained, "a traveler sees the mountains from many sleeps away. Their appearance is like a low cloud bank, blue in the distance. But the clouds move, and tomorrow the mountains still look the same. You travel toward them, and the blue appearance seems the same day after day. You begin to think, *It is only a day or two now.* But then you sleep and wake and the mountains seem no nearer."

"Then how are these different, Walker?" asked Pipe Bearer.

"I have not seen these little mountains either, my friend," Walker admitted. "I am curious, too. We will see when we get there, maybe."

The Lakota with whom we had visited had referred to these low mountains as "black." This we did not understand. These "Black Hills" must be of black rock, we thought. We had seen black stone. Traders sometimes carry arrow points of a shiny black stone, you know. It is very hard, like glass beads. We thought maybe these hills were like that, black and shiny.

Our first sight of the Black Hills of the Lakota was not very impressive. We saw a dark strip along the earth's edge to the north of us. Lone Walker said that it was probably the hills or mountains we sought.

"But it is darker," he added.

It did seem a long time before we came closer. That part was as Walker had said, though I think he was surprised. These were more like mountains than he had thought, and even he was impressed.

As we came closer, we began to see pine trees. Scattered, lone pines at first, then small clumps. In a day or two we could make out distant features in the mountains that lay ahead. They still looked dark, and we were puzzled, because all of the rocks that we saw were not black, but a light gray. Finally we realized that the dark appearance was from the dense growth of trees that covered everything, like the winter hair of a buffalo. These were mostly pines, and grew very thickly.

"I can see what the Lakota mean," said Lone Walker. "These hills are dark, not from the rocks, but from the trees!"

We asked him more about it, but he shook his head.

"You will understand when you have seen both," he promised.

That was true, but we did not see the big mountains until later.

These Black Hills were beautiful, I admit. The smell of the pines in the sun, the soft song of the wind in their branches . . . I have to admit, though, that sometimes it made me feel a little afraid. When we would be camped in a place with trees all around us, I could not see any distance at all. Everywhere there were trees or rocks. In one place that I remember, there were trees in *all* directions. There was not sky, except for a little patch straight up.

Yes, you laugh, but you know what I mean! It is much like the feeling that we get when we visit others who live in earth-lodges or houses built of mud bricks. *Aiee*, I well remember the way I felt when I first stepped inside the lodge of some growers. . . .

I was a child, we were camped nearby, and I played with a little girl who lived there. We went to her lodge, and when I stepped inside, down a slope *into the ground*, I had a moment of panic. I was trapped! I turned and ran.

Forgive me. . . . That is not the story I tell tonight. But I only wanted to explain my feeling about the heavy forests in the Black Hills. I am a daughter of the open prairie, and I feel closed in and trapped if I cannot see the horizon. How can one even have a sense of direction? I feel the same way in the mountains. There is great beauty, and I enjoy the experience. But I am always glad to escape back to the open. There I can stretch my eyes toward earth's rim, and can tell in which direction I am looking. And it is good.

I have no apology for this. It is our way. I am sure that those who live in mud-brick houses feel insecure in our skin lodges. But they have not grown up in the clean breeze of the open prairie, and do not know the sound of rain on a dry lodge skin in the summer. . . .

Yes, Pup, I will go on. I only wanted to explain our feelings . . . all right, *my* feelings. *Aiee*, do you want to tell this? Yes, in a little while. This is my turn. . . .

We did enjoy these Black Hills of the Lakota country. There was game and water, and beauty, of its own kind. People? Yes, we saw others. Lakotas, because that is largely their country. We had no trouble, of course. Because of Plum Flower's Lakota connections, we were well accepted.

What sort of game? Elk, deer, some scattered buffalo, antelope out on the open grassland. But, ah, I nearly forgot . . . bears! We do not hunt or eat them, of course. That is our way, our agreement with Bear since Creation. But the Lakotas do, and there are many bears in those Black Hills. A necklace of bear's claws is highly prized as a symbol of manhood. That is *their* way.

Of course, we had not forgotten why we were there, to find out about the significance of the medicine hat horse. We tried not to make it too obvious, but still to inquire. We met with much the same idea as we had before: Yes, there is great importance in this. Yes, this is an animal of exceptional quality, as well.

Beyond that, there was only the vague idea that such a medicine hat might have even greater meaning for others. We had seen only Lakotas so far. Well, Cheyenne, earlier. Maybe we would find that the Absarokee or the Blackfeet or the Shoshone could be of help in this.

We talked to the Lakotas with whom we had become friendly, and they thought maybe so.

"You will meet Crows first, going west," we were told. "Absarokee, they call themselves . . . Bird People. They are our enemies, of course."

Of course, everyone in that area is an enemy of the Lakota, or Sioux.

20

Otter has told you of our reaction to the mountainous Black Hills. And she mentioned bears. Yes, there are a great many bears there, and this made us uneasy. There are not only the small bears in several shades of color, but many real-bears. We see those sometimes here, following the buffalo herds . . . the great bear with white-tipped fur who stands on two feet and walks like a man.

I mention this because in that area many of the tales that we heard around the story-fires told of bears. More of that later.

But, yes, Otter has told well of the forests of the Black Hills. I felt much as she did, probably. Plum Flower, similarly, because the country of her own band is in open prairie. However, she had traveled more widely than we had. Lone Walker, of course, had grown up in a mountainous area. He was not bothered as much as the rest of us. The trapped, closed-in feeling that a child of the prairie has when surrounded by trees . . . *aiee*, friends, it is not a pleasant thing!

Even so, even surrounded by forests where we could not see anything, and, yes, knowing they were filled with bears . . . Yes, we can laugh about it now. . . . Even with all that, I have to admit that there are places that we thought were beautiful. A different beauty from that of our own land, but worth visiting for a little while.

While we were there, we met and camped with a band of people. . . . I cannot recall who they were, now. Absarokee, maybe. We camped and traded with so many, and there were so many more important happenings, you know. And it *was* three or four years ago. What? Yes, Otter, I will get on with the story. I am only trying to be accurate. *Aiee!*

We met with this band, who had pitched their lodges among scattered pines at the edge of the denser forest. I found that most of the people who live in skin lodges and hunt the buffalo can understand each other's ways. Even though their tongues differ, it is so. Their customs are the same, because the sun, the grass, and the buffalo are their life, as it is with us. And so it was with these people.

We camped, traded, exchanged stories around the fire. I think they *were* Absarokee . . . Crows. They were a little farther east than usual, and were a bit anxious about the Lakotas. Yes, that was it! I think so, anyway. They had no problem with us, because we were traders, and Otter and I were of a distant people. They understood quite well about Lone Walker and why his garments were Lakota. His wife . . . You remember, no?

I am telling you of this particular band of people because they had a very strange story, which they shared around the fire. We had not heard it before.

Some children, back in long-ago times, were playing in the pine woods in the hills, when they were frightened by a great bear. I mentioned that there are many bears and bear stories in that region. This was one of the best . . . the best stories, not best bears. . . . It was a very *bad* bear. The white-tipped fur indicated a giant real-bear. It rose on two legs and came after them, roaring horribly. As I said, this is a good story to tell at night around the fire. It certainly keeps the attention.

These children in the story screamed and ran, but the bear kept coming. They climbed onto a big rock, even knowing that it was not tall enough to help them escape.

But now a strange thing happened. This, you remember, was in long-ago times. All creatures spoke in the same tongue.

"I will help you," said the rock, and it began to grow. Taller and taller it grew. It seemed very slow to the frightened children. But when the bear reached the rock, it was taller than his head. The bear jumped but failed to catch the edge of the rock's flat top. His claws ripped great furrows down the rock's side.

The bear leaped again, and again the giant claws slipped from the rock's edge and scraped long grooves from the top to the ground. The creature roared furiously and clawed at the rock as it grew. Time after time he jumped, while the frightened children huddled on the rock's flat top and the rock continued to grow.

Now, it was much like a giant tree trunk. Yes, I know, bears climb trees, no? It is true, the black bear does. But, remember, this was the great, grizzled real-bear. He is too big to climb. So he continued to roar and claw at the sides of the rock. It continued to grow until it reached the sky. The seven children became stars as they stepped off the rock, and are still there. The storyteller showed us which seven stars represent those children. What? The same as our Seven Hunters who circle the Real-star? No, I am made to think not. . . . That is a different story.

Anyway, we asked where this rock stands. I supposed that its location had been lost. It is so with most such stories, but we were told no, it was not far from where we were. It is called Bear's Lodge, or Bear's Rock by the people who live in that area. A few sleeps, no more. They gave us directions and urged us to go and see for ourselves.

Well, it was to the west of where we were camped with them, and a little bit north. It was in the direction that we were going anyway. We, the four of us, agreed that to see this thing would be good.

We were finding by this time that it was easy to make such decisions. The thoughts and feelings of the four were easily spoken and easily seen. There was no wondering about how this one felt, or that one, because we did not hesitate to tell each other. Sometimes one would feel a hurt or a hope or a good feeling more than the others, but such is the way of things. It is like Otter and the scalps on lodge poles, that she told you of. . . . I did not quite understand that at the time, as close as Otter and I had come to be. But she talked of it with Flower. There are things and feelings that women must talk of together, sometimes.

It is so with men too, I think. Men and women are different, in the way they think and feel and do things. It is good that there is this difference, no? If we were the same, life could become quite boring. And my life has never been boring, as you can see.

Yes, Otter, I will get back to the story. . . .

We decided to go and see this great rock that reaches the sky. We were going that way anyway. The people with whom we were camped told us more about it as they gave us directions. We should be able to see it, they said, from a half day away.

What? Yes, that big! But let me tell you . . . we asked the same thing. How tall? So tall, they said, that you could not shoot an arrow halfway up, toward the top. I was finding this hard to imagine. Even more so when they said that you could walk all the way around at its base, and that it was straight up on all sides. This sounded like a tale for children. *Such things do not exist*, I told myself. I considered that this might be a local joke that the people there play on outsiders.

You can see how we would think so. A scary tale to be told at night around the fire to frighten children into good behavior. Well, yes, to teach them. I overstated it, of course.

Many stories told to children are to teach, are they not? *Aiee*, let me go on!

Bears . . . always a fascination for the People. Our covenant with Bear since Creation is a special thing. We do not kill Bear and his people, so he does not kill us. We avoid each other. Yes, there is the occasional exception. My own grandfather . . . But that is another story, one you have heard, I am sure.

Still, there is a fascination with bears among the People. Something dark and sinister, a little evil, maybe. Maybe it was this suggested hidden danger that made us want to go and see this Bear's Rock, to say we had touched its scarred surface. I cannot say. I had in mind that we would approach it until we felt that its dark spirit was too powerful, and then turn back. It was an adventure, and we were like children, urging each other on.

Even with all we had heard, I was not prepared for the appearance of this Bear's Rock when we first saw it. Lone Walker was riding in the lead and reined in suddenly.

"Look!" He pointed.

There, sticking up into the sky above the dark pines in the distance, was this huge rock. No others around it. . . . It looked flat on the top, light gray in color. There were no other rocks or hills anywhere near. Bear's Rock just stood there, gleaming in the morning sunlight. It was exactly as we had heard it described.

We turned our course in that direction and had reached it by noon. Now, as I have said, I expected its spirit to be threatening. Instead, we found it warm and pleasant! That bothered me a little at first. I was suspicious. Was there something deceptive here, lulling a stranger into a false security? You know how some of the streams in our western regions are? The dry streambed looks solid but is really a sort of sucking sand, in which horses can become trapped. These things were going through my head as we looked. But my own medicine felt good, and we drew nearer.

Ah, how can I describe that rock? You would have to see it for yourselves. It is perfectly round, shaped much like a tree trunk, and about three times as tall as it is thick. The top appears flat, but of course we did not see the top. At the base it is no thicker than two or three bow shots. Eagles fly around its top.

Now, in the story, you remember that the bear clawed at the sides of the rock? *Aiee*, that is how it looks! Deep grooves run from top to bottom, all the way, all around the great rock. And, listen. . . . All around the base are piled the rock splinters that the bear ripped away! Some of these are as thick as my leg, here, and longer than I am tall. They lie in piles where they have fallen away from the rock itself. What a giant real-bear that must have been!

Yes, only a story, but what a story! And what a place. We camped near that rock, because it seemed to us that its spirit was good. We offered tobacco in our first fire and asked that whatever spirits live there look with favor on our quest.

No, we had not forgotten the quest. It is hard to describe, but it seemed that this was a part of it, somehow. The Bear's Lodge seems to have little to do with a horse that wears a medicine hat. Still, it *did* seem that it was so. There was such a powerful spirit living there. . . . We hated to leave, and stayed part of the next day, even. To see the rock change in appearance as the sun strikes it at different angles is a thing of wonder.

And I have not even mentioned its wonder at night. The moon was past full, and had just risen when Lone Walker wakened me to stand watch. We stood watch every night, of course, because we were in unfamiliar country. That night, though, with the stars so close and the rising moon on that tall rock . . . *aiee*, it was good. Walker and I decided to wake the women so that they could share its beauty. Its spirit was very moving at that time.

The four of us sat for a long while, not talking much. There was nothing that we could say that would not seem unimportant compared to what we were feeling that night.

Forgive me. . . . You would have to be there to understand. Even now, I would like to go back again. . . .

21

I agree with my husband. It was a special time and place. One of our best times ever. And, yes, the power of the spirit that we felt at the Bear's Rock cannot be told about. It must be *felt*. And, yes, I too, would like to go back again.

There were some things while we were at that camp, though, that I wanted to tell about. I was afraid that Pipe Bearer would tell them. So, thank you, my husband! It is good of you not to tell my stories.

The next morning when daylight came, we started to move around. Plum Flower and I went a little way from the camp and behind some trees to relieve our bladders, while the men went another direction. As we were so occupied, Flower gave a sudden squeal of surprise.

"Look!" she said, pointing upward.

There in a pine tree, about the height of two men above the ground, sat a bear cub. It was holding tightly to the tree, watching us and not moving at all. There was a movement a little higher, and a second cub stuck its head around the tree trunk to stare at us. The first was black, as most bears are, but the other was much lighter in color, a nice yellow-brown, like real-grass after the first frost.

It was a nice sight, but we knew that we were in danger. The mother of these cubs would be somewhere near. We did not want to find ourselves between her and the cubs. We quickly rearranged our garments and started back toward the fire. We did not encounter the mother, for which we were thankful.

The men were already back, building up the fire. It is cold on those fall mornings, there in the hills. We told them excitedly about the bear cubs, and both wanted to see. Lone Walker picked up his bow.

Now, this is hard to explain. I felt a great sadness that filled my eyes with tears. The People do not hunt bears, of course, because of the covenant. It has never bothered us that others do. That is between them and Bear and is *their* problem. Many times I have seen some of the Head Splitters, who are our allies, eat bear meat while they camp with us. It is their way.

But now it bothered me that Walker was prepared to shoot one or both of those cubs. I knew that it was a silly thing, but my eyes were full of tears as we walked along. No one seemed to notice, because we were all thinking of bears and not of each other.

We showed the men where the cubs were, and they watched a little while. Walker had an arrow fitted to his bow but did not raise it. Finally he turned away.

"We do not need meat," he said.

At that point I nearly broke down in open tears. I was a little frightened, because I did not know what was the matter with me. I felt sick, and wondered if I had somehow angered the spirits of the place.

We turned away, looking carefully around us. We still did not know, of course, where the mother bear might be. We soon learned. . . . As we came in sight of our camp, we saw her. A large, fat, very black bear, circling and sniffing the unfamiliar people-smells of the camp. The thought crossed my mind that we were between her and the cubs. Walker raised his bow.

"Wait!" whispered Pipe Bearer. "If she is only wounded, she will come this way."

Walker thought for a moment and then motioned. We started to circle to the left, keeping downwind of the bear. She was still sniffing, smelling our food but unsure about the fire, probably.

Then she seemed to sense our presence. Her head swung, she uttered a low growl, and her fur seemed to stand on end. She turned to face us and took a step or two.

Now, I have heard it told that a bear cannot see very far. I do not know *how* far. None of us wanted to find out. Walker prepared to shoot.

"Wait!" said Pipe Bearer.

He was made to think that this was dangerous. He could not help to kill the bear, because of our covenant. It would be hard to be sure of a kill with Walker's one arrow. There would not be time for a second shot. The animal was only about thirty paces away.

Thoughts were racing through my head. . . . Plum Flower could shoot, but she had no weapon. My husband's bow might be too heavy for her, and she was unfamiliar with it anyway. It would not do to have wounded the bear with Walker's shot and to have our safety depend on a woman with an unsuitable weapon.

"Let me try," Pipe Bearer said softly.

He took a slow, deliberate step toward the bear, and she snarled, showing sharp teeth. Then he gave the hand sign for peaceful greeting and began to talk.

"We have never met, Mother, but we mean you no harm. My people have a promise, a covenant with yours, since Creation. We do not harm you, nor do your people harm us. Let it be so!"

The bear seemed confused, turning her head this way and that. But in a few moments, much to my surprise (I think to the surprise of all of us), the bear seemed to relax a little, to become calm. Maybe it was only the *tone* of my husband's voice that calmed her. He affects me that way too sometimes, no? But, seriously, I was made to feel that his medicine was good, and that somehow the bear understood.

"We are moving on, now," Pup continued. "We will move this way, away from you, so that you can rejoin your cubs."

He took another step to our left and paused. The bear growled again, but she did not seem so aggressive. She took a step away from our camp, waited to see our reaction, and took another step.

"Come," Pipe Bearer said to us. "Move slowly, now."

Very carefully, we circled on to our left, as the bear moved to her left, avoiding each other's path. When our positions had changed enough to convince her that it was safe, the creature turned and trotted away to rejoin her cubs. She was not retreating, and her pace showed that it was not from fear that she left. Her movements showed confidence. I was made to feel that the covenant of the People with Bear had been renewed. And once again I was impressed with the power of my husband's gift of the spirit. Of course, also, I felt a great pride in his skill. Yes, you laugh, but you know that I am serious. That is how I feel, and am proud to say so, too. It is good.

Now, after the incident with the bear, I felt no urgency to leave. Oh, I kept looking to see if the bear would return, of course. But our preparations were unhurried. We were still feeling the calming spirit of the Bear's Rock, as we prepared to go. It was tempting to stop and sit, and stare again for a time at that great scarred rock. I watched the eagles circling above its top, and my heart was good.

It was about that time that Pipe Bearer spoke to me, a bit impatiently.

"The horses are uneasy about the bears," he said. "I am made to think that we should go."

Now, that was the way that he said it. Nothing more. And you know him. He speaks calmly. Yes, my anger rose at him, and I spoke harshly to him. I seldom do that.

"What do you want me to do?" I snapped. "Catch and saddle the horses?"

I would have, of course, if he had wanted me to. Usually, he and Lone Walker did that. This was a silly thing.

Pipe Bearer looked at me as if I had struck him. He looked so sad. . . . *Aiee*, I wanted to take back my words. I wanted to hold him in my arms and to tell him that I did not mean to speak so. Even more, I wanted *him* to hold *me* and tell me that he understood. Though I admit, *I* did not understand. But he turned away, and I burst into tears. I did not know the meaning of my feelings. Ah, it was hurtful.

Plum Flower came to me, sat down on the rock beside me, and put an arm around my shoulders. For a moment I was even angered at her for approaching me so. But it was a comfort, and Flower was being a good friend.

"What is it, my almost-sister?" she whispered.

Then I really broke down, and the tears came more freely.

"I do not know!" I told her. "I have no reason to feel so."

"You can think of nothing?" she asked.

Her smile was gentle and sympathetic, and even that irritated me, though I appreciated her concern.

"No . . . nothing," I said. "What is the matter with me, Flower?"

"Maybe there *is* something," she suggested.

"But what? I have never felt this way before."

Plum Flower nodded knowingly, and I was about to speak sharply to her. I cried some more, instead. After all, she *was* trying to help.

"Otter," she said to me gently, "you remember when you were telling me about the people to the south of your country? They have a special lodge at the edge of the camp for menstruating women?"

"That is true," I nodded. I sniffed a little. The distraction slowed my tears a bit.

"All right. . . . Why were we talking of it?"

"Because of the danger."

"Yes! The danger of a menstruating woman to the medicine of those around her, to her husband's medicine."

"Yes, but . . ." I still did not understand.

"And your people and mine do not banish a menstruating woman to a special lodge. They only take great care not to touch a weapon or things of someone's medicine. Is it not so?" she asked me.

"That is true."

"And why were we talking of that?" Flower demanded.

"I could not help pack my husband's things, the things of his position as a holy man. I was menstruating. . . ." I still did not understand, you see.

"And when was it?" she kept on.

"Last moon . . . *Aiee*, Flower . . . let me think," I answered. "It was before the full of the moon, no?"

"I am made to think so," she agreed. "Before the full of *last* moon. Before mine. And now there has passed another full moon, and I have menstruated twice."

I was relieved to have a reason for my tears and my irritability.

"Of course," I agreed. "With the travel and all the changes in my life, I have not had time to menstruate. This makes me feel full and heavy, and I am hard to be with. . . . Ah, I have been unreasonable, Flower. Thank you for helping me to understand!"

Plum Flower stared at me in amazement for a moment. Then she began to smile. It was a warm, happy smile, and since I did not entirely understand it, this, too, irritated me.

"What is so amusing about it?" I demanded angrily.

"Otter, my almost-sister," Flower said softly, "you still do not understand. I have seen your moods, your stomach bothering you. I had not realized the rest until now. But there have been *two* full moons since we talked of the menstrual lodge of your neighbors. Otter, I am made to think that you are pregnant!"

22

She was right, of course. I felt stupid that I had not thought of it myself. It would account for all of my strange behavior. My tears and sudden anger, the way my stomach was not right. The soreness in my breasts. But all of these things are also true of a late menstruation, no? So how is one to tell? As I had said to Plum Flower, I had never felt this way before. Not to this extreme, anyway. There was good reason. I had never been pregnant before, so how could I know? And we had not been around any women with experience to whom I could talk. One does not discuss such things with strangers. Even friendly ones . . .

This raised some big questions for our quest, though. I was not particularly concerned about it, but I could see that it was bothering my husband. It was necessary to think of a number of things now. How long could I ride a horse? How long *should* I? Where would we be when my time came?

Plum Flower and I counted and decided that it would probably be late in the Moon of Growing, or possibly the Moon of Roses. It would be a good time, because of the variety of food available at that season. To me, and to the child.

There was one other factor that was quite clear, though. The birth would not take place among the People. This was of concern to me. I was still very emotional because of the early pregnancy, you know. It seemed that to winter among strangers and then to deliver a child in some place that I had never seen . . . *aiee!*

But there was no other way. We could not reach the People before winter, even if we started that day. I cried, and Plum Flower put her arm around me.

"I will be with you, almost-sister," she said.

I do not know what I would have done without Flower. She was, indeed, my almost-sister. I could depend on her to understand my moods and to give me comfort and support. Not that my husband was deficient in this, you understand. There was never a better man to be gentle and understanding. But there are some things that need another woman, and this was one.

"I am told," Flower comforted me, "that the moods are better after a few moons."

I laughed. That is a strange thing. At that time, early in the pregnancy, I could be crying big tears and laughing at the same time, laughing at myself for crying. I am sure that I was not very much fun to be with.

Pipe Bearer, as I have said, was concerned for me. I think he would have abandoned the quest if it seemed he should. We talked about it, and I assured him that since I would birth among strangers anyway, it made no difference. I meant that to be a comforting thing to him, but it did not come out that way. *Aiee*, I must have snapped at him like a trapped wolf.

I could see that he was hurt, but Lone Walker took him aside and talked to him. Walker told us later that he himself had been born among strangers. His parents, traders, had been wintering far from home, much as we planned to do. He saw no big problem, and that helped both Pup and me.

I learned later that Walker also knew of the moodiness of a woman at this time, and comforted Pup greatly. He may want to tell you of that, for he tells it well.

We traveled on, traded a little, and asked about the medicine-hat horse. Our foal, Good Hat, was growing rapidly now, coming into his first winter. He was smart, throwing himself only once as he fought the rope when we broke him to lead. We had let him run loose to follow his mother at first, you know.

Everywhere we asked, the colt was admired, both for his quality as a horse, and for his strange markings. Everywhere we were congratulated on our good fortune. Still no specific story or legend that would go with it. I began to think that this was not to be answered by a story. Maybe, like some other things, this was not to be understood. It was a thing to be experienced, instead. Maybe the goal was the quest itself, though I had not thought of that yet.

Several people, as we met different tribes and nations, offered to buy or trade for the colt. Pipe Bearer refused, of course. Those who seemed to understand, however, made no such effort. To have such a foal born to one's mare, it seemed, was like a powerful spirit-gift. It is an honor to be chosen so. One does not give away one's medicine, or try to sell the power it bestows. Those who tried to bargain for the colt were only showing their own stupidity and ignorance of things of the spirit. But let my husband tell you more.

Otter is right. Those who would bargain with spirit-gifts do not understand their nature. But I was thinking also of something else, too. There were a few who did seem wise, and still spoke of trading for the horse. One old Shoshone holy man comes to mind. Shoshone, we found, are very closely in touch with things of the spirit. This old man, when he tried to bargain, seemed more interested in whether I knew. Or *what* I knew of spirit-things. When he saw that I was humbled by the gifts of the spirit that are mine, his manner changed. We visited much and, in time, became good friends. It was his band with whom we spent the winter, in fact. Winter Skins, his name.

But I am getting ahead of the story. I wanted to comment on some of the things Otter has said about the pregnancy. It was difficult for all of us. The two women could talk to each other in great detail about their feelings as women, but had no older woman to consult. But I, too, had no man with experience. Lone Walker, my almost-brother, had never been through this experience, either.

Now, Otter has told of her moods, her unpredictable feelings. Those who have been through this will understand. Those who have not *cannot* understand that of which we speak.

Now, think of this from the viewpoint of an unsuspecting young husband. Where I once had a soft, warm body to share my sleeping robes, I now found a great difference. How does a woman do that? From one moment to the next, she can change. The warm body that cuddled so deliciously is now made mostly of knees and elbows, which jab his ribs and stomach . . . his back, even!

Of course, during the waking time things are different. There is no way to prepare a young man for the attitude of a newly pregnant wife. She is very emotional and cries easily. Even someone as strong as Otter does so. Now, this is so unlike her that he is startled.

"What is wrong?" he asks.

She then wipes her tears, shakes her head, and answers quietly.

"Nothing."

Well, obviously, one does not act in this manner over "nothing." He loves her and wishes to help her, so he attempts to help. He puts an arm around her, but unsuccessfully. She pulls away.

"What is it?" he asks again. "Is it something I have done? Or *not* done?"

Now, at most times in their life together, this would have been well received. Not at this time. For reasons that he does not understand and probably never will, she flies into a rage.

"If you do not know," she snaps, "I will not tell you!"

Ah, I see a young man in the back of the lodge, there, who is greatly disturbed by this story. Do not worry, Gray Squirrel. There are answers to this problem. And the others, there, who are laughing . . . they are not laughing at you, but because they have been there, have had this experience. Let me go on.

In the usual situation among the People, the young husband would seek out an older man who has helped him in the past. A grandfather or an uncle, maybe. He would blurt out his grief and confusion and ask for help and explanation. Then the uncle would think a while, light his pipe, maybe, and try to explain. Of course he cannot do so. Some things cannot be explained. So he only reassures the young man that this is to be expected, and that it will be better later. It is the way of things.

But at the time of which I tell you, there was no "uncle" to talk to. I had only Lone Walker, who had never experienced it either. We talked about it, and both of us thought that we had heard the men talk and make jokes about it. It seemed no joke, though, I can tell you, there in strange country. My heart was heavy to see my Otter behaving so strangely, sometimes crying and laughing at herself for crying, all at the same time.

Of course, the women talked of this between them, too. They were better prepared for it than we were, maybe. But you can see how it must have been. During that time, the first few moons of Otter's pregnancy, we had only each other in whom to confide, because we were among strangers. One does not talk of such personal problems with strangers. So this was one of the ways in which we grew closer together, the four of us.

Now, a word of reassurance to our friend, young Squirrel back there. I have been making jokes of this, though it was serious at the time. We have all laughed about it, and I have teased the women a little. I have no doubt that Otter will have some comment when she resumes the story. So to head off part of that counterattack, let me go on for a little while, here.

There did come a time, after we left the Bear's Rock, when things seemed to change. Otter became herself again. She was Otter, my friend and companion, and the one with whom to share my bed. It was almost as if she thought that she had neglected me and was trying to make it up to me, somehow. She was as eager as ever in bed. Maybe more so. Her moods were still unpredictable, and she tired more easily, but is that not to be expected when a woman is with child?

I am telling all of this so that you can understand how it was going with us. Well, yes, for some laughs, too. There must be laughter in our lives, no? But this was a time when our lives were changing. One's life is always changing, of course, though it does not seem so at the time. We look back and think *aiee!* When did *that* happen?

What was happening there was that we were growing through a difficult time, drawing apart and then back together and finding ourselves closer than ever. And it was good.

And during that experience we had drawn closer to our friends for help. We had no one else. I have said before that people who have shared a threat or a tragedy or danger feel a bond that is very powerful. It cannot be sought or learned, but it can be appreciated. It was this sort of bond that kept drawing us together in friendship, the four of us in strange country. We were sharing many things which involved powerful feelings, and were depending on and trusting each other.

Yes, these are deep thoughts. We did not realize much of this at the time. We were occupied with travel and contact with different bands that we met, asking about the medicine hat horse, seeing new sights. . . .

And, of course, Cold Maker was coming. We needed to find a place to winter.

23

My husband has told it well, that part of the story. He has made it seem laughable, though, and in truth it was not at the time. There we were, four young people, inexperienced yet thinking that we were wise in the ways of the world. It was hard, not to understand the quick swings of my moods. Hard for me, and even more for Pipe Bearer, I know.

Girls are taught some things, of course. Looking back, I can see that the way I felt and behaved during the early part of that pregnancy was exactly as I had heard described. But I had not recognized it.

Also, as I look back, I am thankful that my husband and I were not alone during that time. It was difficult enough with my almost-sister to comfort me and reassure me. Of course, she had no experience either, but she could be more sensible. Her moods were not distorted by a pregnancy. Not yet. So she could help to keep *me* steady, and keep me from being too cruel to Pup.

Lone Walker, also, helped *him*. Men traditionally comfort each other in such times. They like to pretend otherwise, and I think they largely talk of other things, but it is obvious. They, as well as women, have a need for sympathy when things seem dark.

As I came out of the moody confusion and the crying spells that had bothered me, I realized that here was something meant to be. We had met Walker and Plum Flower at exactly the right time. They were in need of help, and we were able to help save them from the fire. It seemed an accidental meeting, but are there really accidents?

Later these two, now our brother and sister, almost, were there for us. I was made to think that it was meant to be, in the strange way things happen. Who knows? Maybe their presence kept me from scaring Pipe Bearer away entirely! He could have just left me there for the bears, no?

Not really. I am joking, teasing him. Bears would not eat me anyway, because of the covenant, I guess. And even if he left me, I would have . . . No, no, I will stop, Pup. But it is amusing, looking back. *Aiee*, we took ourselves so seriously then. And many things that seem important at the time become a joke when we look back.

So enough of that part of the story. Let me only say that, yes, after I got past the crying and moody part of the pregnancy, I *did* feel sorry for my husband, and the way I had treated him. Yes, I probably did try to make up for the "knees and elbows" treatment in the robes which he tells of. But I was also feeling sorry for myself, you know, and trying to make up for that. It takes two, Pup.

Now, let me go on. He has mentioned the Shoshone, and that we wintered with them. No, we did not meet in any exciting way. It was just another of those things that seemed meant to be. I think Pipe Bearer was getting ahead of the story considerably, there. We did not meet Shoshones for some time.

When we left the Bear's Rock, we were moving into the country of the Absarokee, or Crows. They are enemies of the Lakotas, so we were careful to identify ourselves as traders to anyone we saw. This gave us the special status that traders carry, which we have mentioned before. With the Crows, it was sometimes difficult.

When Crows and Lakotas meet, it seems that they would *expect* to fight. *Prefer* it, almost. *Aiee*, I did not understand it! That seems to me a very big country, with a great amount of space. Yet when men of two different nations meet, they would rather fight than eat, or make love, even. Well, maybe not. It probably depends on how their women handle the situation. What? Yes, Pup, I will go on. I was only making a comment. . . . Women do have a great influence. *You* know. . . . Yes, I am going on.

My friends, recall how it is when we are traveling with the entire band. Sometimes we meet another column of travelers. Head Splitters, maybe, our allies. But it could be Cheyennes or Snakes, or Kiowas, even. We are not at war with any of these just now, but we have been with some, and may be again. Now, what happens? Neither group wants a fight. Both have their women and children, and all their property is strung out across the plain. It would be too dangerous.

So a few leaders meet between the two groups, to talk. In hand signs, usually. It is understood that there is a truce. They talk of the weather and the game and where they intend to camp. There is no need to try to mislead each other on that. It is hard to hide a summer camp of forty lodges or more. An enemy will find it anyway. So they talk mostly truth.

It is much the same there. Blackfeet and Crow, Shoshone, Lakota. The same meeting takes place, just as it is here. But suppose two hunting parties meet. That is different. If the two are enemies, they will fight, and the larger group probably kills most of the smaller. If they are friends, they probably sit down for a smoke. Maybe camp together, or join in a hunt.

I mention this all because it becomes important later. But in this same line of the story, remember the trader. He is welcome to anyone's camp. He carries goods and stories that are of interest, and brings news. This gives him a special position. You are aware of all this.

But in that north country the trading itself is important. They have little contact with the French. They love to trade, so they trade with each other. With their enemies, even! We heard of times when there would be a battle, and after all the counting of honors (or coup, as the French now say), the survivors of both sides sat down to trade weapons and horses. It is true!

So we found it to be that way in that north country—they love to fight and they love to trade. Fighting comes first, probably. I tell you all of this so that you can better understand some of the things of which we will tell you later.

Now, we mentioned trading earlier, and how useful it had been as we met new people. When we started on the quest, we had been thinking in terms of using the trading as a deception, I think. It was to be a disguise, a thing to make us seem something that we were not. To do this well, of course, we had to *do* some actual trading. We learned much about that from Lone Walker, who was, of course, a *real* trader.

Very quickly we had confided to Walker and Flower that the trading was only to conceal our true purpose, the quest. By that time Walker had already realized it. But he had also suggested that if we were to be trading, we should do it well. It would be ever so much more convincing. We began to learn some of the tricks of a trader.

This is not to say that Lone Walker was a dishonest trader. Far from it. In fact, he felt strongly that a trader must give value in trade.

"You might want to come back sometime," he explained. "If you have cheated someone, he tells everybody he sees for the rest of his life."

Yet all this is not to say that he would not use a clever trick now and then. If you were wanting to trade a horse, you would groom him well to make him look his best, no? There are ways to make a trade look desirable.

The first time we saw this skill in use by Walker did involve a horse, in fact. One of his pack horses. She was a clever old mare and was hard to catch. Many a morning we spent extra time trying to find that bay mare. She could hide from us like no horse I ever saw. After one such morning, when we had been searching long and hard, Walker determined to trade her at the first opportunity.

I do not recall what was being offered. Furs, I think. The man really seemed to want the mare, but was in doubt. He seemed to suspect some trick. Walker had told him that the mare was sound, but a little lazy, which was complete truth. They were still haggling, and I thought that the trade was nearly done. Walker looked disappointed, although that, too, can be a trick.

At about that time Plum Flower walked past and stopped, with a look of amazement on her face. I did not understand, because they had talked the night before of trading this mare. Flower proceeded to scold him angrily in their own tongue, in case anyone present understood it. She accused him of stealing her mare, the best she ever had, the joy of her childhood. She spoke of the marvelous colts the mare had produced, fine buffalo runners, and the disposition of all her offspring. She pointed indignantly to the pile of furs being offered.

Walker let her scold and finally retorted angrily. Then he turned to his client.

"My heart is heavy, my friend," he said sadly. "My woman says I must not sell her mare for only this many furs."

"But you have agreed," the man protested. "We are only talking of how many, now."

"But you see her anger," Walker answered. "I have to *live* with that woman."

"Maybe," the man suggested, "you could soften her anger with this."

He drew out a beautiful fox pelt, dark and shining, one of the best I ever saw, and added it to the pile on the blanket between them. Walker seemed to deliberate a long time and finally agreed to take the risk of Flower's wrath. The trade was done.

Now, I knew that he would have happily taken the skins that were offered before Flower intervened, just to get rid of the troublesome old mare. Yet the other man was certain that *he* had made a clever trade.

What? Yes, I learned to do that, too. We had, after a while, come to a point where we no longer *pretended* to be traders. We *were* traders. We were doing well at it. We had a good crop of furs, trading for only the best, and had added an extra pack horse.

It helped, when we encountered a town of people who were doing some growing, to try to make a kill of buffalo or elk, and to offer them meat and the skin. Yes, I am proud to say that we were successful at trading. Much of it, of course, due to Lone Walker's skills.

But this quest concerned the horse, the colt who wears the medicine hat. Good Hat. There is so much to tell that it is easy to forget that this was the reason for the journey. As my husband has told you, we were working with the colt from time to time. He showed signs of growing into a big, strong horse. Not too big. A big horse is hard to climb upon, and he eats too much. When I say *big*, I mean big in muscle and in heart, not just tall. This colt would be the right size for a buffalo runner, and strong enough to do it.

Why do I tell you of all this, instead of letting Pipe Bearer tell it? Well, he was *not* telling it. No, I know he was telling of other things. But another reason . . . I had been riding the roan mare, the mother of the colt. He was always near her, and I would watch him. When we stopped, and the colt came to nurse, I would pet him and play with him. As you know, a horse that is handled from the time he is small is easier to work with. So by the time we left the Bear's Rock, we could slide a rope all over and under him, tie him to hold him. . . . All that was needed to begin to teach him to be ridden was his size. It would be another year, at least, before he could be ridden. Meanwhile, he could learn much. I could put my hands all over him, rubbing and scratching him. There was a special place on his back, behind the place where a saddle would be, that Good Hat loved to have me rub. I would scratch him there, and he would close his eyes, lift his nose in the air, and wrinkle his upper lip with the pure pleasure that he felt.

It was not all just play, though. I tried to teach him useful things. He would come when I whistled, a special whistle that my grandmother taught me when I was small. She used it, she said, to call her children from play when it was time to eat. I do not know why I happened to use it to teach Good Hat to come. Just for amusement at first, maybe.

I also taught him the use of hobbles. That was unnecessary, of course, but I thought it might be useful someday. A hobbled horse, with his front legs tied loosely together with a short, soft rope, can move around well to graze. It keeps him from wandering too far, because he cannot trot or run. You are familiar with this, I know. The People often use hobbles. I do not know how I happened to teach hobbles to the medicine hat colt. It was just something to do, like the whistle. It is much easier for a colt to learn about hobbles than for an older horse. Good Hat responded to this lesson much as he had to the rope. He fought and fell only once, and then understood. As I said, we seldom used the hobbles, but we could, when and if we needed. Anyway, the learning of the colt continued.

24

We were working our way farther to the northwest. The country is good there, with wide skies and good grass . . . cold, clear rivers. . . . There are places that reminded us much of our own Sacred Hills.

It was a good season, and we were happy in our great adventure. Otter was now past the time when she was made difficult by her pregnancy. It was good to see her feeling better. She tired easily, but we were in no hurry and did not push our travels. Looking back, I am made to think that the other three of us were trying hard to see that her needs were met, without saying anything to each other about it.

It was good to see her playing with the colt, Good Hat. I knew that she was teaching him a lot. Otter is skilled with horses, and here was a highly intelligent colt, a special animal. He learned easily.

The weather was good, too. After the first cool nights here at home, you know, there is often the Second Summer. Days are warm and sunny and calm, and nights are cool. It was like that. Geese were moving south across the bluest skies we could imagine. We were in areas near the mountains, and we were made to think that the elk come down to winter at lower levels. Some of the people we met said that, yes, this is true.

They do migrate, like geese or like the buffalo herds. Not so many, of course.

Autumn is truly a beautiful time of the year in that high country, as it is at home. If it were not that it means winter is coming soon . . . The leaves were turning colors. . . . There is a tree much like our cottonwood but with smaller leaves, which covers many of the mountain slopes and foothills. They turn a bright yellow, like cottonwoods, and a distant hill will be a beautiful sight, with the patterns of this bright yellow and the dark blue-green of pine and juniper. When the breeze stirs the leaves and they quiver, it is a sight to see.

We were heading into mountains now, because it seemed that it would be a better place to winter. Walker reminded us that our own Mountain band does this. So do his people.

The idea is to go into the shelter of the timber in the foothills, without going much higher. I had never realized how much difference that makes, how *high* you are. Once when we were traveling along the edge of a range of mountains, a little storm came up. Now, that is interesting to watch, particularly to one who watches weather. My medicine, you know . . .

A line of clouds rose behind the mountain range to the west and moved eastward. We could see those clouds as they hit the ridge of peaks. They caught there for a little while and then came pouring and sliding down the slopes, like a thick, foamy liquid. Then the clouds or fog began to layer out as it continued to move. When they reached the area where we were camped in the shelter of some pines, they were high over our heads. We could no longer see the peaks.

A drizzling rain set in and lasted part of the night. Next morning it was sunny but cold, and we could see snow among the peaks. It had not been there before. But there had been only rain where we were camped.

This reminded us that we should be thinking of a place to winter. We were depending heavily on Walker to guide us in that. He was the only one of us who really had experience in the mountains, you see. He kept saying that it should be no problem. We had done well at trading, we were prosperous, and would be welcomed by almost anyone. He seemed to think that Shoshones would be good to winter with.

"They are interesting people," he said.

I did not know, still do not, if Lone Walker actually knew that, or if he had only heard it somewhere. We had been told by the Crows that there were Shoshone in the area to the northwest. We kept asking, which was logical for traders to do, of course.

Now, we have been talking as if all of the people we met were pleasant and friendly. But there had been times when we were anxious. Even a little afraid. People were suspicious sometimes. It was no problem if we could just ride into a village or camp. We were obviously there to visit and to trade. The uneasy times were unexpected meetings with a hunting party. Or sometimes a war party. A hunting party in that area *becomes* a war party when they meet others who are traditional enemies. So there would be a short time while they decided that we were no threat to them.

Meanwhile, there was a clear threat to *us*. More than once some individual would become arrogant and pushy until we had satisfactorily identified ourselves. It is merely their way, though hard to understand for us. But we learned, with Walker's advice, how to handle such situations, and became more comfortable. The main thing was to remain calm and not make any moves that could be interpreted as hostile. That means *any* moves, actually. If someone with a question in his mind has time to think, he may figure it out for himself. The secret was to appear confident, display the hand sign for peace, and move very slowly, to allow the stranger to evaluate the situation. Obviously, two men with their women and with pack horses present no real threat for a little while. There is time to think. Still, an uneasy moment or two sometimes.

I was made to think, though, that we had one other advantage. The medicine horse, Good Hat. It is possible, of course, when we meet strangers, to tell much about them by their horses. A party, or an individual, who has animals of poor quality, few in number, poorly treated and underfed . . . well, you know how you would consider such a stranger. Either he has been having a run of incredibly bad luck, or he is one of the never-do-wells that any band has. You know them . . . Sometimes impoverished by gambling, often just lazy. . . .

On the other hand, if we encounter a stranger with good horses, sleek and well cared for, we say to ourselves, *Ah! Here is a man who is skilled with horses.* There is also the idea that this stranger is capable, probably intelligent. He has possessions of value, so his medicine must be strong.

It is this last idea that I felt was helping us. We *did* have good horses. If one was not working out, or kept going lame or was a problem in any way, we traded for a better one. Always we traded up, because we had to. So our little band of travelers would be seen by strangers immediately as one with good horses. This gave us a little prestige from the start.

Even more when they saw the colt, with his strange medicine hat markings. More than once someone would take a quick glance, look away, and then back again to be sure: *Did I really see that?* Sometimes they might try to pretend that they did not notice, but we could always tell. That we had such a remarkable animal gave us as a group a degree of honor. And, I finally realized, a degree of protection. Here was an animal that by his appearance suggested the presence of very powerful medicine. A stranger seeing us would not immediately know whose medicine . . . maybe the whole party's. One is cautious about things he does not understand. Especially things involving powerful medicine. So anyone we met had a tendency to treat us with respect. Even a degree of honor, maybe, because of the horse. *I must be careful*, they would probably tell themselves, *not to offend these people who have such powerful medicine.*

It took us a while to understand this, but I am made to think it was working for us before we knew it. Then it became amusing to watch. Otter would whistle for him to come to her, would play with the colt and show off his little tricks. Some people whom we met seemed to consider her a powerful medicine woman. Well, she always has been for me. Since we have been together, life is good. What? Yes, Bull, that *is* part of my story, is it not? *Aiee*, let me go on!

Bull is right. I do become distracted. But this story has many parts. I am trying to give you a feeling for how we *felt* about ourselves, and how others felt about us when we met as strangers. And, of course, how they felt about the remarkable colt that had started his whole quest.

I mentioned before an old man called Winter Skins. He was a great help to us. We met quite by accident, and he became a big part of our lives for the next few moons.

It was one of the sunny autumn days of which we have spoken. Crisp mountain air, sky a clear blue, the colors of the pines and the yellow trees . . . the ones like our cottonwoods . . . Did I tell you that their leaves flutter, like those of a cottonwood? Yes, they quiver in the most gentle stirring of the air. From a little distance, a hillside covered by those seems to be moving . . . like water rippling, maybe. That day the yellow color was at its best. In another day or two those quivering yellow leaves would be falling. But that day they were painted in their finest colors.

We were beginning to look for a place to camp. We came over a little rise. . . . Walker was in the lead. . . . And he suddenly reined in and lifted his right hand in greeting. I could not yet see the people he was signing to but moved ahead to join him, in case he needed help. It was always an uneasy time, the meeting of strangers in this country where there was constant fighting and distrust.

This, however, seemed to be no great threat. A party of several families, it appeared. Maybe five lodges . . . an older couple, and several young families. Children, from toddlers to youths approaching manhood, and a girl beginning to flower in the first flush of beauty as a woman.

Two young men rode forward to talk to us, returning the hand sign that Walker had given.

"Shoshone," Walker whispered.

It did not take long to identify ourselves and to get past the uneasy first meeting of strangers. As Lone Walker said, they were Shoshone, headed for winter camp. The young men, four of them, were all sons of the older couple.

I was immediately impressed by Winter Skins. He was a dignified old man, yet instantly curious about us. The day was growing late, and we quickly decided to camp together, visit, and possibly do some trading.

That was when, as we made camp, old Skins tried to bargain for my horse, Good Hat. I was astonished, because I had thought that here was a man of great knowledge and dignity. Possibly a holy man. He should have known that to bargain for a horse with the medicine hat marking was inappropriate.

As it turned out, he was testing *me*. He suspected that, since I was being so noncommittal about the horse, we did not know its importance. When I refused to consider a trade, or even to talk of it, he realized that I knew at least something of the animal's unique status. He then took a different path.

"You are a holy man among your people?" he asked me.

"Not really," I answered, as is proper in such a situation. "I do a little medicine."

His eyes twinkled, and the crow's-feet wrinkles around the corners tightened as he smiled.

"And you?" I asked him.

I had begun to realize that there was something about the spirit of the man. I have come to think, through all the people that we met that season, that one person blessed with the gifts of the spirit recognizes another. It was that way between me and Winter Skins, though he recognized it first. It is a thing that is *felt*, in spite of differences in language, age, or anything else. Our spirits touched, and it was as if we had been friends for a long time.

At first, of course, we had only hand signs. We learned some of their language that winter. But I knew, that first evening, that our spirits had touched, mine and that of Winter Skins. In a way he reminded me of my grandfather, Singing Wolf.

25

Some of you have known me since we were children together in the Rabbit Society. Others, not so long. But those who knew me before remember that I was always close to my grandfather, Singing Wolf. My childhood name, in fact, Wolf Pup, came to be because I was like him. "This one is the Wolf's Pup," they joked.

I was well grown when I decided to become his apprentice. He renamed me Pipe Bearer when our summer camp was destroyed. . . . But that is another story. What I am trying to explain just now is the way in which I came to realize the gift of spirit. I am sure that there are those who are struck suddenly with the idea that they have such a gift. Apparently, it sometimes is that it comes like a spear of real-fire from the sky, and the recipient says, "*Aiee!* I have been given the gift. What do I do now?" To himself, of course.

Sometimes, maybe one does decide, after receiving the spirit-gift, maybe through a vision-quest, that he must become a holy man. Or *she.* There are many very powerful holy *women.* There was once an owl prophet in the Eastern band. . . . Never mind. That, too, another story.

I have been trying to say that the spirits approach people in different ways. I have mentioned some. It is also possible for a devout holy man, or woman, to pass on some of the power of his medicine gift. I have come to think that my grandfather did some of this for me, as his assistant. I am sure that the realization of such a gift came to me very slowly, rather than like the spear of real-fire.

There did come a day when I was forced to say, *Aiee, I could not have done that by myself! I must be receiving some help from somewhere!* In addition to that from my grandfather and from my wife, of course. Ah, I probably would have amounted to nothing without Otter.

But allowing a guide to help you is something that must be learned. For me, at least. It is a matter of trust, maybe. An ability to ask help, and to give thanks for it when it is received. For me this came very gradually, the ability to loosen up and enjoy it.

Forgive me for being so serious, friends. And I know you cannot understand why I am speaking of such things as spirit-gifts. It is because we are now beginning to tell of our time with the Shoshones, and I am made to think that this is important. It is very important to *them*.

I have mentioned the old man, Winter Skins, and how he quickly saw things of the spirit in me. And, yes, I in him, after we got past the horse-trading start. I have said that it seems to me that those touched strongly by the spirits recognize each other quickly. It is because of the open and receptive mind that one comes to have, maybe. That is surely a help, anyway. Sometimes I have been wrong. Sometimes, as with Winter Skins, but that was because *he* was testing *me* with his talk of the horse trade. No matter.

All of this only to begin to suggest something that I noticed about our Shoshone friends. *Many* of them are offered the gifts of the spirit. Maybe even half, I do not know. Many more than among any nation I have ever met. Many are women, too. This gives their women better status and prestige than among some groups. Of course, the women of the People have always been respected and treasured.

But about Shoshones . . . Many are offered the gifts, and in many different forms. Some can find lost things. Some can tell who will win a horse race, or at gambling. Some seem to be able to see the future. Some are healers. There are even those who have several, or all, of these gifts. The longer I live, the more I am astonished at the wide differences in the way the Spirit speaks to us.

Another interesting thing about the Shoshones, though. At least I found it so. Many *refuse* the spirit-gifts. That is no disgrace. Even among our own, the People, it is a personal thing, and some refuse it. My grandfather mentioned it to me as I was making my decisions. "You do not have to accept the gift," Singing Wolf told me. "There is much honor to a holy man, but much that is duty . . . very demanding duty and responsibility. If you are unwilling to assume that responsibility, you can say no, and it is no disgrace."

Of course, talking of "duty," maybe my grandfather *was* pressuring me a little. He made me *feel* the call of duty. There may be some of that in the Shoshone way of thinking, but not much. Those who are offered the spirit-gifts seem to feel free to refuse it, with no shame or criticism.

One thing I noticed, also. I think that this is true among Shoshones or the People or anyone else. If one does not *use* the gift, he loses it . . . loses its power. It must be exercised and kept active. Not only that, it must be used without regard to personal gain. I mentioned the ability to predict a horse race, or the toss of the plum stones in gambling. But if such a person would use that gift to win, he would surely lose it. Not only that, he might also be punished. It is well-known that to use a holy man's gifts to *harm* others can result in his own death.

So, you see, this gives us a high regard for the limits one takes on to accept the spirit-gifts. It also gave me a better understanding of why these Shoshones, though frequently offered the gifts, often refuse. I respected their right to do so. Much of this I discussed with Winter Skins during that long, dark season, and came to a great understanding.

We had been with Skins and his family for only a day or two when the decision was made to winter with them. We were traveling in the same general direction. They planned to meet others of their people at a predetermined place to establish winter camp. We had found these pleasant people to be with, and as I said, Winter Skins and I had quickly begun to talk of common interests. Their tongue was not difficult for us, being quite similar to that of the Snakes, or Comanches, whose range borders ours on the south. Apparently they were once one, in long-ago times.

Winter Skins and I had talked long and seriously over the campfire one evening. The others had already gone to bed. I knew that Otter was probably impatient for me to join her. . . . Well, the night was cold, Bull. It is much warmer . . . Ah, whose story is this? Otter knew that Skins and I were learning much from each other, and had made no complaint. But I felt that she would be glad for me to come and warm her feet. And she would warm mine, no?

The fire was dying, and it was time to close the conversation or to build up the fire a little. Winter Skins knocked the ash from his pipe into the palm of his hand and tossed it into the fire. He put the pipe into his pouch, and I took this as a signal that our conversation was over for the evening. He rose, a little stiffly, and stood for a moment, stretching his legs.

"My friend," he said suddenly, "you have said your party will winter in the mountains. . . . You are meeting someone? Walker's people?"

We had told of Walker's background, of course, to explain his vocation and his Lakota dress, due to his Lakota wife.

"No. . . . We know of none of his people this far north. Are there some?"

The old man shook his head.

"None that I know. Maybe one or two, like Lone Walker. What of your people?"

"None," I told him. "This is new country to us."

He nodded, seemingly lost in thought for a moment.

"Would you consider," he finally asked, "wintering with us?"

"Your band?" I asked, unsure.

"My lodge. Mine and that of East Wind, my wife."

East Wind had impressed us as a quiet, kind woman, much loved by their various grandchildren. I assumed that the two of them must have talked of this. Still, I was greatly surprised.

"But . . . there are four of us, Uncle!"

"I know. But, look . . ."

He swept an arm around to indicate the number of people. I realized that he was indicating that their lodge had once been filled with children and was now empty.

"I am made to think that Wind would enjoy the company," he went on.

So they *had* talked of it.

"I am honored," I told him. "But I will have to discuss with the others."

"Of course." He nodded. "There is no hurry. But we, too, would be honored."

We turned away to our respective beds.

"*Aiee!*" said Otter as I slid beneath the robe. "Your feet are cold!"

"So are yours," I told her. "Let us see if we can warm them."

I did not mention Winter Skins's invitation that night. We would have probably stayed awake talking of it. As it was, I stayed awake for a long time, thinking about it. This seemed an ideal arrangement, to be guests of a respected holy man of these people, one who could teach me much. A motherly, kind woman, to whom our young wives could talk. Others who were close families, with their own lodges . . . I did not know how the others of our party would react, but it seemed to me that it was good.

Their reaction, too, was favorable.

"It is good!" exclaimed Lone Walker. "I was hoping for this!"

Aiee, Walker had already thought of this possibility. But he was experienced, of course. We were all honored. We had become friendly with the sons of Skins and his wife, and the prospect of a winter with this family band was favorable.

Another thought occurred to me.

"How many in their whole band, with whom they winter?" I asked.

"Maybe forty lodges, their women say," Plum Flower said.

The four of us were a little aside, discussing the generous invitation of Winter Skins.

"Much like the People . . . our Southern band," Otter said.

None of the four of us had any hesitation. We could contribute by hunting and by sharing our supplies. In a way, we would become a temporary part of this loyal family. Yet at the same time, we would fill empty spots in the lodge of this interesting couple who had raised four capable sons, and whose lodge was now empty. A daughter, too, we learned later, who had a husband and a lodge of their own. They had summered with his mother's family.

We told them that evening, at the evening camp. The four of us went together, the few steps to the fire of Skins and East Wind.

"We would all be honored," I told them, "to winter in your lodge. We will do our part to make it a good season."

Winter Skins nodded, pleased. East Wind smiled, a beautiful, motherly smile that would become very familiar in the coming moons. This smile occupied her entire face, narrowing the eyelids almost closed.

"I am happy for this," she said. "My heart is good."

This woman became like a mother to all of us. I might mention something about her name, though. East Wind . . . As you all know, the doorways of our lodges always face the east. The rising sun may enter. . . . Any people using lodges such as this, the tepee, face them so.

Aside from the religious symbolism of the rising sun, there is good reason. The smoke flaps are on the same side, above the doorway, no? The flaps are moved to quarter downwind, so the smoke will draw out and not fill the lodge. In summer the winds are from the south, in winter from the north. Storms may come from the northwest or sometimes, in summer, from the southwest. All of these allow for easy adjustment of smoke flaps.

But what if the wind comes from the east? Well, as you know, it seldom does, and then only for a short while. We keep the fire low and close the flaps across each other to keep out the rain that usually comes with the east wind. East wind is contrary. I was made to think that this may have been the reason for the name of Winter Skins's wife. She was kind and thoughtful, a mother to us all, but she always spoke her mind. Sometimes contrary, mischievous, like the east wind . . .

26

My husband is teasing me a little, maybe. He came to think that I was much like East Wind, the woman in whose lodge we wintered. Well, I could do worse. She spoke what she thought, as I do, and though he may tease me about it, I think it is what he likes about me. One of the things, anyway. So his comments about East Wind are really something of a compliment, no?

Yes, it was a good season. We moved into winter camp with the Shoshones a few days later, very comfortably.

During a long winter people do become irritable with each other, but it is expected. Besides, these people did much visiting and playing games and gathering for social smokes and stories. This helps greatly to avoid the problems of winter, with its long, dark nights and gloomy days. After a snow there was no time at all until the paths from one lodge to another were beaten down again and people were moving around the camp.

When the weather was good enough, many of the men were out setting traps or running their trap lines.

It might be thought that the people in that area would not be trading in furs very much yet. They are far from the forts of the French. Not so. I am made to think that when there comes word that someone wants furs, the trapping and trade begins. Many of the Shoshones had metal knives and fire strikers. A few had guns. Blankets were common, as well as beads and ornaments.

It took us a little while to realize that in our role as traders, *we* were part of this. We were beginning to gather a few furs, trading for only the finest. We would need to go to a trading post somewhere, next season. We had not realized until then how complicated this quest could become. And in a way, we still did not even understand what our quest was about.

When the weather was bad, they stayed in the lodges. It was at those times that the smokes and games and stories and gambling would take place. It goes without saying that friends gather with others of similar interests. Some families' lodges were known for their preference for gambling, some for stories, and so on.

Usually, we found, the visits to the lodges of others were by invitation at first. We had invitations because we were new, had new stories, and people were curious. After a while that died down some, but we sometimes went to the lodge of some friend or another, just to give some privacy to Winter Skins and East Wind. It was a very generous thing, for them to winter us.

One thing bothered us about our visiting. Having no lodge of our own, we could not return an invitation. This could have become a problem, but we were careful not to allow it to do so. We were also determined not to become involved in local politics. That, Lone Walker assured us, could be very destructive for a trader. And not very smart. Walker was a great help that winter, because of his experience in living with others as he traveled with his parents.

You remember, of course, that we were staying with an older couple. That was because of the understanding that had developed quickly between Winter Skins and Pipe Bearer. They had much to talk of. It became apparent, though, that to be guests in that lodge brought us prestige and respect. We might be invited by those of any age, who wanted to share some of that prestige. That is how we could have been led into their political maneuvering. It was good that we had Walker to help us avoid any pitfalls.

I do not want to give the impression that these people were any more obsessed with politics than others. It is only that when you live with people, it is easy to be drawn into any power struggle that is going on. We were fortunate that Winter Skins, as a respected elder, seemed somehow above all of that maneuvering. This helped us, too, to remain above it.

Many of the friendships that came about, though, were with people more nearly our own age. The sons of Skins and East Wind, their wives . . . We had become well acquainted with them during the few days' travel after we met. Lone Walker could talk to anyone, almost, and that established a friendship with those families. Then, after we joined the larger band, we met *their* friends. This introduced us quickly into the structure of the camp. We spent many enjoyable evenings in various lodges in their circle of friends.

Sometimes there would be smokes in which primarily the men would gather. They would talk of horses and weapons and past hunts and battles. And women, probably. When they had those events, the wives would gather at another lodge and talk of woman-things. What things? Ah, Pup, that would be to give away our secrets, and one of those is to keep our men guessing, no? Let me go on.

There was gambling, as in most winter camps. And as among our own people, some of it was serious, expensive betting. On horse races and contests of different kinds. That sort of betting was done by a small number of men, who are usually poor because of it. Then there was the gaming, with small bets on the roll of the plum stones, as among the People. They also use the sticks, drawing from several in a closed hand, to see who draws the shortest or longest.

There is another game, too, related to the stick game, maybe. It can be played by any from two to maybe ten people, men and women, divided into two sides. There are several small objects, and these can be simply a stone or a stick, an elk's tooth or a carved bone, small enough to be hidden in a closed hand.

One side has the "sticks," and they all put their hands under a blanket or robe and pass the sticks around to confuse the other side. They then all bring them out, hands closed and held forward. The other side has chosen one person to guess who has the sticks. Sometimes there are bets and side bets.

This is an enjoyable game. There are always one or two who have a reputation for skill at the guessing. I was made to think that it is a spirit-thing, almost like the gifts of which Pipe Bearer spoke. I have wondered, though. . . . If such a person were in a game where the bets become large, would they still have the skill? *Aiee*, I do not know.

But I do agree with Pup. These are a people who seem very close to the spirit-world in their daily life. The large number who are offered the gifts, yes. I do not mean to suggest that other people whom we met had *less* contact with things of the spirit. Lakotas surely do feel things of spirit strongly, as do Crows, and our own People. Blackfeet, too. I was made to think that the spirits speak to each in a slightly different way. In our own tongues, maybe. Though, in truth, such things seem to me to be not in any tongue, but in our heads and our hearts.

Forgive me. . . . I have probably made it more confusing in trying to explain. Some things are to be experienced, not understood. Did my husband say that, before? It is a favorite saying of his.

I wanted to tell you, though, of a conversation one evening in the lodge of Bright Fox, the youngest son of Winter Skins. He and his wife are a little older than we. Only a few seasons. . . . Their children were small.

There were four couples of us, visiting and making small talk. This was shortly after we arrived at the winter camp. We had helped with the setting up of the lodges, and they had invited us to eat with them. We were talking of the similarities in lodges. Theirs, the Crows, Lakotas, Arapahos, and others. They had never seen ours, those of the People, and were asking about them. Mostly, you know, the differences are in the shape of the door and the smoke flaps. The decorations, of course . . .

Someone mentioned that there are more differences in moccasins and shirts than in lodges, and we began to note these.

"Walker," said Bright Fox suddenly, "had you thought that it might be well for you to use different dress and hair style?"

They had become good friends, you see. Even so, Lone Walker was startled.

"Why would I do that?" he asked. "I follow the customs of my wife's people, the Lakotas. She makes my garments."

"Yes, I understand that. It is good, when you are among *them*. But here . . . Walker, everyone is a Lakota enemy. Someone might shoot before asking questions. Could you not follow the dress and hair of your own, the Trader People? It would mean less danger. Pipe Bearer and Otter follow their customs. They are not known here, so strangers see that they are far from home, probably traders."

It was a thoughtful argument, but Lone Walker laughed.

"Your worry is appreciated, Fox. But look . . . who would make my shirts? The pattern is not familiar to Flower. Besides, I honor her people in this way, which brings honor to her."

"You could carry a shirt of your people and wear it in this area," Bright Fox suggested. "You probably carry an extra shirt and moccasins anyway."

"That is true. But what about the hair?"

It appeared that Walker was half joking, not really taking the discussion seriously.

"The cut is not so different," Fox went on. "You could change the plait and the combing, maybe."

"It is too much trouble," Walker said. "Thank you, Fox, but I have traveled and met with strangers all my life with no trouble. Look at our horses and packs. . . . Can there be any doubt that we are traders?"

"No, maybe not. But what if a stranger sees you and not the pack horses?"

"Ah, that would seldom be, my friend. But I will think on what you have said. And I thank you."

The talk turned to other things, and no more was said of that. There was nothing to do anyway, at the time. We would not be traveling. There was no place that Walker could have obtained a shirt of Arapaho design just then. We were preparing to winter.

It did cause some concern to me. I was still a little emotional with my pregnancy, and was concerned for my own husband's safety. It seemed a pretty thin protection, the hope that someone would *not* shoot Pipe Bearer simply because his dress was unfamiliar. Besides, Walker was skilled in meeting people, and he was not concerned. It was not so with my husband. He is good with people, true. But not experienced in the sort of meetings with strangers that we expected to encounter.

To Pipe Bearer, there seemed to be no problem. He had taken on much of the attitude of his friend Walker. He was on a quest, to which he had been called, and he seemed to feel an immunity to danger. He laughed at my concern.

Well, I finally reasoned, if they, our husbands, are not concerned, why should we be, Flower and I?

We talked of this some and found that it helped. We were young and inexperienced, and still felt immortal. Both our husbands were strong and capable, and had proved themselves so. The medicines of both had proved strong. Why should we worry?

But I did. And in my concern for my own husband, it did not occur to me that I could be of help. I could have shown Plum Flower the pattern for a man's shirt which we use among the People. I could have helped her make Walker's shirts. It is always easy to look back and say *I could have. . . . I should have. . . .*

27

I was growing larger with my pregnancy now. East Wind was becoming more like a mother to me, looking after my needs and comforting me when my heart was heavy. And it was heavy, sometimes. I wished for my own mother, and for the familiar customs of the People. It bothered me, maybe more than I realized, that I would give birth among others.

That was a strange feeling, because certainly these kind people were far from strangers now. They were like family to us. I probably would have had the same feelings anywhere. It is only that this event is such a big part of a woman's life. It is to happen only a few times, and to bring another human being into the world . . . *Aiee*, there can be nothing else like it.

It was good to have the advice and comfort of East Wind. I am made to think that it was good for her, too. She had only the one daughter, who had a child a few moons of age. Now, with her own experience behind her and the recent helping of the daughter, Wind was ready to be my almost-mother.

The Moon of Snows had passed, and the Moon of Awakening. By the Moon of Greening there were some things apparent that required decisions. I was growing so big that I doubted that I could travel. Not very well, anyway. To get on and off a horse seemed a huge task.

We had talked at length to East Wind about when I might expect the birth. That is, Flower and I had. We told her all that we could remember about when I might have conceived. Wind thought about it and counted on her fingers. She agreed that, as Flower and I had estimated, I would probably give birth late in the Moon of Growing.

"That seems to be true," my husband teased when I told him. "You surely *are* growing!"

I thought about that with mixed feelings. It was hurtful, a little, to have him say it, but it would have hurt more to have him pretend that he did not *notice* how big I was. He found other ways to be nice to me, and he was fascinated when we could see the kick of tiny feet poking up against my belly. He could feel it with his hand. . . . "Our child, yours and mine, Otter," he would say in wonder. In that way I knew that his teasing about the Moon of *my* growing was just that, a tender joke, and I loved him for it.

There was another thing that I felt and thought about. A silly thing . . . You know the part of our Creation story, how the People came into the world by crawling through a hollow cottonwood log? And, finally, a fat woman got stuck in the log and no more could come through? Yes, it is one of the jokes of the People, mixed with the Creation story.

Sometimes, though, that is told as a *pregnant* woman. Mostly in the Eastern band, I suppose, because they are noted for being foolish people. Well, that story has always bothered me. Why a fat woman, anyway? Why not a fat *man*? And to have the person stuck in the log a *pregnant* woman . . . *aiee*, that always worried me. That is a cruel story! How did she get out? Did someone have to grab her feet and pull her back into the underworld? Where was her husband, and what was *he* doing? Well, think about it, now!

As I said, it had always worried me, that story. Now it became even more worrisome. The increasing pressure around my belly . . . I began to feel as if *I* were the one stuck in the log. I even dreamed, sometimes, that it was happening to me.

Ah, you laugh, Bull, and you other men. It would be interesting to see how you would behave with a growing creature in *your* belly. Maybe you do have one, there. It *does* stick out a bit!

Seriously, friends, I am trying to share with you how I felt at approaching this special time of my life far from home. It was good to have a husband who understood, and friends who had become like family, and East Wind, who treated me as she would a daughter. It helped very much.

I am not sure that I mentioned that we had decided for me to bear the child there among the Shoshones. I do not remember that we talked about it, or when we came to know that it would be so. It was one of those things that requires no discussion. It had simply come to be assumed. Actually, looking back, we had little choice. By the time the weather had opened enough to allow us to travel, I could not have done so.

There arose another problem, though. This band with whom we had wintered was preparing to move to summer camp. A day had not been set, but it became a matter to think on. If I had not yet birthed the child, what would we do? I did not believe that I could ride a horse. I could still walk, but I hesitated to think of the long distances involved in a day's travel. My feet were swelling when I stood very much. Moving around made them not quite so bad, but I hesitated over a long walk.

"When will the move come?" I asked East Wind.

She smiled, her beautiful motherly smile. "Ah, you are wondering how you could travel," she said. "Look, Otter, there is nothing to decide yet. Maybe you will make a move before the council does. If they decide it is time to move, you can choose. You could ride on a travois, or walk. . . . You could stay here until your time comes. We would stay with you. But you may not need to make that choice. Wait and see."

Now, I had no desire to consider bouncing on a travois. It would be bad enough in our plains country. But we were in mountains. In the foothills, anyway. It was rough and rocky, and a travois over rocks . . . *aiee.*

Pipe Bearer was not much comfort with his remark that if I had not started labor, bouncing on a travois would do it. But I knew that he was teasing. He was excited about our child, too. During the winter he had made a cradle board, like those of the band with whom we stayed. They were pleased, of course, and I was, too. It helped to show how he felt about it, and it made my heart glad.

The day came when the leaders met and decided that it was time to move. Three days . . . The band would move eastward, out onto the plain, where the buffalo would be more plentiful. There was a scurry of activity. Have you ever noticed? Whenever such a move is to take place, it comes as a surprise to some. They have known all winter that when the season opens up, the move will come, but they are never really ready for it. There are always those who seem surprised. Always the same ones, maybe. We expect their howls of protest that it is too soon, that there is not enough time before the announced day. It is like that among the People, and among every other people with whom we ever happened to be when they prepared to move. They begin to scurry frantically, like ants whose lodge has been damaged.

And now, too, it was time for me to make a decision. Stay here and wait for my labor to begin, or go with the band? I was very big and clumsy now. I knew that if I tried to travel, it must be on a travois. I was still fighting that idea. Aside from the discomfort of a jolting, bumping ride, there was a certain indignity in being transported on a pole-drag. To begin with, it was for baggage. Sometimes for children too tired to walk or ride one of the pack horses. Or for the old and infirm.

Now, I did not feel that I was any of these things, and even to think about it irritated me. I resented that I had to make such a choice at this time in my pregnancy. I was not helpless, I told myself. Yet I knew that I *was*, and even that irritated me. I could feel the child, very low. . . . Sometimes I felt that it was between my knees. I must be close. . . .

I had not decided yet whether to go or stay. I was trying to help by staying out of the way, and was frustrated by the feeling of uselessness. I was standing alone a little way from the lodges of East Wind's family, watching the flurry of activity. I was feeling guilty at my uselessness, when Rabbit Woman, wife of Bright Fox, approached the place where I stood. She had a child a few moons old.

"Here, Otter," she said, "you can help me!"

She was carrying a cradle board and her child, and had hardly enough hands.

"You hold the baby a moment, while I ready the cradle," she requested.

Now, I had held babies before, but this time a strange thing happened. As I took the infant from her arms, it seemed that it was such a natural thing. . . . You men cannot understand, but the women do. Yes, I see nodding heads. I held the baby next to my heart and felt a satisfaction. The warmth of its small body as it snuggled against me, moving against my breasts . . . I knew then that I truly was a mother in spirit, and that soon I would be in body, too. I could feel my belly tighten and relax again. . . .

Rabbit Woman finished readying the cradle board, thanked me, and took her child from my arms. I would have gladly held it longer. . . . My breasts still tingled, and I looked down. . . . *Aiee!* A wet spot . . . two, actually, soaking through my buckskin dress. I was confused for a moment. Had the baby's bladder emptied? No, two spots, one on each side. Rabbit Woman was laughing.

"Otter, you are truly ready to be a mother," she told me. "Your milk is ready."

It was true. The stimulation of handling the baby had made me let down my milk.

"It is a good sign," said East Wind when I told her. "Here, wash it out before it dries."

She handed me a waterskin.

"My time is near, then?" I asked her.

"Maybe. Maybe not. But it is a good sign, anyway. You have the *feelings* of a mother. Is your belly hard and then soft?"

"I do not know. . . . Yes, it feels hard sometimes."

"Good. Feel with your hand when it tightens. . . . Up on the round part, with the flat of your hand, so. . . . Yes! It is hard. Now, let us see how it softens."

It was not until two nights later that I began, for certain. Nearly morning. I waited as long as I could and then woke my husband, who roused East Wind. She took charge of the lodge instantly, sending the men out to do whatever it is that men do at such times. The three women of us, Plum Flower, East Wind, and myself, waited. Flower built up the fire, and Wind sat by my side, talking calmly, crooning a song of her people, sometimes placing a hand on my tightening belly.

I was filled with mixed feelings. Part of the time it was uncomfortable, but there was a great satisfaction that it was happening. I was to be spared the need to make a decision.

Our daughter was born about noon, and Plum Flower went to bring Pipe Bearer and the other men back to the lodge. We had not even thought about a name for the baby yet, and did not do so for a little while. I was glad to see my husband, and he to see me, and to hold our child.

Now some of the decision making was over, but there were decisions of a different kind. We had to decide whether to stay with our friends a little while and move with them. Or should we stay behind when they left this place of their winter camp? We could move on, but in the other direction, northwest while the band traveled east.

But I did not have to think about it yet. I was tired. I put the baby to breast, and she seemed to be a good feeder. Pipe Bearer smiled at us, and I could begin to see the lines of worry leave his face. He, too, was tired.

I held his hand, and we watched our child as she moved her hands and legs and stared around her at this strange new world.

Is this not one of the most wondrous experiences of one's life, to see and hold a new human being? One that is the product of our love together?

And it was truly good.

28

Otter is right, my friends. The joy of such an event, and to hold one's child . . . *Aiee*, but you all know this.

Now, however, we had, as Otter has mentioned, other problems. In another day the band would move on. In our minds I think that we had all decided that we would stay here for a few days, until Otter was better able to travel. Then we might as well head to the northwest, where it seemed that our quest would lead. There was no real purpose in going in any other direction. We could see how it was going for Otter, and match our pace to her needs.

This, of course, created a decision for Winter Skins and his family. Would they stay behind when the band moved on? We felt that we owed them so much. . . . I hoped, almost, that they would move on and not allow us to interfere with their summer season.

It was not long until we found out what they intended. East Wind had decided.

"We will stay a few days," she announced. "There is no hurry."

And so it was. Bright Fox and his lodge decided to stay with his parents, and the others of their family quickly agreed. Five lodges.

"We had decided to camp apart from the band as we did last season," Fox explained, almost apologetically. "This is no different. A few days here . . . It is nothing."

But we were very grateful. They would stay, just long enough to be sure that Otter was doing well, and then be on their way. It was a thoughtful thing, not to leave us until they were sure that we would be able to continue our journey.

They stayed about seven days, after the band left. When the day finally came, it was like parting from family. East Wind had talked to Otter and Plum Flower at great length, giving advice about the care of our infant daughter, and for Otter's recovery.

Winter Skins, meanwhile, had told us much about the country and the people ahead. Lone Walker asked many questions, and seemed satisfied that we were well informed.

We were cautioned again by Bright Fox to be careful. Then he laughed.

"Ah, *I* am telling *you*," he chuckled. "You are more experienced than I in dealing with other tribes, Walker. And Pipe Bearer, with your medicine . . . This will be a great quest. Maybe it is that I envy you this adventure!"

We helped them take down and pack the lodges, and they were on their way. We were alone again, the four of us . . . now *five*, with the addition of our daughter. She was a good baby, quiet and uncomplaining. Her wide-eyed gaze seemed to take in everything with wonder, yet understanding. We still had no name for her. Her disposition, accepting but definite in her wants and needs, reminded us of East Wind. We sometimes called her Little East Wind. But the same traits also reminded me of her mother, and I teasingly called her Little Otter occasionally.

The hungry way that she took to breast finally settled it. Otter was starting to feed her one morning, and the babe approached with mouth wide-open, searching eagerly for the milk.

"*Aiee*, in a moment, little bird," Otter said to her. "It is good that I do not have a nest full of hungry mouths like that."

We laughed, and the child became Little Bird. She still bears that childhood name. Many babes are called such names, but this seemed so appropriate. . . .

The horse, Good Hat . . . *aiee*! He was a yearling now, and marvelous in his muscling and in his way of going. Every gait was even and effortless. He had a running walk that appeared so smooth, I longed for the time I could try it. His trot, too, was like the bending of a willow, springy and without the jarring bounce that many otherwise good horses inflict on a rider.

His lope was as soft and easy as that of a cougar. When he extended it into a run, it only emphasized the power and grace. I did not want to begin to break and train him too quickly. His bones were not yet hardened enough, and I did not want to damage his back and spine. He would require very little "breaking," actually. Otter had handled him so much that he enjoyed it. Maybe we could start to put a saddle on his back and let him carry a small pack, to get him used to a light load. Then *next* year, as a two-year-old . . . his real training could begin.

These were the thoughts about him that were running through my head as I watched him that summer. I was also dreaming about him some. The night-visions were puzzling. I would see the horse, as I saw him when I was awake. Nothing special. He stood or ran or just grazed. The dreams seemed to go nowhere. They were also mixed with dreams about our travels, the others of our party, and, of course, Little Bird. Sometimes there was a fear, a dim, unformed fear of danger. I would waken, and it would take a few moments to realize that there was no danger, that it had been in the dream. I decided that it was because of the new responsibility that had come to me. We now had a child to consider.

It is odd how that changes a person. Until it occurs, the birth of the first child, one can follow any whim. Well, marriage does lend a sense of responsibility, of course. Even so, the coming of a child into that marriage may be the most sobering experience of a young man's life. From this time on, he has a greater duty to others. He must grow up quickly, if he has not done so already. Yes, you laugh, but you know. Some have grown up, some have not. Some never do. But all of these *think* that they are mature and responsible. It is only as we look back that we find it embarrassing, sometimes, to see how childish we were in many ways.

I do not mean to say that any of the four of us on that quest were guilty of poor judgment. Not really. But as I said before, we were young. We were learning. And the birth of this, the first child to any of us, had a profound influence. I am made to think so as I look back, anyway. It was truly a changing point, a bend in the path that had become the trail for the lives of all four.

Our first few days of travel were very short. Otter would walk a while and then ride some. Our pace was set by the rider in the lead, either Walker or myself. Usually Walker, because he was more experienced in meeting strangers of other tribes. Besides, he was more familiar with the country. That is to say, it was more like his than ours. It was apparent that both of us, Walker and I, were setting a very slow pace out of concern for Otter's well-being.

Finally, when we stopped for a rest, Otter spoke.

"Look, you two! I am not old or crippled. We can move a little faster. Let *me* tell you when we should slow down."

We felt a little foolish, maybe, but it was good to have her tell us. And, yes, I admit, that is one of the things that I have always admired about Otter Woman. She always says what she feels and walks her talk. Except, of course, when she feels there is a need to carry out some clever plan.

Then she goes slowly, a word or an idea here and there, until she accomplishes what she wants and lets me believe that I thought of it. Ah, yes, Otter. You did not think I knew that?

Yes, the journey . . . After Otter explained to us, we traveled faster, but still not as far as a usual day's journey. She did tire easily and had to admit it, even though resentfully. Since none of us knew what to expect, we were all cautious about Otter and the baby. Probably few women have had so much hovering and concern during that time.

We would meet people on the move from time to time, and we camped and traded with them. Always we were interested in their reactions to the horse, Good Hat. Some still asked about trading, but most did not. They recognized his importance, and his powerful medicine. Yet there was nothing specific about it.

The best information was from those who seemed to be medicine men or women . . . holy ones among their own people. These we could sort into two kinds. Some eagerly told us all they could, which was not much. The medicine hat was important, sometimes "sacred," and should bring good fortune. We heard stories *predicting* such a horse and its importance, but the tales were very vague. Winter Skins had told me of this. He had also said that although such a marking is unusual, it is not extremely rare. He had seen several. "Although none as good as this," he added.

The other reaction from the holy ones we encountered was odd. Some seemed fearful and defensive. Suspicious, maybe. We finally decided that they feared that my medicine, that of the medicine hat, was more powerful than their own and presented a threat. When someone has such an idea, there is no use to try to convince him, of course. We did not try. Tell him once, "We mean no harm," and then go on with trading and move on.

For people who were not really traders, we were doing well at that. I can see how it could appeal to some. We had the advantage, as I mentioned before, of Lone Walker's skill. He had helped us to outfit ourselves with some practical items while we were with Plum Flower's people, and had given us advice as we went. Our packs had increased in size, number, and, yes, in value. We had traded horses, too, except for our best. We now looked, and actually *were*, a prosperous party.

We jokingly attributed our success to the medicine of Good Hat. Only partly joking, maybe. We had certainly had good fortune.

But there still remained the big question in my mind. *What was the purpose of the quest?* Surely not to make traders of us. It was challenging, at times amusing, and enjoyable. We had met many good friends. But through it all we had the feeling that we were only playing a part. I was still Pipe Bearer, student of Singing Wolf, the holy man, and aspiring to such status as his. This quest, though it was important, seemed to me to be diversion. I did not question it, really. There must be a purpose to my dreams and visions. But *what*? Every quest that I had ever heard of had more direction than this. Our ancestor, Red Horse, traveled far in search of the white buffalo bull. Another, Horse Seeker, searched for his dream-horse even longer ago. The blood of that great stallion still flows in the veins of our horses. Maybe even in this, the medicine hat. I had thought, even, that that might be the connection. But surely I would find a more reasonable purpose, somehow.

How much farther? I thought sometimes. I even carried out a ceremony, offered a little tobacco and a prayer, hoping that I would be given an answer. . . . Nothing.

I was beginning to have some guilt. Had I misinterpreted my visions? Was I dragging my wife and newborn child into unknown dangers because I misunderstood my dreams?

No, that could not be it, I decided. I *had* seen such a horse in my night-vision, *before* the birth of the foal. I had talked of it with my grandfather, the holy man, who was convinced that this was a call to a quest. Surely, with his great insight and experience, he could not be wrong. I certainly could, but Singing Wolf would have seen the error in my thinking.

In the end I decided that I must wait. I remembered my grandfather's parting words.

"When the time is right, you will see how it is meant to be."

But it was difficult, sometimes, to find comfort in that as we traveled on, apparently aimlessly.

29

Crow, Shoshone, Blackfeet . . . we met them all, traded furs, stories, and visiting. There is a fascination with a person of another tribe or nation, one that helps the trader. If he has good stories, so much the better. I could see how the trading could become the biggest thing in one's life. Not for me. . . . It was an interlude in our lives, Otter's and mine. We learned much. . . . There were times of pleasure, success, and joy, even though the times when things were not so happy. . . . Did you ever notice that it is easier to *forget* the bad times? Yes, we remember the bad, of course, but not in such detail.

Think, for instance, of some of the *best* memories of your life. We remember every sensation. How warm or cool it was, the feel of the breeze on the skin, the sound, maybe, of rustling leaves of the cottonwoods or the whisper of running water. The smell of a warm stand of pines and *their* whispers . . . different from the song of the stream or the cottonwoods.

But the bad memories we remember in less detail. We remember that it was *bad*, yes. That we were cold or hot or in fear or pain, yes. Yet much of the detail is gone, wiped away from our memory. I am made to think, my friends, that it is meant to be this way. At the times our hearts are heavy, we are protected. We are allowed to think, later, to remember the bad times, but much of the way it felt is forgotten. It is a generous thing, then, that we are allowed to remember all the details of the good times. The feel, sound, smell, taste . . . That way we can live it again in our heads.

And we do that about this quest-journey. There were many good times in those seasons, and we remember those with warm hearts. *Aiee*, I can still think of the smell of the lodge of Winter Skins and East Wind, sitting and sharing a smoke on a cold night. Skins mixed some leaves into his tobacco, a plant that they call bear berry. It gave a pleasant smell, like nothing else, and I remember that when I think of that winter.

Forgive me. The memories come crowding back, and most are pleasant.

Little Bird grew rapidly and was quickly a joy to us. Not only to Otter and me, but to the others. Plum Flower adored her. She gave the baby the loving attention that only a woman of childbearing age but without one of her own knows how to bestow. Lone Walker was like an uncle to her, in the best ways. We were *family*.

But I started to tell of an event that happened that summer, one that seemed to end our quest. We came to a summer camp of about ten lodges. They were bright and well constructed, and the camp was orderly and clean. Well, within the expected for a summer camp. The children were fat and the women were happy, as our saying goes.

As we rode in, we noted their horse herd. These were animals of exceptional quality, maybe three hundred of them, carefully herded by the young men. This was not unusual, you understand. We saw many fine horses that summer.

As we entered the camp, however, there was a reaction to *our* horses. More properly, the one horse, Good Hat. Children ran, pointing excitedly, calling to each other, and following our party. It was apparent, though, where their interest was centered. *The medicine hat horse.*

Of course, there was often interest in the horse when we entered a village. People would stare quietly as he passed. This was something else. We had never encountered a place where there was a reaction like this. The adults were more reserved about it, but we could see in their eyes that here was a different sort of understanding.

And the children, *aiee!* In most camps the children show curiosity for strangers. We have all seen that. Again, this was quite different. They hardly looked at us. Their interest and excitement was concentrated on the horse. It was quickly apparent that we had found a band of people who knew something more than others we had met. They had an understanding about the horse who wears a medicine hat. Even the children . . .

We tried not to react to this, but it was difficult. Was our quest about to be fulfilled? With hand signs we inquired about the leaders of this camp, so that we might pay our respects. We were directed to a big lodge on a little rise at the edge of the camp. The crowd of children and quite a few adults followed us. There was an air of excitement that we did not understand.

"What is happening here, Walker?" I called to him.

"I do not know. I feel no threat, do you?"

"No. But they know more about the horse. More than others we have met."

"I am made to think so," Walker answered. "Let us see. . . . Stay alert."

"They would not let the children approach us if there was to be trouble," Otter noted. "This is a *happy* occasion for them!"

It was quite puzzling. We drew up in front of the big lodge where their leader lived, and paused. It seemed useless to call out the usual greeting. There was so much noise that anyone within a bow shot could not fail to be aware of our presence. We had hardly reached the lodge when the doorskin lifted and a tall, dignified man of middle age stepped through and straightened to his full height.

Walker gave the hand sign in greeting, and the man nodded.

"We come to trade in peace," Walker went on.

He gave our names and our nations and asked permission to camp. The leader nodded agreement.

"I am called Broken Tree," he signed. "You are welcome in our camp."

He appeared somewhat puzzled and kept looking around and beyond us. Just then the colt, Good Hat, stepped into his line of sight from behind one of the other lodges. Now, I have said that this man appeared dignified. His reaction, then, at the sight of the medicine hat horse, was quite remarkable. All pretense at dignity was lost for a moment. . . . Only a moment. His mouth fell open, his eyes widened with wonder, and he actually gasped. Then in another instant his dignity returned.

"What is this?" he signed. "Is this the horse the children shout of outside my lodge?"

"I do not know, my chief," Walker signed. "This colt belongs to my friend here, Pipe Bearer."

The man turned to me.

"You are a holy man?" He signed the question.

"Not really," I told him. "I do some medicine."

Broken Tree nodded an understanding of my expected denial.

"What of the horse?" he asked.

I tried to appear ignorant of the special status of the animal, to learn all we could. I shrugged.

"He was born to one of my mares," I signed. "What do you ask about him?"

He gave me a rather indignant look, as if he saw through my pretended ignorance. Which, in fact, he did, of course. He turned to one of the older boys, spoke a few words, and the youth trotted off.

Now the conversation turned to small talk. Broken Tree and Lone Walker visited in signs about the weather and the season's game. Walker skillfully discovered that the man knew some of the Arapaho tongue, and this helped with communication. The chief seemed to be waiting for something.

Then there came a flurry of excitement among the onlookers, and we could see someone, or maybe a small group, approaching from outside the camp. People were moving around already with all the excitement, you know, but this was something else. I lost sight of the source of this special attention for a little while as it drew nearer. But finally the crowd turned to look, and I did, too.

Now it was my turn to be astonished. From between two of the other lodges came a strange procession. At its head was the young man who had been sent on an errand by the chief. He was leading a horse and was followed by an excited column of younger children.

But the horse that he led . . . *aiee*, what an animal! A mare of about fifteen hands, deep-chested, well-muscled, and clean-legged. She appeared to be young, in the first bloom of maturity.

Yet it was not the obvious quality of the mare that caught my attention. At least, at first. It was her color and markings. The base color was white, shading to red roan in some areas, that is, the lower legs, mane, and tail. The overall effect was that of a white horse with bright red-gold markings that glistened in the sunlight. Well, like a sunset. And I began to see the cause of all the excitement. Across the top of the mare's well-formed head, including the ears and the poll between, was *the medicine hat*. Where Good Hat's color was blue, that of this beautiful mare was red, but it was the same.

My head whirled. I knew that this was important, but I did not know how or why. Sometimes I think I still do not understand it. But if you can imagine . . . That entire camp of people gathered to stare and marvel at what was happening before their eyes. There stood the two animals, alike in markings yet differing in color. One a magnificent mare, the other a young stallion.

"This is your mare?" I asked the chief.

He nodded, almost in wonder.

"They are alike," he signed. "The medicine hat . . ."

What more was there to say? Or to do?

Now you realize what any horseman would think when seeing those two beautiful animals together. *Can they be bred?* A horseman's dream. And not only their qualities but their significant markings. "*Sacred,*" someone had said in our travels when he had seen the young horse. This was a feeling that seemed very special as we stood and stared. It was as if this day was a turning point for all the earth. A new beginning, a new Creation story, maybe. I felt honored, yet very humble, to be permitted to have a small part in bringing these two special animals together.

Could they breed? I did not know. Yet even that possibility was such a powerful force, such strong medicine. . . .

The two special animals approached each other, curious, very cautiously. The mare was held by the young man who had brought her to Broken Tree's lodge, so it was Good Hat who stepped forward. Dainty, mincing steps, nose stretched forward, eyes protruding as he studied the mare.

They almost touched noses before the mare suddenly squealed and struck out with a forefoot. It is always a surprise to me, that sudden squeal when a mare is approached by a strange stallion. I am always so startled that I jump when it happens. I did so this time, too. Good Hat did, too. He retreated, almost in a panic.

After all, he was not yet mature. He was just beginning to be attracted and excited by mares. He did seem to be unsure of how he was reacting. It is questionable whether he could have done anything about it if the mare *had* been ready.

But at that moment, I felt that many of my questions had been answered. This must have been the reason for my quest.

30

It was too much to expect, I suppose, that a breeding of those two sacred animals would result. Good Hat was very young, to consider such a thing. But we could hope, Broken Tree and I.

The young stallion was interested, but not fully developed and was lacking in experience. An old stallion is skilled in the arts of such things. He is quick and dominant, and moves in a forceful way to accomplish his purpose. In addition, he knows how to avoid the painful kicks and even the serious injuries that may result from attempting to mount a reluctant mare. There is a moment during the courtship . . . as he rises, a space of only a few heartbeats, when his soft underbelly and his male parts are completely unprotected. There is only a short while, less than a day, where any mare is really receptive. Many will kick violently at all other times. A stallion must accomplish his purpose quickly, avoiding any deadly kick that might cause permanent damage.

Now, young Good Hat, maybe not even mature enough to sire a foal, had certainly had no experience. He was much more likely to be injured, and he was a little bit afraid of the mare. That was good because he would be cautious.

I viewed this whole thing with mixed emotions. I longed to bring these two special animals together. It seemed to me that this was the purpose of my quest. Possibly the most important accomplishment of my lifetime. Aside from marrying Otter Woman, of course . . .

Yes, Otter, I will stick to the story. But it *is* true. We will discuss it later, no?

Where was I? Oh, yes. . . . There were decisions to make. How long would we be justified in staying with Broken Tree's band to wait for the possibility of this coupling of the two special horses? I was made to think it important, but *how* important? It would be nearly a year before Good Hat came to full maturity. True, there was the possibility that he could breed sooner. Possibly at any time. But would such a breeding result in a foal? Or in an injury? There was no way to tell. It would be necessary to wait and see.

It did not take long to realize that we would have to winter there, even to see if the purpose had been accomplished. Maybe longer. It was possible . . . *aiee!* A year to see whether the young stallion had the ability, and another to be sure whether his effort had been successful? Two years more away from the People? Little Bird might be dancing the Children's Dance with the others of the Rabbit Society by that time! We had already been gone for a year. . . .

As important as the meeting of the two horses seemed, there was something not quite right about this. I wondered for a while if I was being tested. Did I have the dedication, the heart, to handle such a responsibility? I was not sure. There were others involved. I longed to talk to my grandfather.

Another thought . . . Why would I have been led into this situation if the two special animals were *not* able to fulfill the desired result? And just then, they appeared not to be. Why, then, were we here? I spent much time in meditation and prayer. Could there be another purpose to the quest, one I had not found?

Or, again, my own motives. Was I somehow expecting personal gain from this, if the breeding could be accomplished? I did not think so. It would have been exciting merely to be a part of such an event. More exciting than any gain that might result. No, I decided after much meditation and even some fasting, that my heart was right.

Now, while I wrestled with this, the days passed. We were honored by Broken Tree's people, and there were many stories around the night fires. To make *this* story shorter, I might say that we decided to stay a little while to observe how the horses related to each other. I was convinced that the heart of Broken Tree was as right as mine. Neither of us was attempting personal gain, but wanted to be a part of whatever was meant to be.

We talked of it, and Tree could see our problem quite clearly. He urged us to stay for a long enough time to observe the horses. Maybe we could tell whether this was meant to be.

"Stay two moons," Broken Tree urged. "That should let the mare come in season twice."

It was a good plan. If it was apparent by that time that the two were not to be joined, we could leave and return to Plum Flower's people. Winter there, then on home to the Sacred Hills. Even so, it would be a two-year absence from friends and family, and that was enough. Otter and I had decided that, aside from this quest, we were really not meant for traveling. Not on an ongoing basis, or as traders, anyway. It was good to see new places, and good people that we would remember always, but we both longed for the Tallgrass Hills of the People.

At the end of the two moons suggested by Broken Tree, we were not sure about the horses. As you know, a mare comes in season a little sooner than a moon. Usually, anyway. Sometimes it is hard to tell. But it had appeared to us that the time came a day or two after we arrived. There was much squealing and laying back of ears and showing of teeth, anyway. Then again, about twenty days later . . . About as expected. It occurred to me that if we stayed there for the two moons we had discussed, we would have the advantage of *three* times in season for the mare, instead of two. The whole thing was unsure, but it seemed worth the delay.

Was it? I do not know. We left Broken Tree's camp and have never learned whether that breeding was successful or not. I have wondered. Many things happened to us after that. We found ourselves facing events that became more important, more urgent. Maybe I was wrong about the purpose of the quest. Maybe it had more than one purpose. I do not know. I have thought that it would be good to go back and see if the mating of those special horses was successful. Maybe someday . . . But you see how our family has grown. So quickly, too. *Aiee!* Maybe we will learn, someday, whether our attempt to bring those horses together brought a good result.

One thing I *have* heard. A trader told me last season that when two of the medicine-hat horses are mated, the foal usually does *not* have the medicine-hat marking. I do not know. That trader was one who talked much and said little.

Anyway, we stayed for the few days until it would be time for the mare to come in season the third time. She appeared to do so, but you know . . . even after a mare is in foal, there is the appearance of another season sometimes. So we left without knowing, of the success or failure of the mating, and of whether that was really our purpose in being there. All that I can say for sure about it was that we tried. More accurately, Good Hat tried. I really feared for him, but he did escape injury. Just the usual kicks, bites, and bruises. Some mares are like that, more than others. Some . . . No, I will not take that thought on to its logical conclusion. That would not be wise, would it?

Our travel was a bit different after we left the camp of Broken Tree. We were starting back. We did not take so much time, did not try to ask so many questions. We felt that we had learned many of the answers. So we moved faster. We stopped with several of the various bands we had met on the outward journey. We met some new ones. But our whole attitude was different. We knew where we were going, and why. Certainly that had not been a factor before.

Still, there was an uneasy feeling. I could not identify it. Finally, I spoke of it to Otter and found that she felt much the same.

"I had not really thought much about it, Pup," she admitted.

She was occupied with the new baby, of course.

"But think on it," I told her. "What have we really learned from this quest? We know little more than when we started."

Otter smiled. "Oh, *that*. I thought it was only I who felt that way."

"You, too, then?"

"Well . . . I do not know, Pup. It is you who have the spirit-gift. Are you made to know other things about this?"

"I am not sure, Otter. I am made to think that there *was* purpose to the quest. The horses . . . Yet is there another purpose, somehow?"

"Is there a way to find out?"

"That I do not know, either. I can try. . . . The bones, a ceremony or two. Sometimes, Otter, the thing for a holy man to do is nothing. Wait and see. Ah, I wish I could talk to Singing Wolf!"

"Have you spoken of this to Lone Walker?" she asked me.

What? Oh, yes. I did not tell you. We were still together, the four of us. When we prepared to leave Broken Tree's people, we did not even talk about it. We all just seemed to assume that it would be so. Back to Plum Flower's people for the winter, and then on home. I *had* spoken to Walker about that and suggested that he and Flower might like to visit our country as we returned to it next season. But we had decided nothing beyond "We will see. . . ."

At the time of which I was telling, though . . . Otter had suggested that I talk to Walker about the quest. He only shrugged when I inquired as to his feelings.

"Who knows, Pup?" He and Flower had begun to call me by that, Otter's pet name for me. My childhood name, you know. "Who knows?"

I tried to explain.

"Otter and I have wondered," I told him. "Should we not have a better feeling that the purpose of the quest is finished? Or at least understood?"

Walker laughed.

"Ah, my friend! Have you not told me that many things are better *not* understood? Some are not *meant* to be. Maybe this is one, I do not know."

"Then you have no feeling for whether this journey is finished or not?" I asked him.

Walker thought about that for a little while.

"Not really," he admitted. "I am made to think that no journey is finished until one returns to home or family. Or dies, of course. In this matter I had thought . . . Pup, it was *your* vision, *your* quest, *your* horse. And you, though a holy man, cannot tell?"

"Walker, if I knew, I would not ask you!"

"Ah, forgive me, Pup. Now, if *you* cannot tell whether your quest is complete, I am made to think it is *not*. But what could its purpose be?"

I thought of our experiences. There was much that was good. Our spirits had been lifted, mine and Otter's, at such places as the Bear's Rock. We had met and become friends with many people. None quite so close as Walker and Flower, but many others. I recalled again the manner of our meeting.

"Walker," I told him, "Otter and I had talked, soon after we met you. . . . Maybe *that* had some purpose. That we should meet."

He nodded. "Flower and I talked of that, too," he said slowly. "It seemed meant to be. The fire . . ."

"Then . . . is it possible that it was the *reason* for my quest?"

Walker was very serious now.

"I am made to think not," he said slowly. "Not the only reason. If it were, you could have gone home then. And what about the horses? No, there is more to be learned."

He was right, of course. There *had* to be more to the story than we knew at this time. There was still a piece missing.

But *what*?

31

Ah, my husband has told you in great detail about the horses. Why is it that men are so interested in watching horses mate?

What? Well, yes. Women are, also, Pup. Is not everyone? You trapped me, there! Maybe it is that horses are big and noisy and excited in their lovemaking. Excited and *exciting*, maybe. *Aiee*, how did this start? Let me tell my story!

We stayed there long enough for the mating to take place if it proved to be possible. The two special animals were kept near to each other, yet away from the main horse herd. There were plenty of young men who were eager to assist in this, to be a part of a very important event. Each time that the mare came in season, the two were watched closely, to see if there would be a successful mating.

Three times the proper moment came. We stayed there for more than forty days, to be sure of two times. But as it happened, the mare again came in just before we left. *Three* times. We saw that with mixed feelings. If the first matings had been successful, she might not have repeated her cycle. But some mares do, so we were not sure.

What? *Was* the mating a success? We do not know. Ah, I guess Pipe Bearer did not mention that. We left, and many other things interfered. We have not been back and have not heard. Surely we would have, do you not think so, Pup? Such a great event would be told and retold by the traders. Yes, it would be good to know, but I do not want to go back, even to see such a colt.

At the time we all thought that there was a good chance that the attempts at mating might produce a foal. Young Good Hat was cautious and a little afraid, but he tried. Fortunately, he was not kicked or seriously injured by the mare. But the fertility of a young stallion is in doubt. And, remember, he was only a yearling.

Anyway, we do not know. If there was a foal born from those attempts, it probably did not have the medicine hat markings. If it had, I am made to think that we would have heard.

But now we prepared to start home. I was dimly aware that there was something wrong, something missing. I was busy with the baby, and that was a joy. It did keep me from seeing that my husband, too, was concerned about the quest.

It was *his* quest, of course. The others of us knew that but had been drawn in by his excitement. And by the unusual nature of the mystery of this medicine hat horse. Now it seemed that he had found the source of his dreams or visions. The two sacred horses had been brought together, and it was to be understood that we would start back, the quest completed.

We did not talk much of it. Looking back, I now see that in the joining of the two sacred animals, there was nothing of completion at all. We did not know the outcome. We *still* do not. And I had not yet fully realized that there was something missing. When I began to feel it, I was able to see that something of the sort was bothering Pipe Bearer, too. I did not know what it might be.

Finally we talked of it, my husband and I, away from the others.

"What is it, Pup?" I asked him one evening.

"What do you mean?"

"I am not sure. But you should feel good, your heart should be filled with excitement and joy that your quest is fulfilled. Instead, your heart seems heavy."

He looked at me strangely.

"You see it, then?" he asked me.

"I do not know, Pup. See *what*?"

It was a long time before he answered, and there was a sadness in his eyes. He looked at the colors of the distant sunset and took a deep breath. Finally he turned and looked into my face.

"I do not know, Otter. I do not understand. You are right. I should *not* have a heavy heart. I have finished my quest and seen the sacred horse that I saw in my dreams. Why, then, do I feel that there must be something more? Have I been misled, somehow? Is there more to this quest?"

We were several sleeps from the camp of Broken Tree by this time, but I began to wonder.

"Are you made to think," I asked him, "that we should go *back*?"

Again, there was that uncomfortably long pause. I waited. The golds and yellows in the western sky were turning to reds and purple, and the dark shadow of distant mountains marched toward the east.

"No," said Pipe Bearer thoughtfully. "That is not it. That part of the quest is done. But, Otter, there *must* be more. More than one purpose in this long journey we have taken. It has not been given to me to know."

"Can you toss the bones?" I asked.

"We talked of that. Maybe I will try. But I am made to think that it would help little. That ceremony is best used for others. And it is a very broad prophecy. It does not quite fit this problem."

"How do you mean, Pup?"

"Well, we have come to think that there is another purpose for this quest. More than one. There must be a reason why I have not been shown this other purpose. It seems right, though, to start home. Maybe when the time comes, I will be shown."

He seemed more satisfied after that. It was as if he waited for a sign that would tell him what the purpose, the *other* purpose, of this quest-journey might be. Of course, there was a certain amount of doubt still in my mind. I could pick out several possible purposes that had already made themselves known. The fire, and our help for Walker and Flower. The meeting with Flower's people, which was invaluable in learning the languages we needed. The season with Winter Skins and East Wind, and Wind's help with my birthing. And the horses . . . I had to wonder. Which of these were really linked to the quest? And how many purposes may a quest have? My husband had studied this sort of thing in great detail, but I was not sure I should ask him. This was a holy man's territory. Therefore, it bothered me a little that he did not seem to know either. Were all the things that had happened merely accidents? Or as Singing Wolf always said, *Are there really any accidents*? Well, we had little choice. We would learn, at the right time. We traveled on.

Now, this next part is very hard for me. For Pipe Bearer, too. I will start it, but, Pup, you help me if I need you.

We had traveled for several days. We stopped with a camp of Blackfeet, one we had not met before. These bands of several different nations move around a lot, as we do in the Sacred Hills. There was no problem, after their first reaction to Walker's Lakota dress and hair. They understood our explanation.

We should have taken that problem more seriously. It is easy, you know, to look back and say *I should have, I could have. . . .* But things seemed to be going well. How many times have I thought . . . Ah! Never mind.

We were coming down out of a mountain area. There were long, low ridges, running north and south. It would be several days' travel yet to the area where we might find the people with whom we had wintered.

When we topped some of these ridges, we could see far ahead. Probably we could see the area where we would camp tomorrow night, or the next. Then, when we were in the valley between, we could see nothing very far either ahead or behind us. We were using the same plan that we had before. One of the men rode in front, then the pack horses, and Plum Flower and I. The other man brought up the rear. Usually Lone Walker had taken the lead position. He was somewhat more familiar with the country, and much more so with the languages we might encounter. Walker was leading that morning. If only . . . But let me go on.

We were moving up a long, straight slope, through scattered pines. Because of this climb, the horses were strung out. There were maybe two bow shots' distance between Walker and the first of the pack animals. Then came Plum Flower and I, and behind us another bow shot, Pipe Bearer.

Walker reached the top of the ridge, which was a rolling, rounded crest, and drew his horse in to wait for us. Then, suddenly, he seemed to see something beyond and reined his horse around. The animal fought the unexpected rein for a moment, confused and uncontrolled. Walker had both hands on the reins, trying to control the startled animal, when suddenly he was knocked from the saddle. It was as if he had been swatted like an insect, by a giant hand. A heartbeat later came the boom of a musket from behind the ridge. Walker fell heavily, and his horse bolted and ran.

I could hear Pipe Bearer's horse pounding up behind me.

"Stay here!" he yelled as he passed us.

Plum Flower sat staring in disbelief, like a person in a dream. I did not know whether to be more concerned for her or for my husband, who might be charging into great danger.

Now a rider appeared from over the ridge and approached the fallen Lone Walker. He paused when he saw Pipe Bearer charging at him, and turned his horse uncertainly. The two circled each other for a moment, and then the stranger did a very odd thing. He offered the hand sign for peace!

I had not seen Walker move since he fell. Now Flower kicked her horse into a run up the slope, drawing her belt ax.

"Flower! Stop!" I yelled at her. I could do little else, with the baby in her cradle board on my back.

For a few moments there I could see my world falling to pieces before my eyes. I was sure that they would all be killed. Probably Little Bird and I, too. It was almost too much. I could not even defend us. *Aiee*, Pup, will you tell it now?

It was as Otter has said. I am made to think that Walker was dead before he struck the ground. The young warrior on the ridge had a scalping knife in his hand, but paused when he saw me. I pushed my horse to the crest because I did not want to give him a downhill charge. I could dimly see a party of warriors riding up the slope, but I dared not take my eyes off this one.

He was very young, and afraid and confused. He seemed puzzled at my appearance, and surprised me by giving a peace sign, followed by repeatedly signing "mistake" or "accident."

Now, I am no warrior. I had no wish for a battle with however many warriors were charging up their side of the slope. I wanted to see to my friend's wound. I did not yet know that he was dead. Besides, if I was killed, Otter, Plum Flower, and Little Bird would be in greater trouble.

I was just preparing to return the peace sign when I heard a horse pounding up *our* side of the slope. I knew without looking that it was Plum Flower. I had seen *her* in action, and a new fear struck me. If she attacked this youth, who was probably the killer of her husband, she could easily get us *all* killed.

32

Too many things were happening, too fast. My main concern was for Lone Walker. I did not even know yet whether he was still alive. The war party . . . (I had to assume it was a war party . . .) was pounding toward me. Yet I dared not turn my attention from the young warrior who was still circling his horse in a sidestep practically at arm's length from me.

Add to that the approach of Plum Flower. Finally I had to do something. I was already answering the peace sign of the young man before me, and turned to shout at Flower.

"Stop, Flower! Do not try to fight! It is an accident!"

I was not sure of that, but it was as close as I could come to truth. The young man kept repeating it in signs. Whether it was or not, I had realized that if Flower attacked him, his companions would join the fight. I risked a glance to see that there were at least six of them. Capable-looking warriors, well mounted and heavily armed. We did not want a fight with *those*! I continued to give the peace sign as they approached.

Plum Flower jerked her horse to a sliding stop and ran to her husband. That was good. If he still lived, she would begin to help him while I tried to communicate with our attackers.

I was very grateful that she did not try to fight. Still, it was a tense moment. Anything could still happen.

I looked back down the slope at Otter. She was trying to calm the excited horses and to keep them well away from the tragedy on the ridge. I saw that she had placed a rope on Good Hat. As a young stallion he might be the most unpredictable. Once more I was grateful for my wife's calm judgment in emergencies. I could turn my attention to the crisis at hand.

I could not identify the nation of the approaching warriors. That was important, if that was the reason . . . It occurred to me in a fleeting thought that Walker had been taken for a Lakota by some enemy of the Lakota. It was the thing that we had feared. As it happened, that was not far from the truth.

But there was no time now to think of that. The warriors quickly circled us, weapons ready. *Aiee*, my friends, how big the mouth of a musket barrel looks when it points your way! This was at close range now, only a pace or two away. I tried to sit very still, and kept my right hand raised in the sign of peace.

There was much talking between and among the warriors . . . seven of them altogether. They seemed to be questioning the young man who had apparently fired at Walker.

Behind me, Plum Flower was sobbing.

"How is it with Walker?" I asked over my shoulder, not looking around.

"It is not good," Flower answered, half choking through her sobs. "He is dead, Pup."

"Are you sure?" I asked.

It was a stupid question, and she did not answer. Instead, she resumed her crying, and I knew. I was still thinking that she might try to attack her husband's killer, but she made no such move. Another thought struck me. . . . Would she try to harm *herself*? I could do nothing about that just now.

One of the older warriors, apparently the leader, now began to sign.

"Who are you? What is this?"

I was glad to be on this basis. The danger of sudden murderous intent was lessening now, with a start at conversation.

"Pipe Bearer, Elk-dog People, Southern band," I signed quickly. "We are traders. How is it that you have killed my brother?"

The man did not answer my question. Instead, he asked one of his own.

"You are not Lakota?"

"No, no," I told him. "Elk-dog."

"But he is Lakota." The man nodded his head toward the still form behind me.

"No. He is of the Trader People. Arapaho," I signed.

"Then why . . ."

I could see his thoughts as he looked from me to Walker to Plum Flower.

"His *woman* is Lakota?"

"That is true."

The stranger had interpreted the situation correctly. The garments of Walker had been made by Flower.

"Your woman?" he asked.

"Elk-dog People. She is of my own band," I told him.

There was more conversation among themselves as they discussed the new information. Finally, the leader began to sign. His heart was heavy, he said, for the mistake. The young wolf, on his first hunting party, had seen a lone Lakota and had raised his weapon to be ready. It was not certain, but the musket may have fired by accident. Regrettable.

As he signed this, I saw his eyes widen, looking past me. Plum Flower had risen and now made a rush at the young man.

She was silent, which was worse than if she had been screaming at him . . . more deadly.

Now, I had no idea how they would react to this. Among some, it might be that they would think it her right to fight her husband's killer. Among others, they might kill *her* to protect their own. And still another reaction might be to kill us all so that they would not have to worry about it. I had only a moment, a heartbeat or two, to decide what to do.

As Flower crowded past me, her ax raised, I flung myself from the horse, knocking her down. She struggled, but I managed to twist the ax out of her grasp and toss it aside. Then I held her, to prevent her from trying to attack him again.

"Do not fight them," I told her. "You will get us all killed!"

For a little while Flower continued to fight *me*, but gradually began to cry again. I was made to think that it was good. I did not even begrudge her the vile things she had called me in her own tongue.

Now there was an exclamation from one of the other warriors. He was pointing down the slope toward the place where Otter was holding our horses. I could not see well, half lying on the ground with Flower. I spoke to her gently.

"Flower, I will let you go, but you must promise not to fight them. I have your promise?"

I knew that I could trust her, if she would give her word. It was a bit slow, but she agreed.

"Yes . . . for now, anyway."

Well, that was better than nothing.

"You will tell me first, before you take back that promise?"

"Yes."

"Then say it!"

I was taking no chances here.

"I will tell you before I try to kill my husband's murderer."

"*Aiee*, Flower, I am not sure that is enough."

I was afraid, you see, that she would "tell" me just as she made a lethal rush at the young man.

Plum Flower looked me full in the face, through eyes filled with tears.

"You can trust me, Pup. I would not put you and your family in danger."

I let her go, and she walked back to Walker, sank to her knees, and took his hand in hers. She was crying softly, and I knew that she spoke truth. I *could* trust her.

I rose and looked down the slope. Otter was waiting for the outcome of the meeting. I concluded that they must have seen the medicine hat horse and were discussing him.

"That is your woman, your horse?" he asked.

I nodded and motioned Otter forward. She looked to be in doubt, and I called to her.

"Bring the colt?"

That seemed to answer her question. She kneed her mount forward, still leading Good Hat, and approached us. There was excited talk among the other party.

"Where did you get the horse?" their leader asked.

"He was born to one of my mares. The roan, there," I told him. "You have seen such horses?"

"Only one in my lifetime. This horse must give you strong medicine. You are a holy man?"

"Not really. I do a little medicine."

It was at about that point that I began to realize. *They are afraid of us, now.* That idea was reinforced as the leader continued to sign.

"Our hearts are very heavy for the grief that our young man has brought you."

He glanced contemptuously at the scout. I thought he might offer to give him to us, almost, if we would hold no grudge against the rest of his party. I would not have known what to do if they had offered that. More important, what Plum Flower would have done. Fortunately, there was no such offer.

"Is there any way we can help you?" the leader asked.

I could think of none, so I shook my head.

"What will you do?" the man asked.

"Mourn our loss. Prepare my brother for burial."

"Ah! How is your burial?"

"The scaffold," I told him. "We will build one. Then back to his woman's people."

"It is good," he signed, though there was little that I could see that was good.

"We will leave you now," the man went on. "It is not good for us to be here while his woman mourns."

That was certainly true. And if they remained here, I would have to worry about Plum Flower's pledge not to harm them.

"I am made to think it would be better," I agreed.

They moved away, and we turned our attention to caring for Walker's body. I moved his arms and legs into a natural posture and placed his hands on his breast, before the stiffness of death could begin. Then I built a fire and offered a prayer and tobacco.

Plum Flower was beginning her three days of mourning. She cut her hair, threw dirt on her head and her clothing, and gashed her forearms with a flint knife. I was not certain how extreme the deeds of mourning might be among her people. I hoped that she would not harm herself further. I took Otter aside, and we agreed not to leave her alone for very long at a time.

Otter stayed with her while I rode around the area to find a place to build our scaffold for Lone Walker. I found a place on an open slope, where four small pines formed the four uprights that we needed. There were others to cut for the platform. The spot overlooked a wide view of mountains and plains and somehow made me think that it was a place where Walker's heart would have been good.

It was not far from a little stream where we could camp and have water for ourselves and the horses. It would be our camp for at least three days.

I rode back and told the women. Then I cut a pair of poles for a travois to carry Walker to his resting place. But we stayed there on the ridge that first night, and there was no sleep. We mourned Walker, friend and brother.

Just before dark we happened to see, in the far distance, the party whose scout had caused his death. I had no grudge. I honestly think it was an accident. Revenge would not bring back Lone Walker.

I only hoped that Plum Flower would be able to see it this way. At least I did have her promise. She would tell me before starting any mission of vengeance.

33

Three days we stayed there. Plum Flower was in mourning, carrying out the traditional rituals of her people. Pup and I mourned, too. Lone Walker had been more than a friend. I know that he was like a brother to my husband. I cannot remember anyone to whom Pup has ever related that well. To his grandfather, maybe, but that was in a completely different way. No, this had been like the best and closest brother-to-brother team ever.

And I too had come to think of Lone Walker as family. An older brother, maybe. I do not think that Walker was much older than I. It was more a feeling of confidence and calm good humor that always radiated from him. He was a kind person, but strong and capable. I am made to think that he would have given his life for any one of us.

One of my regrets is that Little Bird will not remember him. *Aiee*, every child should have such an uncle. Lone Walker adored her and would have been such a good influence in her life as she grew.

Ah, forgive me. I did not intend to become so emotional. But you can see what an important part of our lives Walker had become. He crossed over far from his own people, yet among loved ones. He was mourned by a devoted wife and by

Pup and me, his almost-brother and -sister, with the mourning songs of our own tradition.

It was a great hurt to see the grief of Plum Flower. I had been afraid at first that she might do herself harm, but I soon decided not. Her ritual of mourning was very open, to let out the grief. Somewhat different from ours, but similar in form. The cutting of her arms was strange to us, but there was no suggestion that she would try to join him on the Other Side. But we stayed close to her, knowing that she could not be comforted. Except for our presence, there was little that we could do. Well, our own mourning . . . Yet that was for ourselves, in our loss of a friend and brother.

But I will go on. . . . After the three days of mourning we prepared to move on. Pup and I had talked about it. We would return Plum Flower to her own people. Maybe stay a little while to make sure that she would be recovering from her loss. Then on home.

I knew that my husband's heart was very heavy over this. Not only the loss of his friend, but the way his quest had gone bad. Something seemed wrong. He did not talk about it very much, but I knew what he felt. A wife knows. Especially when they are as close as Pup and I. He had been concerned that he could not see the purpose of his visions and his quest for the medicine hat horse. Now he was filled with grief for the loss of his friend and almost-brother. I knew what Pup must be thinking: If Walker had not joined us on the quest, he might be alive. But we had talked very little about it. Not yet.

When we moved on, it was very hard to leave that scaffold against the sky, with the wrapped body of the man who had become such a part of our lives. I did not want to look back, but I did, just once, and tears came again to my eyes. Pup had chosen the place well, the sort of spot that Walker loved. I could see an eagle feather fluttering in the mountain breeze at the tip of one of the poles. A raven flew across the slope below, and I knew that Walker was at peace with the world.

I took Plum Flower aside at our first rest stop. I helped her to wash the dried blood from her arms, and the dirt and ashes from her hair. I had been afraid that she would not allow me to do those things. She might want to wear them. But she seemed to be doing well. She had eaten nothing since Walker's death, and I did not urge her yet. She would know when to break the fast.

I wrapped some of the deepest of the wounds on her arms, using an ointment that Pipe Bearer carried. Flower thanked me. I felt better about my fears that she might harm herself. It was probably past the time when she might have done so. I wondered what she would do when we reached her people. I recalled that among our People, there was a custom that would be appropriate. A party returning from a long journey will sometimes paint their faces with black to show that they have suffered a death. Well, Flower would tell us what might be appropriate for us to do, when the time came.

My real concern was for where she would live. It was so soon after her loss that I doubted she had thought much of it yet. Well, that too she would tell us later. I was not familiar enough with their customs to know what would be expected. Maybe she would move into her mother's lodge.

Plum Flower ate a little that night, but it did not sit well on her stomach. Dried meat sometimes does that after a fast. It grows too quickly in the stomach, maybe. I made her a little soup with strips of the meat and water, and she kept that down.

Yet the next morning her stomach was upset again. Well, she was still recovering from the shock of her loss. It was understandable.

In another day I was beginning to wonder about it, though. Since we had known her, Plum Flower had been completely healthy. Never a sick day. This was foreign to anything we knew of her. Besides, there was her behavior. I had attributed that to her great loss, of course. We would be riding along, saying nothing, and Flower would suddenly break into tears and sobbing.

What could I do? It is a logical thing, for someone who has sustained such a loss, but what is there to say? A time or two when I tried to comfort her, Flower turned on me angrily and reined her horse away.

It was several days before the reason became apparent. We were riding side by side, and Pup was ahead of us, beyond the other horses. Flower was crying quietly, and I was saying nothing, to avoid the anger she had shown before.

"Otter," she said suddenly.

"Yes?" I answered, surprised.

"Otter, I carry Walker's child!"

Aiee! This would explain some things! I did not know what to say. My head whirled. Was this good or bad? Or *both*?

While I was still trying to think of something to say, she spoke again.

"Walker did not know."

"You had not told him?" I asked.

"No. I had only just realized. . . . I was to tell him that night when we camped."

Ah, how my heart reached out to her, my almost-sister. To lose a husband whom she loved as I know she loved Lone Walker . . . Then to realize that she carried his child and had not been permitted to tell him . . . On top of all that, to fight the mood swings and the squirming stomach of an early pregnancy . . . I did not know whether I could have borne so much, all at once.

I reached out a hand to her, and she gave it a quick squeeze.

"Thank you," she said.

Now *I* broke into tears. Flower was thanking *me*, when I was in the midst of despair that there was nothing I could do for *her*. But I . . . Maybe just being there was a help.

"Will you tell Pup?" she asked me.

"You wish me to?"

"Yes. He should know."

"That is true. Do you feel like traveling, Flower?"

"Oh, yes. I can be sick on the trail as well as in camp," she said with a wry smile.

It was then that I knew she would be all right. Her spirit was showing through, and her sense of humor.

"I have little experience, Flower," I told her, "but that part did not last long for me."

She only nodded.

I told Pup that evening as the three of us sat by our night fire. His eyes widened, but he said nothing for a few moments. Finally he spoke, softly and thoughtfully.

"It is good," he said. "You will have a part of Walker always."

Then the three of us cried together for a little while. I was glad that we knew, because it would help us to plan our travel around what we thought Plum Flower was able to do. Not much was said about it, but I could see that Pup was trying to make it easy for her. At least, as much as possible.

That is one of the things about him. . . . Pup is a thoughtful man, gentle and kind, and I love him for it. Ah, I embarrass him, I see! No matter. It is true, and he knows that I say what I think.

By the time we reached the area where we might find Flower's people, her stomach was better. We had traveled well, considering the heaviness in our hearts, and the changes in Flower's body and spirit.

But life is for the living and must go on. We inquired from a town of growers about the summer camp of Flower's band. They pointed us to the east. A chance meeting with a trader and his wife let us know more. When he began to describe the place, Plum Flower spoke.

"Yes," she said. "I know the place. We have camped there before."

It is much as it is with our people. A good site for summer camp is remembered with pleasure. It will be used again. Not every year, of course. The place must recover. The paths of the many feet and the places where the lodges stood must grow green again. A few seasons . . . Flower thought that it may have been five seasons since they had summered there.

"I was still a child, almost," she mused. "I thought I was a grown woman, but . . . Ah, much has happened."

There came the day when Flower told us that we would reach the camp. We painted our faces in mourning to indicate our loss, and rode toward the area where Flower believed her people to be.

Our first contact was a young man, one of the wolves. It is much as it would be with us. He expressed sympathy and then rode ahead to give the information.

When we came in sight of the camp, people were beginning to straggle out to meet us. Some sang parts of their Song of Mourning. It was a difficult time.

Plum Flower's sister came running, tears in her eyes. She rushed to Flower's horse and reached out to her. I knew how she felt, because I had felt the same way since Walker's death. There was little that could be done to help our sister.

Bluebird walked beside the horse as we moved on into the camp, holding tightly to Flower's saddle thongs.

Pipe Bearer was looking for a place to make our camp, talking to one of the men, the wolf who now rode with us as an escort.

"We will camp over here," he called to us, turning his horse aside.

We paused, and I spoke to Flower.

"Will you camp with us, or join your family?" I asked her.

"I had not thought . . . ," she began. "Bluebird, where is the lodge of our mother?"

I saw from the look of surprise and shock on the woman's face that there was something wrong. It was one of those tense moments when no one wants to speak, or knows what to say.

It occurred to me in that moment that Bluebird looked older than I remembered. She was surely not more than a few years older than her sister. But the face that looked up at Plum Flower's was old and drawn. This woman had seen much grief.

Finally she spoke.

"Ah, Flower, I had forgotten. You did not know. . . . Last season . . . our mother crossed over in the Moon of Long Nights. Our father followed her in the Moon of Snows."

My heart was very heavy for my almost-sister. How much more grief could Plum Flower bear?

34

Plum Flower camped with us, and I was pleased with that. I had mentioned, I think, that the husband of Bluebird was a man I did not like. Bull's Horn, he was called. He was loud and haughty and conceited, and he mistreated Bluebird. At least, I was made to think so.

When we had stayed with this band before, he had leered at me. I do not know why it is . . . sometimes an admiring glance from a man is welcome, even though both know that nothing will come of it. It makes a woman feel good about herself. Others, *aiee*, their gaze makes my skin crawl! Yes, you men laugh, but the women know. It does not matter whether the man is handsome. Not much, anyway. It is the *way* he looks at a woman. Sometimes it is a compliment . . . an honor, almost. Sometimes it can be a repulsive thing. My reaction to any looks that I ever received from Bull's Horn was revulsion. I always felt uneasy around him. There was something threatening and unclean in the way his eyes wandered over a woman's body.

I think I mentioned before that Bluebird may have had a happy lodge. Every marriage is different, of course. Some women seem to enjoy a man who is domineering. I could not live with a man like that.

You are laughing. . . . Forgive me, but I become angry when I think of it, even. But I am trying to explain to you the whole situation that now faced us. More accurately, what faced Plum Flower.

This new loss, that of both her parents, placed her in a very unfortunate situation. She would normally move in with relatives until she decided to take a new husband. I knew that she felt about Bull's Horn much as I did, though. She politely declined the invitation from her sister to stay with them for the present.

"You are busy with children, Bluebird," Flower told her. "I could not impose. I will stay with Otter Woman."

Her sister might have suspected the real reason for her refusal. Surely Bluebird knew the way most women felt about her husband. But maybe not. Maybe she loved him, though I cannot see why. Or maybe she was trapped. Bluebird was not nearly as pretty as her sister—was older, and had several children. Maybe she was trapped in a bad marriage.

Anyway, there was no one else. These women had had a brother, Flower told us. But he was killed in an accident on his first buffalo hunt. He had been the only other child.

There were friends who would have taken her in. No Tail Dog, a close friend of Lone Walker's. But this brought out another problem. Flower would be eligible for remarriage after a reasonable time of mourning. It would be assumed that if she moved into any lodge now, that she would become a second wife, or third, to that man. That was part of her problem with moving into her sister's lodge. Everyone would assume that she was to become the wife of Bull's Horn. *Aiee*, my flesh crawls . . . Never mind. But that would discourage the interest of eligible young men.

It was a real problem. Flower's next move would determine the rest of her life. And no one but Pup and I knew of her pregnancy, either. That would make her less eligible in the eyes of some suitors.

For her to camp with us was a temporary answer. It would give her a little time to think and make her decisions. There was little choice, though, unless some unexpected handsome young subchief suddenly appeared to carry her away. A girlish dream . . .

From the other point of view, Flower would make a highly desirable wife. She was a beautiful woman, intelligent and strong. She owned a lodge, though a small one, and a share in the trade goods that we had. Except for her pregnancy, everything about her was favorable. I am sure that there were those who would not have been bothered by that. There are men, though, who would not take kindly to a bride who already carried another man's child. Such a man might not be the best husband material, either, but . . . *Aiee*, I get too much of my own opinion into the story.

But you can see the problem faced by Plum Flower. There was no real urgency to her choosing to accept a husband, except that with each passing moon she would become more pregnant, and her choices more narrow.

There was one other matter. Flower was staying at our camp, Pipe Bearer's and mine. . . . We had to be thinking of how long it would take to travel home. I was afraid he would be restless to start on while Plum Flower still needed us. I was not certain about when winter might begin here. Pup had said nothing about it. He hunted a little with No Tail Dog, and seemed to settle into a daily routine.

Finally I decided to ask him about it.

"Pup, when do you think it good to start back to the People?"

He looked at me strangely. "When the time comes," he said. "Why?"

I was confused. Did he know something that I did not?

"Do you know when winter comes here?" I asked him.

"No. I had not thought of it."

"But, Pup . . ."

"What is it, Otter?" He smiled. "Were you afraid that I would not realize that Flower needs us?"

I suppose that was it, and I felt foolish for doubting him. But he went on, speaking softly and thoughtfully.

"It is hers to decide," he said. "She will have her choice of many suitors, but Flower will have to decide *when* to choose, too. She must finish mourning, in her heart."

"That is true," I agreed.

"So we can wait, Otter, until she does not need our support. If it is too late to travel . . . well, we could even winter here, and go home in the spring."

I loved him for understanding. Then he surprised me.

"Otter, what do you know of her sister's husband, Bull's Horn?"

"What do you mean?" A stupid question, of course.

"Well," Pup said thoughtfully, "you have been in her lodge. How is it there? Is the spirit good?"

So he was thinking along the same lines I was!

"Pup," I told him, "this does concern me. Bull's Horn seems to be a good provider. He is respected as a hunter, is he not?"

"Yes, that is true."

"But I am made to feel that most of the women do not like him."

"Ah! I wondered," Pup exclaimed. "He is a braggart, hard on his horses, but it is not easy to know another's marriage."

I could have thought of a clever remark, but this was no time for such teasing.

"Some women are better with such a man," I told him. "I could never be. "Why do you speak of this?"

"Well, you know the reason why Flower camps with us. So that she does not have to commit to anyone yet."

"Yes, she has spoken of that to me," I told him.

"Do you know their customs in such a situation?"

"Not entirely. Much like ours, or others of the plains, I think. The husband of her eldest sister takes a widowed woman as his second wife."

Pup nodded. "That is as I understand it. If there is another suitor, she may choose him, but if not, it is assumed to be the *duty* of that sister's husband to provide for her, no?"

"I am made to think so," I told him.

"Aiee," Pup said tiredly, "will the troubles never stop for her?"

We were made to think later that among these people, that duty was a stronger custom than among our own. Maybe it was only because Bull's Horn made it seem so, as he became more insistent.

Half a moon had passed since our return now. In another half a moon we would have had to make our decision about the winter. We hated to inquire of the climate there from Plum Flower. We did not wish to give her the impression that we wanted to force her into a decision. That was furthest from our minds. She had enough concerns without our adding more.

Flower's active period of mourning was over, and she was gradually recovering her more normal attitudes. At least it seemed so. It was hard to tell. We had never known her except as the wife of our good friend, Lone Walker. To add to that, we had never known her when she was pregnant, either. She had not yet started to show, and we had said nothing to anyone. It was hers to tell when she saw fit. Her worst mornings of sickness seemed to be past, and she had not mentioned it lately.

It was at about this time that a few suitors seemed to turn up. It was not good manners to press it when there was no real urgency. In winter, for instance, or in time of hunger or wartime. So the advances were more subtle. A young man would stop for a visit and a smoke with Pup. Then he might casually speak to Flower, offering condolences and inquiring about her welfare and how things were going for her. This would provide some idea as to whether she was ready to consider accepting suitors.

Flower was polite but distant. Not enough to frighten them away, but not much encouragement, either. She did not appear ready.

No Tail Dog stopped by one afternoon and brought a bundle of choice cuts of buffalo. He had gone hunting alone, he said, and thought we could use part of his kill. He visited a little with Plum Flower and, after a little while, strode off cheerfully toward his own lodge.

"That is odd," Pup said as we watched him go. "Why did he not ask me to hunt with him?"

Plum Flower giggled. "It was not about hunting, Pup. It was about courting."

"*Aiee!* No Tail Dog?"

"Yes, my husband's friend. It is good of him to be concerned, no?"

"You will go to his lodge, then?" Pup asked.

"Not so fast, Pup," Flower told him. "He has not even mentioned it."

"But you said . . ."

"Ah, Pup, I do not even know whether I would be interested. Dog has only indicated that if I need him, he is there. It was a gesture by a friend, that is all."

I was aware of most of this already, but it was not apparent to my husband. I am made to think that women are much more aware of such things. Maybe it is because we *have* to be. For many lifetimes, since Creation, maybe, our men have killed each other or died in the hunt. They face more danger, so there are more women. Woman have *had* to be aware of the subtle hints. Men blunder along, without noticing such things. No offense, my husband. It is only the way of things. Even one as sensitive as yourself will not see as quickly as a woman the small mood changes. . . . Ah, this is too complicated to tell. You women already know it, the men will never quite understand.

Yes, we have had our joke. I will go on. It was good to know that Plum Flower had someone. If it came to it, No Tail Dog would probably be a good husband to her. Flower knew him well. Better than we did, of course. She had known him since childhood. But she gave little indication as to whether she would be interested or not. Maybe she was simply not ready yet.

The quiet stream of potential suitors continued. There were a few young men, not yet established, who came mostly to let their availability be known. There were a few lecherous older men, eager to proclaim their affluence, who were quickly rebuffed by Plum Flower. This was not a woman to be impressed by wealth.

It seemed unfortunate that few of the men of her own age showed much interest. We finally realized that while the interest might be there, these young men were just starting out. A new lodge, a new wife, maybe a child or two . . . most of them could not yet afford a second wife.

But at least it began to appear that there would be choices for her. It was good, too, that her husband's friend, No Tail Dog, was ready to be supportive. He would not push it, but would be there if Flower needed him.

So far, he would have been *my* pick.

35

Pipe Bearer and I had decided from the first that we would try to stay completely out of Flower's deliberations. That was impossible, as we might have known. Not only did we have to be polite to anyone who might stop by, but Flower was staying with us, and she often shared her thoughts. It was good for her, probably, that we were there. We could listen to her voicing her thoughts, remain apart from her problems, yet still give her a chance to think aloud.

One thing of interest, we found, was the constant stream of women who stopped to chat. It was very transparent, I thought. They were looking for gossip. No, not all, of course. Some came out of genuine concern. But there were those whom Flower hardly knew, talkative and prying, probably trying to size up any potential competition. Flower graciously visited with them all, like the sweet and thoughtful person that she was. It was harder on *me*, maybe, because I wanted to tell them what I thought of them, and they were Flower's guests. Between her and Pipe Bearer, they kept me from insulting the visitors. Most of them, anyway.

Bluebird came sometimes, but as a sister would. As far as I can recall, she rarely if ever inquired about Flower's plans. She was pleasant to have around. The two of them talked of childhood memories and laughed together, and it was good. Maybe it would turn out well, I began to think. These two could live together, share a lodge. . . . But then I would remember who they would be sharing it with, and the thought would turn to ashes in my mouth. Bull's Horn. Possibly Bluebird could live with him, and even be happy, in a strange way. What is the saying about "Do not judge anyone until you have walked in his moccasins?" *Aiee*, there are some moccasins in which I would not want to walk, even long enough to judge.

Yet as I watched the two, I began to think that maybe they could work it out together. Bluebird seemed to have done so, and was happy with her children. Theirs was a big lodge, well provided. . . . Maybe the problem was in *my* head, not in that of Plum Flower.

My feelings were beginning to lean in that direction. I was not totally pleased, but thinking that maybe there was a possibility it could work out for Flower. That was until the day Bull's Horn approached our camp.

Pipe Bearer was not present. He and No Tail Dog were out somewhere, and Flower and I were at the fire at the lean-to, doing daily busywork or something. We had been considering setting up Flower's lodge. Both of us were avoiding, maybe, any talk of that. Sometime before Cold Maker arrived, other decisions would have to be made. Probably the band would move to a winter camp anyway, and it might be better to wait. As I look back, it seems that we were trying to postpone decisions, but we did not know it then.

Bull's Horn swaggered up to our camp, planted his feet wide apart, and folded his arms over his chest. He was a big man, muscular, a little fat, maybe. Some women might have thought him attractive.

He smiled. At least I think so. It impressed me as a mixture of a sort of leer and a haughty smile, which looked to me like a silly grin. For a moment I wondered how I could have been thinking that maybe Flower could be happy in her sister's lodge with this man.

"Where is Bluebird?" he asked.

There was no greeting, no *How goes it with you*, nothing. He was addressing his question to Flower, ignoring my presence. Now, realize, this was *my* lodge, even though a temporary camp. Anyone should be polite enough . . . Let me not be distracted from the story, here. . . .

Plum Flower answered him politely, looking him straight in the eye.

"We have not seen her this morning, Bull's Horn. She was here yesterday."

"Yes, I know," he snorted. He was no longer smiling. "She wastes too much time here."

I was astonished at the crudeness of the man. His wife was coming to try to be of help and comfort to her widowed sister, and he resented it as a waste of time! I said nothing. I was not a part of the conversation. Flower, too, was apparently caught off guard, and struggled for an answer.

Not waiting for one, Bull's Horn changed the subject.

"When are you ready to move to my lodge?" he demanded of Flower.

It was a display of incredibly poor manners. Now, this was a nation not my own. I did not know their ways. But some things cannot be misunderstood, even others' customs. This was crude and cruel, and my temper boiled. If the question had been asked of me, I would have had an answer. *When snakes fly, dung-eater!* Yet I managed to keep my silence.

Plum Flower was silent for a moment. She seemed to be searching for an answer, or maybe just choking down one similar to mine.

"That is mine to decide, Bull's Horn," she said politely.

He grunted. "It has been long enough," he said. "It is time for you to stop playing like children."

I was sitting in the open lean-to and had been nursing the baby. With the way my temper was rising, I wondered if my milk would be souring or turning to gall. I shifted Little Bird and covered the breast, not looking at Bull's Horn. Finally

I could be silent no longer. I placed the baby on the robe beside me.

"Bull's Horn, this is her decision," I told him, "and this is my lodge. You are very rude."

I should not have challenged him, I suppose. Yet I thought that he was taking advantage of a situation. Though I did not know the ways of his people well, some things are wrong. A man should have no right to approach *any* lodge and challenge the woman and another woman who is her guest. True, the temporary camp did not have quite the sanctity of a real lodge, but the insult was the same. And in the absence of the man of the lodge, I thought this unforgivable. I would probably have gone on with my tirade, but just then Pup and No Tail Dog rode up and dismounted.

"Good day to you, Bull's Horn," Pup said cheerfully. Then he noticed the looks on our faces. "What is it?" he asked, concerned. "Something wrong?"

Bull's Horn answered quickly, smiling. "No, no," he said. "I was looking for my wife, but she is not here."

It must have been apparent to the other men that something *was* wrong, but there was nothing to say. Bull's Horn turned and sauntered away.

"What is it?" Pup asked again, this time directly to me.

I blurted out the whole story. Oddly, when I told it, it did not seem so bad, so irritating. Even in my anger I could not explain the way it was.

"So . . . ," Pup said with a puzzled look, "Bull's Horn asked about his wife and then invited Flower to stay with them?"

"You do not understand, Pup," I almost shouted at him.

Flower said nothing.

"He is a strange one," suggested No Tail Dog.

"That is true," Pup agreed, "but I do not understand what happened here."

"You would have had to *be* here," I told him.

Flower had said nothing, but now spoke. "I am causing trouble for you," she said sadly. "Maybe I should move."

In all her troubles I had never seen Plum Flower so discouraged. She looked tired and depressed and older. The thought passed through my head that now she needed us more than ever.

"No!" I said firmly. "This was nothing that you could help. Bull's Horn offended the hospitality of my lodge!"

I was not quite sure that Pup understood that, but he did appear sympathetic. I felt somewhat better.

"What was it that he said?" asked No Tail Dog. He was showing more interest now.

"He was rude," answered Flower. "He said that Bluebird was wasting time coming over here."

Dog shook his head, puzzled.

Flower went on. "He wanted to know *when* I was coming to his lodge."

"You are going to *him*?" Dog asked.

"No, no. . . . I mean . . . ," Flower stammered, confused. "It had not been mentioned. I have not made any decisions."

"Ah! Then he *was* rude!" said No Tail Dog, as he turned away from our camp.

It was not until later that we talked of it, the three of us.

"Flower," Pipe Bearer asked, "is this the way it should be? I do not know the ways of your people, but . . ."

"But I do, Pup," she said emotionally. "No, it should not be so. Bull's Horn could ask or invite me, but he should not demand."

"He did not invite!" I broke in. "Pup, he asked when she was moving in with him."

"And that should not be?" he asked.

But it was not really a question. I could tell that Pup was disturbed about this.

"Flower," he said seriously, "since we do not know the customs of your people, you must tell us what is right. But the choice is yours, is it not?"

"Yes. I am made to think, though, that Bull's Horn thinks I have no other choice."

"But you do. . . . You will. You have said that No Tail Dog has hinted . . ."

"That is true," Flower answered. "But, Pup, he is only showing that he is a friend. I do not think that his lodge would be my choice. His wife would not take kindly to a second woman."

Now, I am not certain that Pup fully understood what she was saying, but I did. Any second wife would be just that. A *second* wife. The first wife would own the lodge, would manage it, would tell any others what to do.

Now, I had met the wife of No Tail Dog. I had been in her lodge. Though I did not know her well, I could tell something about her. A woman can see the ways of another woman very quickly, I think. That is another of our defenses. Men are slower to see the qualities of a woman, maybe. They look at other things. . . . Yes, I will go on, Pup. *Aiee!*

Plum Flower had known this wife of No Tail Dog all her life. She knew how that lodge would be managed. Any second wife would be subject to the jealous whims of the first.

Flower confided much of this to me a little later.

"She was always bitterly jealous of all other women, Otter. She could never be one to make another feel welcome in her lodge as a second wife. As guests, yes. You have been in her lodge, and it was pleasant, for an afternoon of sewing. But I think not in this other way. Of course, I have not been asked, either."

She smiled sadly.

"I *may* be," she went on. "Dog was very displeased about Bull's Horn. But if he asks me, I will say no. I could be happy with him, maybe. At least he would be a good husband. But as a second wife to *her*, no. I would be better off in the lodge of my sister."

Aiee, I did not like to hear her talk like that. It seemed that she had given up. Then she spoke again, and I felt even more sorrow for her.

"I must do something soon," she said. "My belly is beginning to show."

It was almost as if it were my own problem. No woman should have to make such a decision at such a time, anyway. Especially not one as important as this, when her judgment is emotionally clouded.

But winter was coming.

36

My friends, it is as Otter says. Our hearts went out to this brave woman. We did not know yet what her choices might be. I was looking over the young men who seemed interested, and none of them appeared good enough for Plum Flower. In a way, I was experiencing the feelings of a father when his daughter reaches courting age. At least, I think so. Little Bird, here, will not reach that age for a few seasons yet.

But we were concerned for our friend. I did not think much of Bull's Horn, either. It seemed that most of the camp assumed that the lodge of Bull's Horn and Bluebird would be Flower's home. But he was a braggart and a bully. I do not know whether he mistreated Bluebird or not. If she was content there, so be it. I did not think that Plum Flower would respond well to such a man. Yet I suppose many women have endured worse. Many men, too, maybe.

At first I had thought that No Tail Dog would be good for her. He was not actively courting her, but he was a friend. I did not understand, until after the two women talked, why that could not be. Otter explained it to me, and then I could see. *Aiee*, I cannot think of a worse fate than to live in a lodge with two jealous women!

Otter has mentioned the pregnancy. She and Flower decided that the way to make that known was to tell someone and let the word spread. They chose Bluebird.

I was present when they told her and was startled at the wide range of emotion in the woman's face. Joy for her sister, sadness, but also confusion and doubt. Obviously, it would take some time for Bluebird to think through all the different things that this new information implied.

"I am happy for you, my sister," she said. "At least, I *think* so!"

Then they all laughed and cried a little, and I felt the same way.

"You want me to say nothing of this?" Bluebird asked.

"No, no!" Flower exclaimed. "I feel that it *should* be known. And I am proud to carry the child of Lone Walker."

Then they began to talk of woman-things, and I went for a walk. The campfire was smoking a little, and the wind had changed so that it was bothering my eyes, maybe.

It seemed that by evening everyone in the camp knew of that development in Plum Flower's story. There were some results that became apparent immediately. Several older men, those who had exhibited a somewhat lecherous streak, dropped out of the game. To ogle a nubile young woman as a possible second wife was one thing. . . . To take a pregnant woman carrying the child of another man was quite a different challenge.

Likewise, many of the young men who had been nosing around like yearling bucks in the rutting season quickly lost interest. Most of those were not ready for such responsibility, and that was understandable.

It became apparent that there were a few potential husbands still interested. There were still visitors who stopped by. Some were very nervous now, and tried to avoid looking at the slight bulge of Plum Flower's belly. One by one, those faded from the scene in the next few days.

But there was one whose reaction was certainly impressive. I had not had any idea how Bull's Horn might react to the announcement of the pregnancy. He came storming into our camp, his face red with anger.

"Why was I not told of this?" he demanded of Plum Flower.

"Of what?" she asked coolly.

"Of your pregnancy!" he almost shouted.

Now I could see Flower's temper begin to rise, though she tried to appear calm.

"Oh . . . that! Maybe because it is no concern of yours, Bull's Horn."

For a moment I thought he would strike her.

"It *is* my concern!" he yelled. "When a man takes a wife, he has a right to know—"

At that point I stepped in and interrupted.

"She is *not* your wife, Bull's Horn," I reminded him.

The man whirled angrily on me. He looked much bigger than I had thought him.

"Nor yours!" he shouted in my face. "You have nothing to do with this. You are an outsider, not even a relative. Stay out of this, or you will have me to fight."

It was apparent that this was a real threat. I tried to stay calm and not to show my fear.

"I do not want to fight you, Bull's Horn," I said, trying to keep my voice steady. "This is Plum Flower's to decide, not yours or mine."

"It is probably your child!" he accused me.

Now I tried to hold in my temper.

"Bull's Horn," I said, my voice shaking a little, "you dishonor not only Plum Flower but her dead husband with such a thought. I will not forget that. But there is no purpose to fighting you."

"You are afraid!" he taunted.

"Maybe. But I have my family to think of. I will not put them in danger because of your stupidity. And as I have said, I am made to think that it is Plum Flower's choice."

"No!" he roared. "The woman belongs to me!"

He whirled and strode away, for which I was very glad. I could not believe the anger and the threatened violence that we had just seen. Dumbfounded, I turned to Plum Flower.

"Is this true?" I blurted. "Is there something I do not know about your customs?"

I was just beginning to realize how close to danger I had just come. This was a big man, a proved warrior with many scalps on his lodge poles. I did not want mine there.

Plum Flower was pale and shaken by the tirade.

"No," she said, "that is Bull's Horn's way. I am sorry, Pup."

"Am I expected to fight him?" I asked.

"No, no. Unless *you* want to. I would not wish it, though. But Pup . . ." Tears filled her eyes. "Thank you."

"But what happens now?" I asked.

"Nothing. Horn's temper will cool. My sister will tell us how it is."

"How can she live with such a man?" blurted Otter.

Plum Flower shrugged. "It may not be so bad. I am made to think that he is mostly talk. Bluebird says he is a good husband."

It was an odd reaction from Plum Flower. She was still pale and shaken, and I had the idea that she was trying to convince herself. That was a rather frightening thought. Was she actually considering becoming a wife to him?

And "mostly talk"? *Aiee*, it was not mostly talk that put the fluttering scalps on Bull's Horn's lodge poles. The thought of facing him in combat still made my knees weak.

"Flower," I asked, "how is it that Horn says you belong to him? Is that true?"

Now some color was returning to her face, and with it a flash of anger. . . . More like the Plum Flower that we knew.

"No!" she said emphatically. "Only in his mind."

"But . . . ," I began, but she interrupted.

"It is a common custom," she explained. "The sister's lodge, you know . . . Is it not much the same with your people?"

"Yes, it is often the way. But you do not belong to him, as he said?"

"No." Then she paused for a moment, looking dejected and subdued. "Maybe it would be easier that way."

I was startled, and looked over at Otter. She was staring in disbelief.

"You would consider *that*?" demanded Otter.

"Do I really *have* a choice?" asked Flower. "He is dangerous."

It alarmed us to have her talking this way.

"Plum Flower," Otter said, "do not make such a decision now. Not yet. Let us think about this. There must be another way."

She smiled sadly. "I do not see one. He will be a danger to anyone I consider."

"Maybe so. But I want your promise . . . that you will not go to him yet. Let us think on it."

"Well . . . all right, Otter. You have my promise. I will tell you before I make any decisions."

I needed to talk to someone else, someone not closely connected with this whole situation. I thought of Lone Walker, and wondered what he would suggest. His calm judgment had always been good. This in turn caused me to think of No Tail Dog. Dog had been Walker's friend, and mine. I sought him out and explained the situation, describing the tirade of Bull's Horn.

Dog shook his head. "Horn is very different! That is what he said? 'She belongs to me'?"

"Yes, he said that. Both Flower and Otter heard it!"

"I do not doubt it, Pup. No, he does not own her, but if he thinks he does, it is much the same."

"But he was very angry about her pregnancy . . . ," I began.

"Yes, I heard about that. The pregnancy, I mean."

"Horn accused me of being the father," I told him.

"Ah, that is a dishonor to our friend's widow, no?" Dog said.

"That is what I told him."

"What did he say?"

"He flew into a rage, threatened me."

"What was Plum Flower's reaction?"

"She is sad. Her heart is very heavy. But, Dog, that worries me. I am made to think that she is considering going to him to avoid trouble," I told him.

"How so?"

"Trouble that Horn might make for others."

"Ah! I see. Pup, she must not do this."

"I know. Otter Woman has made Flower promise that she will tell us before she decides."

"It is good."

"But in your customs, must I fight him if he challenges me?"

"I see no reason. *He* has insulted *you*. But let us wait a little. There may be something we do not yet see. And I can talk to Bull's Horn. I know him. Let me see what I can learn."

The next day No Tail Dog came to our camp and drew me aside.

"Let us walk," he suggested.

Away from the camp a little, he began to tell me about his conversation with Bull's Horn.

"The man is a little crazy over this," Dog told me. "I am made to think that he has wanted this woman for a long time. His anger was great just from talking to me about it."

"Anger at *what? Whom?*" I asked. There was much about this that I did not understand.

"At *you*! Horn thinks that you want Plum Flower as a second wife."

"*I?* No, no, Dog! Flower is the widow of my friend, and we only try to help her. Is it not that this is her choice, where she will go?"

"That is true. Most commonly, to her sister's lodge, though. Bull's Horn was counting on that. Now he is furious that she camps with an outsider. If she does not go with him, you *may* have to fight him," Dog told me seriously.

"Wait! This is nonsense. Maybe I can talk with him, explain that I do not court her."

No Tail Dog laughed. "And maybe the moon will rise in the west! But I have an idea. Bull's Horn is a very greedy man. Maybe you can offer him gifts."

"*Buy* this claim he thinks he has?"

"Not exactly. Comfort him in his loss if she chooses you or someone else."

"Would this not seem strange, Dog? I am not interested in her as a wife, but as a friend. I *have* a wife, and a child. To buy his claim so that she can choose a husband . . . *aiee*, maybe so . . . This hurts my head. Maybe I will talk of this to Otter."

"It is good!" said No Tail Dog. "Are they not almost-sisters?"

Somehow, in the confusion of all the thoughts in my mind, I completely missed the suggestion that hung there between us.

37

I guess I thought of the solution before Pup did. I had witnessed the rage that followed the confrontation between the two men. I was astonished, of course, at the irrational anger of Bull's Horn. *Why?* Why was Pipe Bearer the brunt of his tirade?

When the argument was over, it did not take long to reason it out. A woman senses such things. In this case there could be only one possible answer: jealousy. Bull's Horn had actually assumed that my husband wanted Flower as a second wife. I assure you, nothing was further from Pup's mind, or from mine. As you know, we have always been very close. We were helping a friend who had lost her husband, also a friend. When people suffer danger and hardship together, they become very close, and we felt a duty to her.

Now after the argument between Pup and Bull's Horn, I began to do some deep thinking. I was somewhat confused. It had never occurred to me. . . . *Aiee*, maybe it had crossed Plum Flower's mind, but if so, she had given no hint. Of course, she would *not*. Any such suggestion would have to come from us.

But I began to see how this must look to others in the camp. Flower had returned after a season of traveling and trading with us. Her husband was dead, and she camped with us. It was logical to assume that she intended to stay with us.

In the wonder of this new understanding, I began to discover a strange emotion, myself. When I saw the jealousy in Bull's Horn, I began to understand that there was a little in myself.

Plum Flower was an attractive woman. No, let me be fair. Stunning in her beauty. One of the most beautiful I had ever seen. I had not been concerned about it. Well, maybe a little, when I was very misshapen with my own pregnancy. But I knew what Pup and I had in our marriage. There were things we shared that no one could harm.

Of course, Flower was not a flirt. If she had given any sort of hint that she was interested in my husband, we would never have spent that season together. The thing that had made it successful was that she did not, any more than I would have flirted with Lone Walker. We, Pup and I, were made to think that their marriage was as solid and good as our own. So we could respect that, and each other, as friends, and feel no threat.

Now I began to realize that others around us were failing to understand that relationship. Flower surely saw it, because they were her people. I now realized, too, how hard she was trying not to appear interested in such a solution. This, then, must be the reason for her remark about joining her sister's lodge. Ah, sweet, devoted Flower, willing to subject herself to such an indignity . . . *Aiee*, to be Bull's Horn's wife, to avoid any harm to *my* marriage with Pup. My eyes filled with tears, and I went for a long walk.

I had more than one problem to ponder. Would I be willing to do this thing for the woman who had become like a sister to me? Who had helped me so much in my pregnancy and the birthing of Little Bird, among strangers? Yes, I *must*.

But *could* I? Would *my* jealousy destroy us? That was a harder thought. I had not felt any jealousy until now, but I had felt no reason to. Even now I felt no reason. But until now there had been no hint that someone else might share my husband's affections. And his bed. I finally had to allow myself that thought.

The thought that finally let me look at it rationally was this: That was not the *reason* for this possible alliance, but the *result*. None of the three of us were first interested in the physical part of this. The friendship had come first.

In a way, it was much like the relationship between Pup and me. We had been friends together, before the onset of our maturity. Mine had come first, the onset of physical urges. We had still been friends, and it was a joy to see Pup grow into his manhood. There had still been a few years before we were to be able to marry, but . . . Well, so it goes.

Now I looked at this present situation. We had been friends first. And while I had admired Lone Walker's handsome good looks, I had never looked at him as a potential husband. No more than Flower had done so with Pup. I wondered, if I had been the one who had lost a husband, could I . . . There was no doubt in my mind that Plum Flower and Walker would have been there for me. I could do no less than that for her. I felt almost guilty about my jealousy. One does what he (or she) must. Maybe it helped that I could see that Flower's pregnancy was beginning to show. Her beauty would not be so much of a threat for now. And maybe you think *that* was not a guilty thought!

My biggest problem, maybe, was my husband. I did not think that this solution to Plum Flower's problem would have occurred to him. It was not in his nature. He was concerned with finding her a husband, yes. But primarily as we had talked until now, with keeping her out of the lodge of Bull's Horn. Both of us had seen that as our main problem. I was sure that Pup was still thinking along those lines. That, and whether he would have to fight Bull's Horn. *Aiee*, I did not want that. The man was big, even bigger than most Lakotas.

I knew that Pup would not see that as a valid answer to this dilemma. He and No Tail Dog had talked of it, and other possibilities. Pup's idea was still that if Horn understood, there would be no need for conflict. I doubted that. It is hard to reason with an unreasonable man. Yes, or woman. Bull's Horn was not only unreasonable, but a little crazy.

Pup had told me of the possibility of buying out Bull's Horn's supposed rights to Flower. No Tail Dog thought this the best possibility, Pup said. Of course, it did not make much sense if she chose another man, did it? Well, maybe. Flower did own half of our furs and trading stock. Maybe that could be offered to compensate Bull's Horn for his perceived loss. Maybe No Tail Dog could handle the negotiating.

I was still not really convinced that it would work. The idea that I had now certainly made more sense. Flower could join us, as my almost-sister, and we could give Bull's Horn whatever seemed to pacify him.

I would have to do some convincing. First, approach Plum Flower, maybe. She would probably protest that we owed her nothing, and suggest again that she join her sister's lodge. But I could not let her do that, at all costs. I believed that she could be convinced. Had we not been almost-sisters for a long time?

My real concern was how this suggestion would be taken by Pipe Bearer. Ah! You notice? I called him by his proper name, as a holy man of the People. I have been calling him Pup, his childhood name, my pet name for him, and that which close friends call him. But the situation called for something more serious. Pipe Bearer.

How would he react to what I was now thinking the best answer to the problems of all of us? I was sure that his head would tell him that it was the only way. But what would his heart say?

Would Pup consider this a threat to what we have always had? I must be very careful. I could see the threat of a guilty feeling on his part. I must handle this very carefully, make him know that what we have cannot be destroyed. I thought that maybe under the proper circumstances he could be persuaded of that. And I had a powerful weapon in this game of persuasion: years of experience in dealing with him. I would choose the proper time and setting, decoy him out of the camp, and reason with him.

But it must be soon.

Ah, we men are at a disadvantage, are we not? What chance have we, when women are so adept at these games?

Otter might have been surprised at how soon I realized that the answer to many problems was right before us. I did not realize quite as soon as she did, it is true. I knew that the two women had drawn aside for much serious discussion. But, after all, women do this, as men do. And at the time there were many woman-things to discuss.

It was not until after I had been thinking a while that the significance of No Tail Dog's remark sank home. That of the relationship of Otter and Flower: almost-sisters. He had all but explained to me that the logical thing was for Flower to join us, and that most of their people already assumed so. That was the reason for Bull's Horn's rage.

As I thought of it, it began to seem more and more logical. The two women had been through much together. They had shared joys and sorrows. They had worked well together, laughing and sharing private jokes.

But could I convince Otter that it was not for the purpose of acquiring another wife that I would do such a thing?

I would not be truthful if I said that I had never noticed the beauty of my friend's wife. It could not be otherwise, because there was no denying Plum Flower's stately grace and the look of eagles in her eyes. Any man who would not notice is dead, or at least blind.

Yet I am convinced that this was a secondary reason in my mind—second to our friendship, Otter's and mine, with this fine woman and her husband. And to Walker's memory, of course. Could I convince Otter of this? I was made to think so. She had always been secure in our love, and I had never given her any reason for jealousy. I was sure in my own mind that had Flower been fat or ugly, I would have just as easily done what now seemed the only sensible answer.

I must be careful, now. I see an irritated wifely glance. No matter. She knows.

I did not know exactly how to bring this matter to Otter's attention. Surely, she would be the one to suggest it to Plum Flower. But how could I make it seem to her that it was *her* idea?

By now you realize that all three of us knew but could not bring ourselves to talk of it. Whoever mentioned this solution would be very vulnerable to the feelings of the others, of course. I was outnumbered, and men are at a disadvantage in such matters anyway, I think.

I was very curious, then, when one warm evening Otter suggested that she and I go for a walk just before sunset. She picked up a robe, which was logical either to sit on or to put around our shoulders. I suspected from the sidelong glance that accompanied her invitation that it could be useful for other purposes before the evening was over. After all, a camp with only a lean-to and an open fire is a bit public for much romance.

We watched Sun Boy paint himself and the western sky and slide across to the night side. We were sitting together on the woolly robe, arms around each other. It grew cool after Sun's rays died, and we snuggled closer. Otter kissed me. . . . I would have done anything on earth that she asked. She gently pushed me back onto the robe, joined me, and drew the other half of the buffalo skin over us.

A little later, as we lay half-asleep there under the stars, she whispered in my ear.

"Pup, I want to talk to you."

Well, I could think of nothing for a moment that had not just been said, and quite effectively. Then I realized that I needed to discuss a matter with her, too.

"Yes, it is good," I told her. "Then I have something to discuss, too."

She nodded.

"Mine first," she said. "Pup, would you consider asking Plum Flower to join our lodge?"

38

We talked a long time, reassuring each other. We made love again.

"Have you talked of this with her, Otter?" I asked.

"A little. She was concerned as to whether you would accept it."

Now you can realize, you men especially . . . I was on very thin ice here. I must agree with Otter in her conclusion that this was the best decision for Plum Flower. Yet I must not seem too enthusiastic. But in the warm glow of our romantic evening, I was made to think that it was possible. We had all lived closely together for a year, and were familiar with each other's ways. All of us would miss Lone Walker, but in some ways both Otter and I could help Flower to keep his memory alive.

Already we were beginning to remember and talk about some of the happy times that we had shared. One of us would remember something that he had done or said, and we would chuckle together over it. And, though the idea was hardly settled in our minds, we would soon have a part of Walker with us in Flower's child. I was made to think that the three of us could make a good life together.

"But, Otter, you will have to help me," I told her. "Only you can keep this working well."

She snuggled close and gave me a quick hug. "It will take all of us, Pup. But we can do it together." She tossed back the robe. "Now, we should get back to camp. It will be time to feed the baby."

With the advice of No Tail Dog, we planned how we would deal with Bull's Horn. Dog would approach him and tell him of Flower's decision. Then offer to negotiate any exchange of goods that Bull's Horn thought appropriate.

I did not know what to expect. I was very uneasy over Horn's reaction. He might demand a fight.

"I have thought about this," Dog told me. "You are a holy man among your people and would not be expected to answer such a challenge. Is it not so?"

"That is true," I agreed.

"Then Horn should respect your ways."

"But he seems not to, Dog."

"If he refuses to do so, we can take it before the council. It is really a private matter, but that would make Bull's Horn look ridiculous. No, I am made to think that he will be happy to sell any rights he has, or thinks he has, with Plum Flower."

Dog also pointed out to me in private that in bargaining he could use Flower's pregnancy to good advantage. I was a little upset over that.

"That is a *good* thing, Dog," I told him. "She carries the child of your friend and mine, Lone Walker."

"And for you or me or Flower, it *is* good," he agreed. "But we are bargaining here, Pup. You are a trader. You know how it is, and how Bull's Horn is. Her pregnancy is not only a good thing for us, but a good talking point when I deal with Horn."

I was not present when No Tail Dog went to open the discussion. I did not want to be. We had no idea how the man would react. He might even become violent.

"We can probably hear him from here," Otter suggested.

Aiee, it was a very nervous time, to be waiting for Dog to return. The three of us sat by our fire. Talk lagged. That was odd, because we had never lacked for conversation, the three of us. Or when we had been four.

Suddenly Plum Flower giggled. "Walker would be amused by this," she said.

I thought about it. Yes, he would. It struck me as a very funny situation. I wondered if Walker was watching from the Other Side and laughing at us. Now Otter seemed to be thinking along the same lines as I . . . *that* is not unusual. . . . She laughed, and in a moment the three of us were laughing together. *Thank you, Walker*, I thought. This was what we had needed.

We were still laughing when No Tail Dog returned. He was very sober.

"He will not trade his claim?" Otter asked quickly.

"Oh, yes. I do not think he even wants Flower. But maybe that is good. Yet Bull's Horn is more clever than I thought."

"What is it?" I asked impatiently.

"He says," Dog went on, "that you do not have enough trade goods and furs to satisfy him."

"Even with theirs *and* mine?" asked Flower.

"That is true. I even asked about your lodge. We still have it, you know. Horn laughed and said he was not interested, that he already has a far better lodge," Dog told us.

"But what does he want?" asked Otter angrily.

"I am coming to that," said Dog, a little sadly. "He wants your horse."

For a moment I thought that he was talking about the horse that I rode, but it quickly came to me that it would not be that. Many horses sometimes change hands over a wife. We knew a woman there called Ten Horses, because that had been her husband's gift to her parents for her. But I quickly realized . . .

"The medicine hat horse?" I gasped.

"Yes. That is all he wants."

This was a surprising turn. I was revolted by the thought of this special animal in the hands of such a man, who was known to abuse his horses. But it took only a moment to see that it would be better than to have Plum Flower in his hands. He was also, we suspected, an abuser of women.

"*Aiee,*" I said. "That is *all*?"

"You must not do this, Pup," exclaimed Plum Flower. "I will be all right."

"No," I told her, "let us think on this."

I was beginning to see purpose here. There are no coincidences, I am made to think. Remember, we had set out on a quest, started because of the medicine hat horse. Yet after we traveled for a whole season, there was still the feeling I did not understand the quest. I had been disappointed over the finding of the other medicine hat, the mare. There was still something missing, and I had not known what.

Maybe this was it, the purpose of the whole thing. The horse could be used to save this fine woman, who had become such an important part of our lives.

I looked over at Otter. Her face was pale, but I knew from her expression that there was no real choice here. As much as we loved the horse, Good Hat, when it came to the choice there could be only one. The welfare of Plum Flower was more important to us than that of any horse, or all the horses in the world.

"Let it be so," I told No Tail Dog.

"You are sure?" he asked.

We talked about it at some length, and we were all forced to the same conclusion. This must be done.

"I will take the horse to him," offered Dog.

"No, I will do that myself," I told him. "I need to tell him something."

We brushed and groomed Good Hat, now approaching his two-year spring and the bloom of his youth. Otter petted him and cried a little, and Flower did, too. Then I took his rope and, with No Tail Dog, led him through the camp to the lodge of Bull's Horn.

He was inside and made us call to him two or three times before he came out. He was all smiles now, knowing that he had won in the trade of his life. I was sick, a gnawing hurt in my stomach.

"Ah! You have brought my horse!" he said.

I gritted my teeth. *Better*, I thought, *than to bring you Plum Flower.* But I said nothing about that.

"Bull's Horn," I began, "you know that this is a special horse, a medicine animal."

"Of course. There is nothing you can tell *me* about horses," he sneered. "Or about women!"

Now, I felt it important to warn him about misuse of one's medicine. I was a little bit anxious for myself, actually. This medicine horse had been given to me. I had had to decide whether using its power to save Plum Flower was appropriate. Yet it is even more dangerous to try to take and use the power of another's medicine. I felt a responsibility to warn him of this.

"Bull's Horn, you know the power of such medicine, and that it must not be used to—"

"Enough!" he interrupted me. "Leave my horse and go."

There was nothing more to say or do. Dog and I walked back to our camp, where the women anxiously waited.

"Back so soon?" greeted Otter. "How did it go?"

I shrugged. "That was all. He took the horse. Gloated a little."

"Nothing else?" asked Flower. "Furs? Trade goods?"

"No," said Dog. "We were made to think that the horse was what he wanted."

"And I am made to think," I added, "that *this* was our quest. To use the horse to ransom Plum Flower. It is over."

Plum Flower was crying quietly, holding Otter's baby while Otter was tending the cooking fire. It was good to see, and I thought that the two of them could make this a success, if ever two women could. With their help, I could, too.

We thanked No Tail Dog, and he left us to return to his own lodge. It was growing late now. It had been a day that would not be forgotten.

A glance around our little camp seemed to say that nothing had changed. But we knew. Our world would never be quite the same.

"My heart is heavy for Good Hat," said Otter as darkness fell.

"And mine," I agreed. "But if this is meant to be, it will be. And think of any other way . . ."

"Yes, I know."

We talked long that night, the three of us. Until now we could have done little to discuss plans. Now there were many decisions to make. Where would we winter? I think all of us had assumed that no matter what else, Otter and I would go home to the People after Flower was settled. Now it was assumed that she would go with us. Just to make certain, I mentioned it.

"It is satisfactory for you, Flower, to join our people?"

"Of course, Pup. I have no family here but Bluebird, and I would not enter her lodge now. You *are* my family."

"It is good," I told her. "But we have to decide . . . shall we winter here and then start back?"

The two women looked from one to the other, and finally Otter spoke.

"It is the choice of Plum Flower," she said. "Only Flower knows about how her pregnancy feels, what to expect of the weather here. . . . What does your heart say, my sister?"

Flower smiled. "I am made to think," she said, "that we should start on. We will be traveling south, with Snow Rider behind us."

That was the name they call Cold Maker, you know.

"Besides," Flower went on, "the sooner I am far away from Bull's Horn, the better. He makes my skin crawl."

Aiee, I thought, *yet she would have gone to him to avoid trouble for us.* This was a very loving person, and easy to love.

We began to plan that night.

"We must do something for No Tail Dog," Flower said. "Let us give him some of our goods, and my lodge."

It was a good thought. Dog had done us a great service, and we must thank him. The lodge . . . He already had a lodge, but there are always young people beginning a life together. Some young man would be proud to trade a few horses to Dog for a lodge to shelter his new wife.

So our planning began, for this new life together.

39

In only two days we were ready to travel. Dog was pleased with our gifts. There were few good-byes. Bluebird seemed quite happy with the outcome. I was made to see that maybe she *did* love her husband, though we other women did not see how. I was proud of the way Pup and No Tail Dog had handled the dealing with Bull's Horn. It could have been dangerous.

Now we were on the trail again, as we had been many times before. Just the three of us now, and the baby. I could not help but notice that the three of us were in a much happier situation than the last time we were traveling. Then we were still mourning Lone Walker. There were surely some problems ahead, but we felt confident that we three could handle them.

There was one thing that kept bothering me, aside from that. I kept thinking about our horse, left behind in the possession of Bull's Horn. I could see, as Pup did, that this must have been part of the purpose. Without his vision and the quest, we would not have been there for Plum Flower in her time of need. Nor she and Walker in *our* times of need, either. It must have been meant to be.

Yet it bothered me to leave Good Hat behind. Pup had told us that Bull's Horn mistreated horses, and my heart was heavy for the colt who had been such a part of our lives. I mentioned it to Pup, and of course he was kind and understanding. I knew that he, too, felt it.

We always had to come back to the same way of thinking, though. It was better to leave the horse behind with Bull's Horn than to leave Plum Flower. Still, even that was small comfort. I *worried* about our medicine hat colt.

It was our third day on the trail that we discovered someone was following us. Of course, there are always travelers, but we were puzzled by this.

We first noticed the moving specks when we paused for a rest on the top of one of the long grassy ridges. We thought little of it, but the next stop brought them closer. Pipe Bearer, who had been riding in the lead, watched a long time, and then sketched out a plan. As evening neared, we would show ourselves on one of the ridges. Then he would conceal himself while we moved slowly on with the horses, out of sight.

It seemed that there were only two horses following us. One rider was easily seen, the other was a small person, or maybe it was a pack horse. We could not tell the colors of the animals. As you know, distance blurs color before form. At great distances, all horses are the same color, a dark blur. And so it was this time. We could see that they were horses, but not much more.

Pup chose his spot for what might need to be an ambush very carefully, and we took the other horses on over the ridge and out of sight. Flower and I tied their muzzles with thongs to keep them from crying out. Then I left her to watch the baby and went back to where Pup hid. There would be only one shot in his musket, and two riders. I took my bow in case he needed help.

He was not happy with me, but motioned for me to lie down beside him. We watched the back trail through a low growth of plum or sumac.

"Where are they?" I whispered.

"Not far. They will come around the shoulder of the hill, there. . . . Ah!"

Just at that moment a rider did come around the hill. He was several bow shots away, so there was a little time to study him. Pup gripped his gun. . . .

It did not take long, though, to see that the second horse was not ridden, but led. The object on its back was neither a small rider nor a pack, but a loose bundle of robes. Probably the sleeping robes and provisions of the rider, who held the lead rope. By the time I had noticed all of this, I also saw that we had nothing to worry about. The rider was No Tail Dog, and the horse that he led was Good Hat, the medicine horse.

Pup was already rising, and waved to the approaching rider. No Tail Dog responded with a shout and kneed his horse forward. *Aiee*, it was good to see him.

We were all trying to talk at once, and finally Dog held up a hand.

"Wait, wait! Let us camp, and I will tell you all. Where is Flower?"

"With the horses," I told him. "Come!"

We walked down the slope, and on to a place by the stream which offered a camp site. Dog stripped the saddles and bridles from the horses, and turned them loose to graze with ours. I was nearly bursting with curiosity but managed to restrain myself.

Finally, the first chores of a new camp were completed. Flower and I had a fire going while the men took the packs from our horses and released them. The ritual pinch of tobacco in the fire . . .

"Now!" said Pup. "Tell us!"

"Ah, I hardly know where to start," began No Tail Dog. "After you left . . . well, my heart was sad. Not for you, but for the medicine horse. I have a strong feeling for him! Ah, what an animal!"

"Go on," I urged.

"Yes, yes. . . . I watched closely after you left. Horn tied the horse to keep him from following you. That was right, of course. But I wanted to see what he would do, so I stayed near. Pup had told me of his thought that the purpose of his quest was to have the horse ready to help Flower in her time of need. Yet such a waste! A medicine horse for a man who is such a . . . *For Bull's Horn?* Somehow this seemed a strange part of the plan. I am sure that you felt it, too. A loose end, something missing.

"It was later that same day that Bull's Horn approached the horse. He had not fed or watered it, which I would have if it were mine. But then he began to try to work with it."

"To train it?" asked Pup. "The colt is not old enough to ride!"

"I do not know what he had in mind," Dog went on. "He had a quirt, and when the horse would fidget around, Horn would hit him. There were others watching, too. It seemed that the man wanted to take out all his anger on the horse. It did not take long. The horse flew into a rage. He jerked the rope out of Horn's grip, but instead of running away, he attacked Bull's Horn. Nearly killed him! Horn was knocked down, struck by the hooves. . . . One hit him in his private parts. Ah, I doubt that he can sire any more children. No one could stop the horse. It threatened anyone who came near. Bull's Horn would have killed him, but he could not get up."

"But how did you get the horse?" I asked.

Dog chuckled. "I bought him, while the time was right, and made a good trade. Then I waited until his anger cooled. We understand each other now, Good Hat and I. But he is a sacred horse, and he belongs to Pipe Bearer. So I brought him back to you, holy man."

Now I expected Pup to protest immediately, but he was slow in answering. He appeared deep in thought. Finally he spoke.

"Dog, my friend, my heart is good for what you have done for me . . . for us, and for the medicine hat horse. But I am made to think this: His purpose for us is complete. It is over.

You have said that you and he understand each other. I can see that, in the way he responds to you. Your spirits mix well. So I am made to think that he belongs to you now. Otherwise you could not have bought him so easily. He must have had one more purpose, to teach Bull's Horn the error of his ways. *Aiee*, the spirits enjoy a joke, no?"

We had not expected a joke at the end of such a serious speech, and it caught us off guard. We sat there, laughing together as the sun set.

"What will you do with the horse?" asked Plum Flower.

"I do not know," answered Dog. "I had not thought I had a need to decide. But when I need to know, I will be shown."

Pipe Bearer nodded approvingly, and it was good.

Now, my friends, Otter Woman wanted to tell that part. And as she said, it was good. We spent the night there, and then No Tail Dog started back. This time he did not even have a rope on the colt. There was not the urgency on the journey home. Dog had still not said what he might do with the horse. Certainly he would keep him, probably breed all his mares. As Dog said, he would be shown.

What? No, we do not know. Maybe some day we will go back and see.

But the rest of the story . . . it is not long. We traveled well and were favored by good weather. Even so, we were caught in an early snow before we reached our own Southern band. It was warm and wet and quickly melted, and we pushed on.

Winter camp was already nearly complete when we found them. They were camped in the area to the south of the Sacred Hills, where the tallgrass meets the scrub oaks and the dirt is red. Yes, a favorite winter place for us.

Our relatives were quite surprised that we had brought back not only a child, Little Bird there, but a second wife. They quickly took her into their hearts, and now it seems that it was always so. It seems so to us, too.

It was at about the start of the Moon of Awakening that Plum Flower delivered Little Walker. He too has brought joy to our lodge. We see much of his father in him, yet he is ours, too. Is he not a handsome child, there on his mother's lap?

Now, Flower, they have heard our story. I hope I have told it in such a way as to explain it. Yes, thank you. . . .

So that is how it came to be. The three . . . no, four winters since have been good to us. It was a wonderful adventure, that quest of the medicine hat horse. I would not have given up that experience for anything. Yet I would hate to do it again.

The quest was fulfilled, and, I think, the purpose of the medicine hat horse. Maybe he had more of a purpose for No Tail Dog, too. But we do not know.

One thing I do know. . . . For us, life is good.

Author's Comments

In many widely separated cultures through human history, multiple marriage has been an accepted norm. In most, probably. Ancient Greece, Rome, the early Judeo-Christian tradition, the Mormons, and the American Indians all practiced the custom without apology.

The basic reason seems always to have been the same. In many cultures men have been subjected to dangers such as constant warfare or even the perils of hunting. There was a constant loss of life among the males, resulting in a surplus population of women. The solution has always been much the same. The widow was taken into another home. She became an extra pair of hands, a caregiver, wife, and mother.

The most common relationship, from biblical to modern times, has been as I have described among the People. The widow's new home was quite likely that of her sister. In some cultures it has been *required* that the sister's husband take her in.

This situation has not been dealt with to any degree in modern fiction. It is foreign to our culture, to our ethical codes and our Victorian sense of right and wrong. But such emergency situations *have* occurred through the ages. They may again.

I wanted to depict such a custom through the eyes of characters who are deeply emotionally involved in the situation. I have tried to do so fairly and honestly. Our own background has not, in many cases, prepared us very well for acceptance of customs foreign to us.

But in such a situation, was there really any better answer?

DON COLDSMITH